Mystery on Hidden Lane

BOOKS BY CLARE CHASE

Mystery on Hidden Lane

CLARE CHASE

Bookouture

Published by Bookouture in 2020

An imprint of Storyfire Ltd.
Carmelite House
50 Victoria Embankment
London EC4Y 0DZ

www.bookouture.com

ISBN: 978-1-83888-525-0
eBook ISBN: 978-1-83888-524-3

To Andrea, Shelly and Sarah (and their dogs!)

CHAPTER ONE

Eve Mallow sat amongst marram-grass-topped sand dunes, still in the clothes she'd worn for the drive up from London. She'd spent most of the journey feeling hot, stale and cranky, thanks to the sudden failure of her car's air con. The traffic had been nose-to-tail until she was well outside the capital. How had she still managed to arrive at her destination an hour ahead of time? It always happened – it was as though she defied the laws of physics. Once she had a job on, she could never bring herself to delay getting started. It didn't matter that it was too early to check into the rental cottage she'd reserved – a last-minute arrangement, only finalised the day before. Waiting on the beach wasn't a hardship, and it was a relief to be out in the open air.

She'd taken the time to size up the Suffolk village of Saxford St Peter before she'd walked through the woods and heathland to reach the coast. Apart from the Cross Keys pub and a teashop and craft market called Monty's, there was just a small place selling groceries. The notice on the door announced sternly that it was never open after 5 p.m. and shut much earlier on Wednesdays and Sundays. *Worrying.* Still, it looked as though she'd be fine for beer, cake and pre-packed bread. She guessed she'd have to plan ahead if she wanted to cook something more adventurous. But she'd come prepared; in her car was a box containing pesto, pasta and parmesan cheese, gin, tonic and dog food. The essentials. And then she'd added a few extras too. But she would only be here for ten days, in any case.

Gus, her wire-haired dachshund, had clearly been pleased to leave their vehicle behind too. She'd let him off his leash as they'd approached the beach, snaking their way along the narrow path through the heathland. He'd dashed off up the shingle-strewn sand, wet black nose pointed determinedly into the wind, ears flung back by the breeze and his own speedy enthusiasm.

Eve closed her eyes, enjoying the warmth of the sun in the shelter of the dunes. The last couple of weeks had set her nerves on edge. Ian, her ex-husband, had called round two days earlier – to 'check she was okay'. Again. He did it quite regularly, even though they'd been living apart for a year now. He'd walked out on her – and yes, it had come as a shock at the time. But she'd acclimatised surprisingly quickly. How often did she have to tell him she was fine? Was he hoping he could take her tales of woe back to his new girlfriend, so that they could enjoy feeling sorry for her over a glass of Shiraz?

She took a deep breath and focused on the gulls' cries, which overlaid the sound of the waves slapping against the shore, then pulling back, rhythmic and lulling. It was time to let go, and concentrate on the reason she'd come to the village. Writing an obituary of Bernard Fitzpatrick, the world-famous cellist who'd accidentally drowned in the River Sax, ought to be fascinating. Eve loved her work – interviewing the living to unearth the secrets of the dead was both challenging and satisfying. She slipped off her flip-flops and felt the grains of sand and small, soft pebbles under her feet as she wriggled her toes.

Until she heard voices, hushed and urgent, she hadn't realised how well hidden she was below the level of the dunes. A man and a woman. They must be close behind her – standing just above the beach on the edge of the heath. She sat absolutely still, wondering what to do. Should she leap up like a jack-in-a-box, to make sure they knew they weren't alone? But before she had the chance to decide, she was absorbed in their conversation.

'I saw your face.' The man's voice was hard; barely controlled. 'Just after we heard.'

Eve wriggled down further into the dunes, her stomach knotting. This wasn't a conversation she wanted to overhear – she could already tell it was private – but it felt too late to declare herself.

'What are you saying? That there was something wrong with my response? Hell, Andrew – this isn't the kind of thing that happens every day! I don't have an off-the-peg expression lined up for this sort of circumstance.' The woman spat the words out.

There was a pause. 'You looked upset, but I know you – rather too well. You've been acting oddly for a long time now. I'm fed up with your lies!' His voice had risen, and he stopped abruptly. When he spoke again, he'd managed to rein himself in. 'I could see you weren't one hundred per cent surprised at the news.' It was clearly an accusation.

After a long moment, the woman answered. 'You're on edge. You're reading too much into all this.' Her voice was much softer now, and overlaid with sympathy. It sounded overdone – wheedling. 'I know I haven't been my usual self, but things will be different now, I promise.'

'I've heard that before. I'm not a fool!'

'Ow! Stop it! You're hurting me!' She spoke over his last words.

What was happening? Eve eased round. Her mobile had signal. She could intervene or call the police if she needed to.

But a moment later the man apologised and the woman spoke again. 'I want us to be happy. We were once. We can work at it, can't we, darling?'

For a moment there was silence, apart from the cries of the gulls.

'One last chance, eh?' the man said eventually. 'All right. All right. But don't even think about messing me around again. You know what I'm capable of if you do.'

It sounded as though the woman needed to get out of the relationship – and fast.

At that moment, Gus bounded into view, and her voice rang out, higher in pitch now. 'Who does that dog belong to? Is there someone on the beach?'

Eve sat absolutely still, desperately hoping that Gus wouldn't give her away. She leaned back as far as she could and held her breath.

The dachshund dashed past without paying her any attention, but she didn't relax.

The woman's voice came again. 'We should get out of here. Someone must be about. Come on!'

A second later, the man and woman descended onto the beach a little way north of where Eve was concealed and walked off up the coast – stiffly, with their shoulders hunched. He looked older than her, with thick mid-grey hair. Hers fell in red ringlets, well below her shoulders – the neat top and fitted capri trousers she wore showed off her figure, which was pure 1950s Hollywood.

Only when they were well on their way did Eve slide forward again. She felt shaky after the exchange she'd heard.

Gus, who was bounding back up the beach, spotted her, did a handbrake turn and launched himself onto her lap. *Wet paws. Nice.* He must have been in the sea since she'd seen him last.

She gathered herself, brushing the sand off her jeans and slipping her flip-flops back on. It was time to return to the village. She'd been told she could check into the cottage after four. As she snatched up Gus's leash, she wondered about the couple – and if she'd see them again. She was worried for the woman; the man had sounded so threatening. Yet it had been *she* who'd sounded scared at being overheard.

Eve shook her head. At least they hadn't spotted her; if she did come across them again, she'd have to work out what to do. It felt wrong not to say something to the woman – to pitch in and try to help. As an obituary writer she was well versed in assessing people. She'd interviewed surviving friends and relatives experiencing all kinds of emotions; their reactions to a death could be dramatic as well as fascinating, depending on the dynamics involved. She knew trouble when she saw it. But the situation was complicated, and the woman might not welcome interference. It sounded as though she had something to hide…

CHAPTER TWO

In general, Eve hoped she'd meet the residents of Saxford St Peter under more conventional circumstances. As a stranger in a small community, she guessed she'd be assessed on arrival; she didn't want to stand out any more than she had to. She'd only ever lived in cities – Seattle until she was eighteen, with her British father and American mom, before what now seemed like a daring and independent move to London, where she'd studied, married (far too young) and produced children (ditto, though she'd no regrets there). She'd been in the UK's capital ever since. There'd been no thoughts of moving back to the States, even when her marriage came apart. Her and Ian's twins were independent now, but while they were based in the UK, she would be too. She often thought of the Pacific coast though – of blue waters, and the colour and liveliness of Pike Place Market, with its lush flower stalls and the men hurling the fresh fish they sold from one side of their stand to the other, with laughing friendly faces. Visits back to see her parents were a tonic.

Vast, frenetic London was very different, but she loved it too. In the centre of the city the hubbub never stopped, and walking around late at night, it was as busy as if it were midday. You could get whatever you wanted, when you wanted it, so long as you weren't broke. Folk from all over the world mixed on its crowded streets. For Eve – a committed people-watcher – living in such a place was perfect.

She'd feel more of an outsider in this tiny village. People often saw her as a mishmash anyway: not quite fully American nor

British. Might as well add conspicuous city-dweller, landed in rural Suffolk, into the bargain.

Keep in mind the upsides, Eve – two full weeks with no unwanted house visits from Ian. No need for forced politeness for the sake of wider family harmony…

'C'mon, Gus.'

Her dog looked unconvinced, his melting brown eyes appealing.

'I mean it! We need to go and get sorted.' She had the urge to get everything shipshape inside her temporary home, and curiosity spurred her on too. Elizabeth's Cottage – and on a road called Haunted Lane… What was the history there? And what sort of place would it be? As full of interest as it sounded? Shabby, damp and neglected, or well-kept? Normally, she'd already know. She'd have found the place on the internet and memorised every detail about it. But the reservation had been so last minute she hadn't had the chance – and the place didn't have a web presence anyway. It was only available on a temporary basis; she didn't know why. Instinct had made her want to go and size up the house as soon as she'd arrived, even if she couldn't get in. But if someone else was there – cleaning the place, or moving their own stuff out – she didn't want to breathe down their necks. With Ian constantly huffing down hers, she'd come to know just how irksome it was.

Eve half suspected that Haunted Lane had been named by the local authority to attract tourists. Not that it would have worked on her; she didn't believe in ghosts. But she was interested in local history, and because of that, she planned to google the background as soon as she had the chance. She'd been assured the cottage had broadband and a landline, which was good, because signal on her mobile was patchy at best.

At last, Gus gave in and followed her back through the gorse bushes, quickening his pace and overtaking her at speed in pursuit of a bird of prey which had just swooped overhead.

Way out of your reach, Gus!

It was comical, the way he seemed unaware of the fact. And it was certainly just as well. She was sure he'd come off worse in any encounter. As she walked on, a flicker of movement on the ground caught her eye. An adder, darting into the undergrowth. She guessed muggers weren't as much of a worry here as they were in her patch of London, but the local dangers might be harder to predict – and of a sort she wasn't used to tackling. For a second, she felt an odd thrill run through her, brought on by the 'otherness' of the place. Stuck in London, in amongst densely packed terraces, around the corner from a local high street full of betting shops, takeaways and pawnbrokers, she was removed from nature. Here, she'd be brushing shoulders with it every day.

She was relieved when Gus came back into view. He was looking over his shoulder at her, waiting for her to catch up, poised to scamper ahead again as soon as he was reassured. And here were the first seaward houses of Saxford St Peter. She called him and put his leash back on for the last bit of the journey. It wasn't like walking down Kilburn High Road in rush hour, but she'd noticed a nippy red Jaguar zipping through the village earlier, having left the Cross Keys car park. She wasn't going to take any chances.

The lane had no pavements, but in reality she found it didn't need them. Everything was quiet now. They passed a worn red-brick wall, inset with cobblestones and covered with sprawling purple wisteria, its sweet scent made stronger by the warmth of the early summer's day. She had to admit, it made a change from the smell of exhaust and other people's overpowering vape fumes. She stood there for a moment, just breathing it in, letting her lungs inflate. It was probably the first time she'd taken a deep breath consciously in months. It never felt like that much of a good idea, back in the city.

A second later, she and Gus passed a byway she hadn't noticed on her way down to the beach, appropriately named Hidden

Lane. That was the private road where Bernard Fitzpatrick had lived – the cellist whose feature-length obituary she was there to write. She craned to see down the road. Beyond the hawthorn hedgerow, through the lush green leaves of a lime tree, she could just glimpse tall chimneys and part of a red-tiled roof, which must be his place. He might be dead and gone, but it looked as though the lane had carried recent traffic – she could see several sets of fresh tyre marks in its dusty entrance. Presumably there would be a lot to sort out following the musician's death. For a second, her curiosity made her wonder about taking a diversion, but the desire to see inside her own temporary home tipped the balance. She'd save Fitzpatrick's former residence for the following day, when she was due to interview the dead man's secretary there. She upped her pace again, but the moment she'd crossed the entrance to the lane, she heard the low purr of a car engine behind her. Gus had paused to sniff something interesting, so Eve stood up close to the verge to let the car pull out. There were two men inside, their windows down. As they made the turn, she heard one of them say:

'Like a watchful spider that might jump if you poke it. Do you know what I mean? Not that I should base my—'

The rest of his words were lost as the car accelerated away, leaving a cloud of dust behind it.

It left her wondering what the following day might bring.

Eve and Gus strolled past old thatched cottages, their gardens crowded with delphiniums, foxgloves and phlox. Gus insisted on investigating every gatepost, while Eve tried to steer him to spots where the locals were less likely to object to him lifting his leg.

Her flip-flops slapped along in the dirt, but before long they reached the centre of the village, where the lanes were properly tarmacked. At an intersection, she walked past the Cross Keys pub again. It was a homely looking place, with a mellow red-brick frontage and bright royal-blue paintwork. Dog friendly, so it said, which might be useful. Seeing all there was to see was a compulsion of hers. When she wrote about a person, she liked to understand their wider environment, as well as the finer details of their lives. A gaggle of people, standing outside the pub in a huddled group, caught her attention. None of them noticed her staring, so she took full advantage of the fact. Was it the sort of place that stayed open all afternoon? Or perhaps they had been there for some time after the pub had closed. That seemed more likely; one was leaning on a car, another shifting from foot to foot. They were intent on their conversation, and there was a lot of frowning and head-shaking going on. It was interesting, given it was a weekday. Not all of the loiterers looked past retirement age.

Her rental accommodation was off Love Lane, the same road that was home to the pub. (Once again, she was suspicious, but the streets couldn't *all* have been named to appeal to tourists.)

Gus was at her heels now – he seemed to sense they were nearly at their destination, and maybe even he was tired. Her instructions said there was no parking on Haunted Lane, so her battered old Mini Clubman was just across the road, by the green. She crossed over to grab her backpack from the trunk, and snatched up her box of provisions too. She'd want milk if she was going to make tea. Her father was devoted to the drink and had made sure she was exposed to it too: iced on long summer days, but piping hot from the pot when the weather turned cold. Her mother still wasn't a convert. For a second, Eve looked at Gus's padded dog bed, but that would have to wait for a return trip. She'd get it once they'd looked round the house.

Rather heavily laden now, with Gus's leash over her left forearm, she crossed back and turned to walk up the narrow byway of Haunted Lane. Its entrance was bordered on the right-hand side by a vigorous hawthorn hedge, its white flowers in full bloom, and on the other by a venerable old oak tree on a large patch of grass, its trunk swathed in ivy.

She glanced at the first cottage in the lane, to her left. It was a beautiful, ancient-looking place that had finally given up the battle of keeping level with the road and slumped gently down on one side. Scanning its facade, she saw a sign that proclaimed it as Hope Cottage. Through an open window she could hear someone playing the violin. There were several perfectly executed notes, followed by a bum one, whereupon a woman's voice reached her.

'Really, *not* an aid to concentration, Daphne dear.'

The reply that followed was partly muffled, but ended in: 'get better if I never practise!'

Beyond the first house was a large bit of garden she guessed belonged to it. And a little further along, diagonally opposite, was the next, and only other, dwelling on the lane: a whitewashed cottage, its upper-floor windows peeping out from under thick thatch. Three chimneys topped with terracotta pots rose well above the roof. Between her and it was a waist-high wooden gate set into a thick, wild privet hedge – in flower, just like the hawthorn. Round the back she glimpsed a patch of sun-dappled lawn and a gnarled old apple tree. It reminded her of an illustration from a story book she'd had as a child – the kind of place that seemed to promise peace and happiness – but to be somehow unattainable, except in fiction. Even though there were no other houses, she held her breath as she approached the gate, scanning for a sign.

There it was – next to the low front door: Elizabeth's Cottage.

And Eve's, for the next ten days. A tingle ran over her bare forearms.

CHAPTER THREE

Eve had never imagined she'd land such a beautiful place to stay at a day's notice – and it hadn't even been expensive. Her writing fee would cover it – time to get her work done, with a few days to unwind on top, with any luck. She still couldn't take her eyes off the frontage of the cottage. If Elizabeth had been the original owner, she must have lived there 400 years or so earlier – it had to be that old.

She glanced down at Gus. 'What d'you think? Has to be a catch, surely?' *Mice in the kitchen? Spiders in the bath?*

Gus was wagging his tail and leaping to the left and right, which wasn't hugely helpful. *Mustn't drop the gin.* Or land a can of dog food on his head. She managed to half balance the container on the worn wooden gatepost, so that she could lean down and release the gate's catch with her one semi-free hand.

After that, she dumped the box on the gravel front path, found the key, which was under a flowerpot containing a red geranium as advised (imagine *that* arrangement in Kilburn), and let herself in.

She removed Gus's leash, and he flopped through the door as though he'd already accepted the place as home. Eve strode in after him, having picked up their supplies again.

The sun streamed in through the windows, but it still took a moment for her eyes to adjust so that she could see the darker corners of the living room. Outside, the house's ancient timber frame was hidden under plaster, but here its historic wooden skeleton was laid bare. At one end of the room was a large inglenook fireplace, its bricks blackened by soot. Two generously sized couches sat end-on to it. It would be cosy in winter, but through the traditional six-paned casement window she could also see an ironwork table out in the back garden: the perfect place to sit after she'd finished her day's work, given the season.

She was just about to dart upstairs when she became aware of Gus again, nudging her leg. He'd completed *his* cursory exploration, involving a lot of sniffing, and – now that he had her attention – he went through to the kitchen, his paws pattering on the brick floor. She picked up the box of provisions and followed him. Duty called.

The kitchen was through a door to the right of the main living room, and a proper farmhouse affair, with beautifully crafted units in solid wood. The window and a back door both opened onto the back garden. She dumped the box on the oak table.

Dog bowls – check. Water and food, a moment later – ditto. There was probably a can opener in one of the drawers, but with rented cottages you never knew what you'd get, so she'd brought her own.

Gus ignored her now, his mind firmly on his refreshments. *Typical.*

She went back to her explorations. Opposite the kitchen, off the first room she'd entered, was a dining room and, beyond that, a second living room – all full of period furniture, more exposed timber and intriguing nooks and crannies that she'd have to investigate in due course. On the dining room table was a pretty tin, decorated with a pattern of tiny blue speedwells. She opened it and found the most exquisite-looking shortbread biscuits inside – delicately decorated with tiny flowers that matched the design on the tin. They were handmade, she was in no doubt about that, and they smelled fantastic. The house-owner must be a skilled baker. Her stomach rumbled, and she picked one out, feeling like a character in a fairy tale, doing something forbidden, and likely to lead to trouble. But she assumed they must be meant for her. It was only after she'd finished one – letting the last buttery crumbs melt in her mouth – that she saw the note that must have been with them. It had slipped off the table and lay half hidden under an old sideboard. The handwriting was large and forward-leaning.

Welcome! I hope you enjoy being the keeper of Elizabeth's Cottage for a few days.

Keeper? That somehow implied more responsibility than she'd been anticipating.

Please let me know if there's anything you can't find, or that you need. I'm over at Monty's – the teashop – or in the cottage next door if it's closed. Come along any time for tea and cake on the house. I can fill you in on the village, as well as Elizabeth and Haunted Lane.

Hope to see you soon,
Viv (Montague)

Viv? Eve glanced at the email on her phone which had detailed the arrangements for her stay, as organised by Bernard Fitzpatrick's secretary. The person renting her the cottage was supposed to be called Simon Maxwell. Still, she'd visit the teashop as 'Viv' suggested, to thank her, and find out how it all hung together. Food and information was an appealing mix.

She dashed to look at the upper floor next, with Gus – who'd finished his dinner – at her heels. The stairs were steep, and it took her a minute to find them, hidden as they were beyond a latched door that looked as though it might lead to a cupboard.

The bedrooms were all in the eaves. Exposed wooden beams reached over each of the beds like encircling protective arms. Out of one window she could see a path that started where Haunted Lane left off, stretching to where the River Sax opened out into an estuary, just before it met the sea. At the other end of the house, the view was of the sprawling blossom-laden hedge she'd passed, with the village green beyond, and Hope Cottage and the oak tree across the way.

After she'd finished exploring, she messaged the twins on their group chat, warning them she might be hard to reach on her mobile, and telling them about the house. She included a photo of the exterior, which she took before fetching the rest of her luggage from the car.

Looks cool, Nick messaged back, as she re-entered the cottage.

Good luck with the locals! Ellen added, a second later.

In the end, Eve decided to unpack her belongings and cook supper before she got down to work. Her article about Bernard Fitzpatrick was for a lifestyle magazine, rather than one focused on music. She didn't need to reach the level of an academic expert, but she liked to be thorough. It was curiosity that drove her on, coupled with an absolute determination to make the most of her interviews. She set herself up at the kitchen table, with her laptop and a plate of pasta in front of her. As she raised a glass of Pinot Noir to her lips, she entered 'Bernard Fitzpatrick' into Google's search box and pressed return. After she'd boned up on him, she'd dig for information on Elizabeth and Haunted Lane. Despite the promise of information from Viv, it was tempting to make a start on the research herself.

But in the end, she never got as far as looking up Saxford St Peter's ghosts. The results of her search on Fitzpatrick stopped her in her tracks.

CELEBRITY MUSICIAN WAS MURDERED, POLICE SAY

The headline had gone up two hours earlier.

Eve sat for a long time, reading and rereading the short article on Bernard Fitzpatrick's killing. Her previous subjects had died in many different ways: old age, illness, accidents, alcoholism, suicide… but she'd never covered a murder victim before. She always trod carefully – almost all deaths left someone grieving, and people in pain. The rare ones that didn't were often the most upsetting. But this current assignment took things to a new level. And she couldn't stop a nagging voice in her head, too – warning her. Would completing this job put her in danger? Much of it depended on the murderer's motive. If it had been a random attack, then it would probably make no difference – either to her safety, or to what she'd discover from Mr Fitzpatrick's contacts. But if not… In effect she'd be interviewing the dead man's close circle, just like the police, but without their training. She might stumble across information that revealed the killer's identity without warning. The thought made her mouth go dry and her heart beat faster. Did she really want to do this? However things played out, she wouldn't be able to keep her distance from what had happened. She'd have to work out her approach.

Googling, she found the email address the police had set up for anyone who had information relating to the musician's death. She wrote a very matter-of-fact message, explaining who she was, why she was there, the sort of information she'd be gathering and her contact details.

Butterflies tickled her stomach. Sending the email felt like she was acknowledging the extent to which she might inadvertently get involved. But despite her nerves, and her sympathy for the dead man, she couldn't help wanting to know more. The desire to understand human nature was hardwired in her. If Fitzpatrick had been killed by someone he knew, their relationship must have reached an extreme point, such as she'd never witnessed before. What sort of dynamic could have brought them to that final, awful event? A feeling of anticipation was racing round her veins.

Before bed that night, she took Gus out for a walk, along the dark lane and then up the track that led towards the estuary. The hedgerows she passed still smelled sweet in the warm night air, but knowing what she did now, the idea of the way being haunted didn't seem so far-fetched. She wondered where Fitzpatrick had gone into the water.

Gus looked round at her, as though reading her mind.

She pulled a face. 'I know. And I don't seriously believe in ghosts.' *Unless in the form of ideas in your mind that loomed large, and refused to go away.*

She thought again of the newspaper reports she'd read – the bruising on the side of Bernard Fitzpatrick's head they'd all mentioned. Someone had hit him with something, and hit him hard. By the time he'd entered the water, he'd already been dead. Her background reading also confirmed the impression she'd had previously. Journalists used words like 'charming', 'charismatic', 'approachable' and 'vivacious' alongside the usual epithets of 'celebrated' and 'extraordinarily gifted'. Poor guy. On the face of it robbery, or something like that, might have been the motive. He must have been well off – he could have been carrying or wearing items that were worth thousands. Desperate people killed for a lot less, according to the papers.

It would be a less alarming conclusion, from her own selfish point of view.

But reluctantly, she let the idea go. Surely an opportunistic mugger wouldn't hang around a small village, just hoping to find a rich-looking victim to follow? A more populated area would give a greater chance of singling out someone worth targeting.

Ahead of them, the tide was out. Mudflats stretched down to a narrow channel where river met sea, silver in the moonlight. The smell of saltwater filled the air. Out in the darkness she could hear a curlew's cry.

'Time to go home, Gus.' She nodded back towards Elizabeth's Cottage. The following day was a whole different prospect now. What would she find out by talking to the dead man's secretary? Understandably, he'd never spoken to the press about his boss before, so it was a brand-new source of information. And what might she get at the teashop from Viv, who probably knew the habits of all the locals?

As she washed and got ready for bed, her mind ran back to the couple on the beach. How long would it be before she ran into them again? She tried to remember the man's words. Something like: *I could see you weren't one hundred per cent surprised at the news.*

Had it been the revelation of Bernard Fitzpatrick's murder that he'd been referring to? Her recollections put a final thought into her head, that stayed there as she lay in bed that night, looking up at the beams curving over her.

Maybe she'd already encountered Bernard Fitzpatrick's killer. Things might have been quite different if Gus had given her away.

CHAPTER FOUR

By eleven the following morning, Eve was sitting opposite Bernard Fitzpatrick's former secretary, Adam Cox, in Mr Cox's office at the musician's home on Hidden Lane. She switched off worries about Gus potentially chewing up the couch cushions at Elizabeth's Cottage. She'd taken him for a good run on the beach earlier, but he'd still had a giddy twinkle in his eye when she'd left.

Bernard Fitzpatrick's residence, High House, had taken Eve's breath away as she'd approached it, stepping carefully along the dusty gravel lane in her formal heels and shot silk dress. (The outfit was crazily impractical for the conditions, but important for the job. She wanted her interviewees to know she respected them and the person who'd died. All the same, she'd felt conspicuous. The pack of journalists hanging round in Hidden Lane were all in jeans and T-shirts.)

She could see how High House had gotten its name. It spanned four storeys, not including its attic. The place had tall dark windows and stone gateposts. And the inside turned out to be just as grand – the walls were hung with original artworks, and the furniture looked antique. The whole place smelled of wax polish.

As for Adam Cox, he was a good bit younger than her, in his early thirties, she guessed, but he looked like something out of a Victorian novel, with his three-piece suit, highly polished shoes and round wire-framed glasses.

'Thank you for seeing me.' They each had a steaming cup of black coffee in front of them. He was clinging to the handle of his as though it were a life raft. Whether that was down to upset, stress, or both, she wasn't sure. The hacks outside couldn't be helping. Eve had felt their eyes on her back as she'd been granted admittance. At least Mr Cox knew she wasn't there to pry into the scandal. 'I'm so sorry for your loss.'

He nodded his acknowledgement, and his pale blue eyes met hers. 'It must be an odd job, obituary writing. Quite morbid.'

Eve bristled, even though she'd had to answer the same comment many times before. 'A lot of people think that, but being an obituary writer doesn't spring from an unhealthy preoccupation with death. It's actually people's lives that we're interested in – that's the story we tell.' A 3000-word article about a body, lying there in its coffin, really wouldn't have the same impact. To her, obit writing was the best and most fascinating job in the world. And it wasn't just the obvious stuff that she found captivating; people always had some hidden habit or experience that left her marvelling. For a second her mind strayed to the multimillionaire she'd covered, who'd secretly worked as a cleaner two mornings a week just to see how the other half lived. The woman had had the same bug as Eve: curiosity. She couldn't help but admire her dedication, even if Eve herself might have drawn the line at that level of subterfuge. It was important to try to understand other people.

'It must make you very conscious of mortality, though,' Mr Cox persisted.

In fact, Eve felt at her most alive when she was working on an obituary. She loved looking for interesting people to cover, selling her pitches to newspapers and magazines, then putting her whole focus on doing a good job. Unfortunately, she had to couple her vocation with a part-time role as a school administrator to help pay the bills. It was *that* job that made her conscious of the endless hours she'd never get back. She was still feeling blissed-out at managing to arrange last-minute leave.

'Not generally.' She paused. 'Though of course the circumstances of Mr Fitzpatrick's death make life feel more uncertain.' The matter had certainly filled her dreams the night before.

Cox nodded. 'I had thought I might need to put our meeting back. The crime scene investigators arrived yesterday – a couple of hours before the news about Bernard's murder went public. They only finished this morning.'

'It must be horribly upsetting for you.'

He nodded quickly. 'They were all over the place. It was chaotic.'

Not what Eve had meant – but looking around Adam Cox's office his reaction figured. The place was meticulously neat. His files were arrayed on dark polished shelves that lined the entire room, and his system was something to behold. Eve treated records with respect too; once she'd gone to the trouble of gathering information, she liked to know exactly where to find it. She'd been known to cross reference and colour code. But Adam Cox's study showed her heights she'd yet to reach.

'Of course, I can't really talk to you about Bernard's murder,' Mr Cox said.

'Of course,' Eve agreed, though it wouldn't stop her thinking about it.

'That said, it's bound to bring in the visitors.'

'Visitors?'

Adam Cox nodded, and sat up straighter in his chair. 'Bernard has left High House to a local arts trust in his will. He arranged with them that they should open it to the public, as a museum.'

'A very generous gift.' And an interesting one too, given the cellist was survived by a brother. But to be fair, the brother was a lawyer, and more than solvent, according to her research. That might be why Fitzpatrick hadn't felt the need to keep his wealth in the family.

'Of course, I already have a lot of information about Mr Fitzpatrick.' Eve took a sip of her coffee. 'Things like the major events in his career, his education, key performances and awards are all a matter of public record. Where I'd really appreciate your help is with personal reminiscences. What was Mr Fitzpatrick like to work with?'

The man paused a moment before replying. 'Bernard wore his intelligence on his sleeve. He was very quick-witted – razor sharp.'

She couldn't help noticing that he sounded relieved to have produced some kind of appraisal. And if someone made you very conscious of their superior intellect, it might be because they'd made sure you were aware that yours was *in*ferior. Still, it didn't follow. She was reading between the lines.

She paused. It seemed best to give him more space to talk and see what came out.

'He had strong opinions, of course,' Adam Cox said. He was shifting in his seat. 'His strength of personality meant he was quite happy to fight his corner. He was a man of conviction; impressively forceful.'

She made more notes. She could only quote what he actually said, but the sort of euphemisms Adam Cox was using weren't uncommon. Readers would draw the same conclusions as her. Fitzpatrick hadn't suffered fools gladly, and had probably put most people into that category. The description was markedly different from the one she'd gotten via her background media research. Was this a personal grudge of Cox's? She'd need to cross-check.

She nodded, her pen poised.

'He was very honest and upstanding – never one to duck difficult conversations. If he felt a fellow musician had played badly at a performance, for instance, he'd tell them directly. But equally he would never discuss that sort thing with the press.'

Fitzpatrick would have had a lot of clout – it must have been a mercy for those in the firing line that he hadn't shared his views with journalists. But she could imagine how his victims must have boiled with irritation, each time they saw articles that spoke of how genial and good-natured he was. And of course, if he'd let other people in the business know his thoughts – albeit privately – it had probably threatened a few careers. 'How did you find working for him, personally?'

'It was an irreplaceable experience,' Mr Cox said.

It sure sounded like it. It was as though the secretary had warmed up during the course of their conversation. Everything he said came across smoothly now, without a pause.

'It would be interesting to know what your job involved, day-to-day?'

'I organised *everything*. Secretary is a rather old-fashioned description. Nowadays most people would call me an executive assistant, or a manager perhaps. I organised all the logistics around his tours, recordings and public appearances. Bernard was rightly particular about suppliers, and the hotels he stayed at. Everything had to be carefully arranged in advance – and of course, I made last-minute changes if there were unforeseen problems.'

And based on what she was hearing, Eve guessed that had happened often – even if the problems had only been in Fitzpatrick's head.

'And I oversaw the other staff, here at High House.'

'How many people did Mr Fitzpatrick employ?'

'There's a publicity manager, and a woman who acts as both cook and housekeeper – and a gardener who comes in a couple of times a week.'

'Perhaps I could take their names? It might be worth talking to them too.'

'The publicity manager's new. I'll give you the contact information for the previous one as well; she was in post for longer.' Cox wrote the details down in a precise hand in his notepad. He ripped the page out, passed it over and drew himself up again. 'But for anything personal, Bernard came to me.'

She could tell he was proud of the fact, but everything he'd said indicated that his boss had been high-maintenance. Had he made allowances willingly because of Fitzpatrick's rare musical talent, or was there more to it than that? That was one thing you learned in this job; relationships were complex.

'What's your fondest memory of him?' It was one of her standard questions, but in this case, it might be especially revealing.

A long pause followed. At last Cox said, 'Perhaps, the day Bernard hired me. I remember how inspired I felt, talking to him, and how enthusiastic he was when he offered me the job. He said he felt I was the only person who could possibly manage what he needed, and second guess his wishes well enough to carry out his instructions without constantly asking questions.' He took a deep breath. 'He was extremely charismatic. That first meeting was enough to convince me I'd relish the role.'

So, his fondest memory was also his earliest. She felt a stab of sympathy for him, but he must have been prepared to take the rough with the smooth, given that he'd stayed on. If Cox had found his boss fascinating, though difficult, she could see how he might have made that choice.

'Would it be possible to look around? I'd love to see Mr Fitzpatrick's practice room.'

She watched Cox tense up. 'I hadn't thought you'd want to do that today. It isn't very tidy – not ready to be photographed.'

'Oh, don't worry,' Eve said, standing up, 'the pictures will be taken separately, if that's okay? The photographer should be in touch with you, direct, by Monday. It would just be great for me to see it too. I won't focus on the mess when I write about it.' The descriptions 'homely' and 'lived in' were often a lot of help, and she wasn't there to do a hatchet job – just to produce an honest and engaging account.

'Very well,' Mr Cox said, and got slowly to his feet. He was tall, and thin too, to the point of gauntness.

She followed him into the hallway and up three flights of stairs. The house seemed so still and quiet. As they reached the very top of the building, she glanced behind her for a moment, through the curve in the well-polished banister, all the way down to the ground floor far below. For just a second, she felt dizzy.

'This is where Bernard worked,' Cox said, pushing open double doors at the top of the stairs to reveal a vast room, the width of the entire building. 'It has a climate control system, so that the large windows don't cause a problem.'

The stairwell was on the side of the house that faced Hidden Lane, but from Bernard Fitzpatrick's study there was the most spectacular view of the woods, the heathland and the sea beyond. The sun glinted on the crests of the waves, dazzling Eve. She could see why Fitzpatrick had chosen to make this eyrie his hideaway. In addition to the large standard windows facing east, the room had a Juliet balcony. For a second, she imagined working there herself. The house might be out in the sticks, but there were compensations. The magnificence of the view was so striking that it took her a while to transfer her attention to the room's contents.

Adam Cox hadn't exaggerated; the place was a mess all right, strewn with everything from piles of magazines and books left out on the floor, to crumpled bits of paper flung hither and thither.

Cox must have noticed the direction of her gaze. 'Musical scores,' he said, indicating the scrunched-up paper. 'His own. He was a composer, you see, as well as a musician.'

She frowned. She hadn't heard that. How on earth had she missed it? She'd have to check online again later.

Eve tried to look beyond the jumble of papers and books to see other signs of Fitzpatrick's personality. The desk held some clues: there were several expensive-looking items – a Mont Blanc fountain pen, a gold cigarette case and a Liberty leather-bound notebook. He'd liked his luxuries – presumably for their own sake. No point in having status symbols tucked away up here. Though of course he might not have bought them himself. They were the kind of items people chose as gifts.

Adam Cox scuttled over to the desk, where he picked up the cigarette case and slipped it into one of the drawers. He glanced quickly in her direction and blinked rapidly. After a moment he picked up an overflowing ashtray too, though he didn't seem to have a plan for how to deal with it. 'I'd intended to clear the room, but with the shock of what's happened...' He let the sentence hang. 'And as it turned out, the police were glad to be able to see the place just as it was on the night he left the house for the last time.'

'That makes sense.'

Cox seemed distracted and had put the ashtray back down again. The smell of tobacco was strong in the air.

'So, there's no domestic help? You mentioned the cook doubles up as a housekeeper?'

'Mary cleans and tidies the main bits of the building,' Cox said. 'But Bernard wouldn't have anyone else in here other than me.'

Again, Eve could hear the pride in his voice, but this time, as both their eyes ran over the unkempt space, she thought it was doing battle with humiliation.

'He always said he wasn't capable of keeping things in order himself. He *needed* my help, so I used to arrive at the house half an hour before he got up for breakfast each morning, to make sure this room was ready for his use.'

Eve felt cross with Fitzpatrick, and, try as she might, she couldn't help feeling irritated with the secretary, too, for taking it. As usual, she reminded herself she didn't know the full story yet.

Still, call Adam Cox what you liked – secretary, manager or executive assistant – he had also been a lackey, cleaning up after Fitzpatrick as though he'd been a child.

For a second, Eve imagined Cox finally snapping, following his boss into the night, smashing the side of his head with a blunt instrument, then casting his body into the River Sax. They weren't images she wanted to see, but it was impossible not to. And this might happen with each new interviewee she spoke to.

What if she suddenly saw the truth? Would she be able to hide it? She'd just have to hope she could brazen it out.

CHAPTER FIVE

'Looks as though Bernard Fitzpatrick wasn't as nice as he seemed,' Eve said to Gus as she sat having a sandwich lunch in the back garden at Elizabeth's Cottage. The round ironwork table sat on a thick lawn, surrounded by a glorious jumble of shrubs, climbers, annuals and perennials. She watched as bees hovered by the blue, bell-shaped flowers of the campanula, visiting each of the blooms in turn. The warm air was rich with the scent of old roses, honeysuckle and lavender.

Gus looked suitably solemn in response to her dejected tone. As usual, she thought what a sympathetic companion he was, and how much she loved him, even though he'd arrived in her life without warning. For years she'd argued that she, Ian and the twins should have a family pet, preferably a dog, but Ian had always vetoed the idea. And then, the day after he'd walked out, he'd visited her and presented her with Gus 'to stop her from feeling lonely'. It was one of the most infuriating and presumptuous things he'd ever done, despite some pretty stiff competition. But of course, she'd adored Gus on sight – it wasn't his fault that Ian was a jerk.

As for Fitzpatrick, she'd started to wonder, over the years, if most high achievers in the public eye had a dark side. In her experience, the ones that didn't were the exception to the rule. She was still treating Adam Cox's veiled comments with caution, but when you put them together with his role as a glorified nursemaid for a man in his fifties, they were hard to ignore.

She was interrupted from her thoughts (and her lunch) by the sound of a text coming in.

She felt her stomach muscles tense. Ian.

Didn't know you'd got a trip planned!

Trip? He made it sound as though she'd gone on a frivolous day's outing, rather than dashing off to work. Hadn't he noticed she had a career? And he'd added a smiley at the end of his message – absolutely fine from most people, but not from Ian under the present circumstances. Totally misjudged.

The kids explained about it when I messaged them to ask. I'd tried to call you at the flat and I couldn't get any reply – and then no response when I called your mobile!

Eve thanked her network for the patchy signal in Saxford St Peter. She'd noticed a missed call from him on her way home from High House, but hadn't felt inclined to ring back.

Hope you're managing, up there in the sticks. Do give me a call. This jaunt seems a bit sudden, and a little worrying if I'm honest.

He was treating her like she was ten years old. He couldn't resist interfering. He'd always expected her approach to life to mirror his precisely and found any deviation inexplicable. When he'd left they'd been determined to stay friends and behave like adults for the sake of the twins, if nothing else. But Ian had used their agreement as an excuse to carry on trying to influence her. She suspected he thought it was for her own good; a positive contribution from a wise objective ex who saw things so much more clearly than she did… In reality it was wearing her teeth down – the regular grinding was going to cost her a fortune in dental bills. As she sat there in the garden, she realised it was time to take control – something she should have done a long while ago. Physical distance had given her a sense of perspective at last. She'd text him, but not until she felt she could be polite.

After she'd eaten, she tried to banish her feelings of irritation and went to write up her notes at the polished wooden table in the dining room. She couldn't quite settle until she'd peeked into some tall narrow cupboards on either side of the fireplace there. The sideboard, under which she'd found Viv's note, contained all the glasses, crockery and silverware, so she couldn't imagine what was stored in them. The contents turned out to be eclectic – pebbles that might have been from the beach, maps and books about Suffolk, board games and jigsaw puzzles and, on the top shelf of the left-hand cupboard, a plan of both floors of the cottage. The bedroom she'd chosen to sleep in was marked 'Elizabeth's Room', and an area that seemed to be between the main living room and the dining room was labelled, 'Where Isaac stayed'. She couldn't work it out. And then there was the question of who Isaac had been, and why someone had created a map of his sleeping arrangements.

She walked from the dining room, past the latched door to the staircase on her left, and into the main living room, but as she'd thought, there was no extra space accessible from there. The inglenook fireplace took up the entire wall. Had Isaac slept in the under-stairs cupboard, like Harry Potter? She returned to the dining room to look into the storage space. It contained a complicated tangle of vacuum cleaner, ironing board, folding chairs, an old sewing machine, and much else besides.

At that moment, she made up her mind to visit Viv that afternoon. The curiosity would drive her crazy otherwise, and besides, it would be rude not to show her face, and say thank you for the shortbread.

She needed to write up her interview with Adam Cox first though. If she left it, her initial impressions would fade, and she'd only have her basic notes to rely on. She forgot the room around her as she worked, absently stroking Gus's head as he pottered in at one point. As she finished, she came to her note about Bernard Fitzpatrick's sideline as a composer. She googled, but there really was no online record that he'd created music as well as playing it. Could it have been something he'd only embarked on recently? But she couldn't imagine that. He'd played the cello since he was six. If he was going to compose at all, it seemed likely that he'd have started sooner. He'd been fifty-seven when he'd died. Maybe he'd just never made any headway with that side of his career. If so, she imagined the fact must have rankled. Had he worked in secret? Again, she couldn't see it. No one ever implied he'd lacked confidence, so presumably he'd shared his efforts, but they hadn't been well received.

Her head was full of questions and conclusions, and they had as much to do with Bernard Fitzpatrick's murder as his obituary.

She turned to the contact details of the man's employees, as supplied by Adam Cox. She sent them each an initial email, so they weren't caught off guard. She could follow up with a phone call if they didn't respond. She adopted the same approach for the lawyer brother, and got an immediate out-of-office reply. She'd have to wait until the following week for her talk with him.

At last, she was ready to investigate the teashop. She'd changed her clothes before lunch and was now dressed in a fitted navy T-shirt, a knee-length red skirt with a rickrack trim she was fond of, and pumps. There was no need to do anything to her hair – her pixie crop stayed smart without effort, leaving her time to focus on other things. She snatched up her bag and went to make sure Gus was inside before locking up. He gave her a long-suffering look as she promised him a walk later.

Eve strode up Love Lane, with the village green on her left. Ahead was the Old Toll Road, which led out of Saxford. She'd need to cross it to reach the teashop but paused a moment, distracted by a building to her right. The house looked as old as Elizabeth's Cottage, but was on a much larger scale. Its grounds were spacious enough to accommodate a couple of silver birches, as well as a size-able Scots pine. Well-tended lawn spread out between them, along with relaxed flowerbeds sporting hydrangeas, cistus, buddleia and rhododendrons. She was so busy taking in the scene that there was no time to hide her interest when a man appeared in the garden and caught her staring. His appraising glance held hers. She guessed he might be a similar age to her – late forties? – wearing jeans that had gone through at the knee and a charcoal-grey T-shirt. He was holding a pair of shears and had a smear of dirt down his forearm.

Time to make the best of a bad job…

She smiled and opened her mouth, ready to admire the shrubs he'd been tending, but even though he must have realised she was about to make conversation, he turned away abruptly, removing himself from her line of sight.

She sighed and hunched her shoulders. Okay, so she'd already guessed villagers might not like strangers, but people from small places were meant to be friendlier than those who lived in towns. Was it something about her in particular?

At least Viv's note had sounded welcoming. As she crossed the Old Toll Road she wondered if the man she'd just seen was the gardener that Adam Cox had mentioned – the one who'd worked for Bernard Fitzpatrick. Robin Yardley – that was the name Cox had noted down for her. If so, she couldn't imagine him agreeing to settle down for a cosy chat. Of course, he might just be the owner of the house, but somehow she didn't think so. He'd looked too businesslike, and his tanned skin and muscular arms fitted with a manual job performed outdoors.

It was only a moment before she reached Monty's – the teashop and craft market – opposite the village green and just up the road from the church. It had bay windows decorated with floral bunting either side of its glass entrance door. Outside on the pavement, customers were sitting at white-painted ironwork tables, adorned with ribbon-trimmed jam jars containing bunches of sweet williams. Each table was also crammed with the most delicious-looking food Eve had ever seen. Individual cake stands were piled high with tiny scones, chocolate brownies with stencilled icing sugar on top, miniature lemon tarts with perfectly cut pastry cases and doll-sized sandwiches. The informality of the jam jars tied in with the mismatched crockery, but the varied teacups and plates went beautifully with each other. A lot of thought and creativity must have gone into the relaxed scheme.

Beyond the tables there was a chalk sandwich board which told visitors, in a lively variety of pastel colours, that those who entered could expect food for the soul.

She pushed the door open, setting off an old-fashioned shop bell. The place was busy with customers inside too. They sat at round tables covered with hot-pink tablecloths, which provided an excellent background canvas for the food and crockery. The verve with which the place had been done out made Eve all the more curious to meet Viv.

And, looking up, she saw the woman she guessed must be her – around the same age as Eve, wearing a peacock-blue tunic. The pink dye in her bobbed hair might have been chosen to match the linen. She was standing just behind a counter, talking to a guy Eve guessed to be in his late teens.

'No!' she heard the woman say. 'Absolutely not!'

The youth looked sheepish and put down the cake cover he'd half lifted.

The woman rolled her eyes. 'You'll eat all my profits, you horrible child! The sooner you and Kirsty go off on your travels, the better for my coffers!'

The young guy laughed. 'You'll miss me when I'm gone, Mum, and you know it. A few cheeky slices of cake is a small price to pay for my expert help!'

Eve had reached the counter now and they both turned to her, standing close together, their smiles wide.

'So sorry, let me see if I can find you a table,' the woman said.

'Are you Viv, by any chance?'

'Oh!' The café owner's bright blue eyes opened wide. 'You must be Eve, who's staying at Elizabeth's place?' She spoke as though 'Elizabeth' was only temporarily absent. That possibility had never occurred to Eve.

'That's me.'

'Wonderful! I'm so glad you decided to drop in!' Viv came out from behind the counter, revealing three-quarter length jeans and espadrilles under the tunic. She turned to her son. 'Samuel, my sweet, you are, after all, welcome to that slice of cake – if you'd just take over for a bit so that we can sit and chat.' She turned to smile at Eve. 'Lots to ask, and *lots* to pass on.'

Eve ought to have known that being quizzed would go hand in hand with doing the quizzing, but it didn't put her off. A woman as gregarious as Viv ought to be a mine of information.

CHAPTER SIX

Viv's son gave an exaggerated eye-roll in response to his mother's request.

'Take over serving all this lot single-handed? It's a heavy price to pay for a piece of cake, but I suppose I'll have to wear it.' He turned to Eve, laughing. 'I hope you're not in a hurry!'

'Cheek!' Viv showed Eve to a table outside, on a patio at the rear overlooking a thick green lawn and the River Sax. A multitude of gulls had gathered on a sandbank, bright white against the blue of the water behind them.

Viv's son was still grinning as he followed them out with a notepad. 'Enjoy this while you can, Mum! What would you like?'

Viv did some recommending, and Eve thanked her for the shortbread biscuits she'd left, and assured her she was happy with the suggestion of Darjeeling. People tended to assume she'd want coffee as soon as they heard her accent. Its scent, once it arrived, made Eve think of the leaf tea her father used to buy from a specialist store at Pike Place Market; she guessed it was of a quality that she hadn't bothered with since she'd left home. If she ever elected to order it at her local café, it came in a pint-size cup, drowned in way too much milk.

On Eve's plate, which was patterned with peaches and plums round its edge, were three miniature treats: a pastry tart covered in glazed summer fruits, a heart-shaped chocolate layer cake and a tiny coffee cake, topped with icing and a walnut. A gentle breeze shifted their tablecloth and brought the sweet scent of the lawn with it. It mingled with the smell of the confections in front of her.

'This is awesome!'

Viv smiled. '*You* can come again. I'm on a mission to get people to remember what real food's all about – and to take time to stop for five minutes.' She put her head on one side. 'Sorry – it's my passion. So, what brings you to this neck of the woods?'

Eve told her, and Viv gave a low whistle.

'That explains it. I have to say, I was curious when Adam got in touch to see if we could let you have Elizabeth's Cottage. I assumed you must be a friend of his – or a girlfriend even. Only I can never imagine him getting close to anyone, somehow.' She took a breath. 'Writing Bernard's obituary's quite a proposition, I suppose, given what's happened. I presume you didn't know he'd been murdered until after you'd got here?'

'That's right.'

'A bit of a stunner.'

Eve nodded.

'Do you always have to travel this far for work?'

She hesitated, her mind on Ian for a moment. Would she have said yes, and made such an effort to get last-minute leave from her job at the school, if it hadn't been for his latest visit? But she'd been curious too. 'Not often.'

There was a disconcertingly knowing look in Viv's eye. 'Saxford St Peter's a good place to come, if you want to get away from it all,' she said. 'Though I guess it'll feel very different from London.' She grinned. 'News travels fast here, for one thing. Even my latest hair-dying experiments make it across the village in a matter of minutes. I can't stop doing it though – it's too tempting when I know it annoys my in-laws.'

Eve found herself grinning too.

'Who have you interviewed so far?' Viv asked.

'Just Adam Cox – this morning.'

Viv looked thoughtful. 'He's an odd sort. I've overheard him muttering about his low pay more than once, which must have been frustrating, given how well-off Bernard was, yet he never did anything about it as far as I can make out. It's peculiar. He's passive-aggressive, rather than assertive, but even if he didn't want to confront Bernard, he could have looked for a new role. Still,' her glance met Eve's, 'he's fallen on his feet now.'

'How's that?'

'You know that a local charity will get Bernard's house? The Blackforth Arts Trust, it's called, after the donor who set it up.'

Eve nodded.

'Adam mentioned they've asked him to stay on as custodian. It'll be a while before the trust takes possession of the place officially, of course, but I hear Bernard's executors are letting them access the house, and Adam will help with the set-up. I don't suppose working for a charity pays massively well, but I'd guess it'll be an improvement on what he was getting. And the role's got a better title too. I expect the level of work will be similar, but at least he'll be recognised for it. So,' she took a sip of her tea, 'it's an ill wind that blows nobody any good.'

Eve savoured a mouthful of the fruit tart. It seemed to her that Adam Cox had more than one reason not to miss his boss. But until he knew about the promotion Fitzpatrick's death had triggered, he must have assumed he'd be out of a job. The desire to further his career couldn't count as a motive for murder. She shook herself. It wasn't her job to make that sort of analysis – in theory.

She wondered how the secretary would cope with his new position, welcoming visitors to High House. He hadn't struck her as a people person, but he'd no doubt tackle his new role with ruthless efficiency, and he'd have the right inside knowledge to pass on to visitors. They'd see through his veiled comments about his late boss, just as she had – and maybe he'd relish the fact.

'Did Bernard Fitzpatrick ever come to eat here?' she asked.

Viv pulled a face. 'Not him! He did stuff for the village, but I think he liked to keep a bit of distance too. He wanted to be seen as a patron, or a figurehead, not as one of the gang. I forgave him though, because he liked my baking.' For a second, her look was far away. 'I catered for a charity do of his once, up at High House. Some of the Blackforth Arts Trust lot were there. It was a bit of an odd evening, as a matter of fact.'

Eve raised a questioning eyebrow. *All information gratefully received…*

'The kitchen's down in the basement, and it's to die for, as you'd imagine in such a grand place. I had the run of it for the afternoon. When I first arrived, Bernard invaded my territory and tried each type of cake I'd prepared in turn. Adam was hovering a few feet away, as though Bernard was a grenade that had had its pin removed several seconds earlier. I was ready to fight my corner if he responded with anything less than glowing praise. But it wasn't necessary; he was charming.'

Eve had just swallowed the last of her fruit tart, and was wishing she could eat it all over again. Maybe there was something to the soul food thing after all. 'I'm not surprised.'

Viv grinned. 'Thanks. But, later in the evening, when things were in full swing, Adam came through to the kitchen to warn me that one of the trays of cakes was empty. When I went out with a fresh lot, Bernard told me off for not being prompt enough. He was pretty sharp.' Viv shrugged. 'I was annoyed, but I guessed he was snappy because he was stressed, so I didn't take too much notice. It was Lucas Booth, one of the Blackforth Arts Trust lot, who got angry. It turned out he'd overheard the spat, and he took major umbrage on my behalf.' She shook her head, sending her shiny pink hair dancing in the sunlight. 'He took me aside, and went on about how rare it was for Bernard to show his true colours in public.' She raised her eyes to meet Eve's. 'Talk about making a mountain out of a molehill. I don't know what Bernard had done to offend Lucas, but his hands were shaking as he spoke – he spilt his drink. Do you think you'll interview him?'

'If he's one of the trustees, I guess it's likely.' Eve felt her knowledge wouldn't be complete if she didn't track him down. And what about his attitude towards Fitzpatrick? Presumably he'd had to court the musician when discussing the gift of the house. The cellist sounded quite volatile; had the animosity Lucas displayed been the result of a temporary quarrel – or something more fundamental? 'Does he live locally?'

Viv nodded. 'In a large house on the Old Toll Road, just on the opposite side of the river – beyond those trees. He's got pots of cash – made it in banking.' For a second her eyes were serious. 'Watch yourself, won't you, when you're talking to all these people?' But then she laughed. 'Dangerous lot, we villagers.'

Eve laughed too, but she felt a flutter of nerves in her stomach.

'So,' her hostess went on, her smile broadening, 'what do you think of Elizabeth's Cottage?'

'Amazing. And fascinating.' She couldn't decide what to ask about first. 'I was confused, though. My confirmation email said I was renting the place from Simon Maxwell.'

Viv's blue eyes twinkled. 'Ah yes. He's been away on business, so I took over the reins, but you're bound to meet him soon.' She leaned forward slightly and picked up her chocolate heart. 'Let me warn you, he's the most incorrigible flirt – and you are *just* his type.'

Heck. And what on earth could his type be? Short with mouse-brown hair? Or, if he was that much of a lothario, maybe just being his preferred gender and not a blood relative would count. Eve must have raised her eyebrows, and Viv laughed.

'He's my brother, so I'm allowed to bad-mouth him. I've no doubt he'll say all sorts of rude things about me too – so please ignore his every word. Elizabeth's Cottage belonged to our parents, but they're both dead now.' She shook her head and looked down at what was left of her cakes. 'The fact is, we're going to have to sell the place, and I'm finding that hard to deal with. There are a lot of happy memories bound up with it. But I've got my house here, next door, and Simon's got a place by the riding stables he owns. He wants to stay there, too – they had a theft last year, so he thinks it's safest to be on the spot.' She sighed. 'Anyway, it was handy that we hadn't put it on the market yet, so when Adam Cox was trying to find you last-minute accommodation, we could let you have it.'

Eve picked up her teacup. 'Had you thought about renting it out on a more permanent basis, instead of selling it?'

Viv nodded. 'We considered it, but it didn't seem right for Elizabeth's place. It would probably be empty at quiet times of the year. I want it to be loved properly, by the right sort of person.'

'Is Elizabeth still alive?'

Viv grinned and shook her head. 'Only in the consciousness of the village. She lived in the cottage from around 1720, and she's held in high esteem to this day because of her bravery and sense of justice. A woman after my own heart. She protected a thirteen-year-old boy, Isaac, who worked as a servant for the people up at the manor. They paid him almost nothing, and when his brother fell ill and couldn't work, his younger siblings were starving – quite literally. The story goes that he pinched a loaf of bread from his employer's kitchen. You could still go to the gallows for that sort of crime back then.' She closed her eyes for a moment.

'At that time there was a designated constable for the area, and he was a nasty piece of work, by all accounts. He raised a hue and cry to go searching for Isaac. Haunted Lane is named for the ghosts of his men. If danger presses close in the village, you're meant to hear their footsteps – the heavy thud of their feet as they run to try to find Isaac.' Eve didn't miss the slight shiver that ran over Viv at that moment. 'Elizabeth had him hidden in her cottage. Then, when the search had died down, she rowed him across the estuary in the dead of night, to the countryside beyond where he could escape and build a new life. No mean feat, since she was a tiny person, apparently. About your size, I'd guess.' She nodded at Eve. 'I expect Isaac took an oar too, but she was the one that understood the tides and currents. She sent him to friends of hers who could take him north, into Norfolk. And the story goes that he managed to send money home, saved his family and lived happily ever after, working for a new employer.

'A lot of people were secretly glad that Isaac had escaped. The lord and lady of the manor weren't well liked. Elizabeth's heroism only came to light years later, when Isaac's son came back to the village and told his father's story. Those who still remembered what had happened celebrated. And Elizabeth's grandson, who'd inherited her cottage, renamed the house after her.'

Viv gave a wry smile. 'My mother-in-law is a direct descendant of the people up at the manor. I'm not saying you can tell, but I would argue that some of the character traits *have* passed down the generations.' She nodded at the teashop. 'This was my late husband's business to start with, and she and my father-in-law keep a very close eye on what I do with it, even though it's officially mine now. Oliver wrote in his will that I should keep them involved if he pre-deceased them, so I'm duty-bound. I had almost daily visits when I added the extension with the craft market.'

Eve had noticed it to her left as they'd made their way to the rear of the teashop. 'I'm so sorry that you lost your husband.'

Viv waved a hand that currently held her fruit tart. 'It was awful at the time, but it's ten years ago now. The village rallied round, in its slightly oppressive, deeply interested but generally well-meaning way, and we got through it. I've two older sons as well as Sam.'

Eve had the impression Viv wanted to move the conversation on, so she nodded and changed the subject. 'I found a plan of Elizabeth's Cottage in one of the cupboards.'

'That's right. My parents used to open the place up to visitors, a couple of times a year – just before Christmas, and in mid-summer.

They'd take donations for young people's charities in exchange for a tour – and tea and cake, which I laid on. Simon and I are hoping the new owner might continue the tradition.'

Eve was starting to see why Viv had referred to her as the 'Keeper' of Elizabeth's Cottage. Being there obviously carried responsibilities. They might take a while to find a buyer with the right feel for the place.

'Where did Isaac hide?'

Viv had finished her tart. 'There's a trapdoor under the stairs – leading to a space beneath the cottage. That was where he waited until Elizabeth could take him over the estuary. Must have been terrifying. According to legend, some of the men from the search entered the house, but they went away empty-handed, of course.' She peered into Eve's cup and then reached to top her up from the teapot.

'I'm so glad. Thanks for the refill.' For a second, Eve was lost in thought, imagining the child holding his breath, down in the dark below the cottage. At last she roused herself. 'Going back to Bernard Fitzpatrick, is there anyone else you think I should speak with for informal anecdotes?'

'You're certain to get something out of Moira at the village shop. Bernard might have been aloof, but he needed somewhere to buy his milk, just like the rest of us. And besides, she's bound to have picked up on your presence by now.' Viv grinned. 'She'll have you down as a townie that brings their shopping in from London if you don't put in an appearance soon.' Eve was glad Viv couldn't see her emergency provisions box. 'And it'll be worth it, anyway,' she went on. 'Spend enough time ingratiating yourself with her and her husband, Paul, and they'll order your favourites in for you. It takes a while to wear down their defences; it's best if you treat it as a game. Oh, and if Paul acts oddly, don't take it personally.'

Eve could hardly wait. 'I'll pop in – but I'm only here for ten days.'

Viv just smiled at that. 'Why don't you come to the Cross Keys this evening and I'll introduce you to the crowd there,' she said, after a moment. 'Adam mentioned you'd brought a dog with you? That's no problem. Toby, who runs the place with his brother and sister-in-law, has a schnauzer.'

As Eve walked home, she wondered what chaos Gus and the resident pub dog might create in the bar. She hoped the schnauzer was a miniature one.

But after a few moments her mind was back on Adam Cox and his stroke of good fortune: a new job, hot on the heels of losing a boss who'd tested him to the limit. Was it a coincidence? And then she pictured the mysterious woman on the beach, who hadn't been surprised at a piece of shocking news, and who'd sounded so scared at the thought of being overheard.

If there was a killer in the village, she'd rather try to work out who it was than discover the truth by accident, sitting opposite them in an otherwise deserted house.

CHAPTER SEVEN

Eve was cutting her way across the village green with Gus, en route to Saxford St Peter's only grocer's.

'Proper walk soon,' she said, looking down at him. She had a mission in mind for that too. Some searching online had led to a news report that pinpointed the place where Bernard Fitzpatrick's body had been discovered. She wanted to find out all she could about his murder. Taking time to maximise her background knowledge was second nature; the more you knew, the better you understood things. And it guarded against the unexpected.

Gus looked slightly disgruntled to find himself attached to his leash, and not dashing off into the woods or up the beach.

The store was housed in a squat building, painted in one of the traditional Suffolk pinks. Its upper-floor rooms were set into the eaves, just as they were in Elizabeth's Cottage. The building was topped off with red roof tiles. In the store's box bay window were numerous handwritten notices, advertising items for sale, babysitting services and the like. There was a full bowl of water outside for dogs, as well as a series of hooks so that pets could be left safely while their owners popped inside.

'Won't be long,' she said to Gus, in an undertone. 'And from what Viv said, you're lucky you can wait outside.' He looked mournfully at her as she secured his leash on one of the available fixings. She bent to ruffle his fur and was rewarded by a quick conciliatory lick.

As she walked inside the store, a bell that matched the one she'd heard at the teashop jangled loudly.

There were two people ahead of her in the queue to be served, so she took the chance to have a look round before introducing herself. Behind the counter she could see a woman of around sixty, buxom and well turned out, with short, layered auburn hair. Her mouth moved quickly and her darkly lipsticked smile was ever-present. To the woman's left, close to a side door which Eve guessed must lead to the storeroom, was a guy of a similar age, leaning against the wall. His wavy grey hair touched his collar, thanks to the way his shoulders were hunched inside his dogtooth jacket. He had the air of a tortoise that would like to withdraw into its shell as soon as possible.

Eve ran her eyes over the store's contents; better than she'd expected, if she was honest. At a glance she could see eggs, newspapers, wine, jars of preserves, olive oil, cereals, and a wide array of canned food. At the front of the store, on a table set into the window, was an array of fresh produce – not a massive range, but what there was looked good. She could smell the ripe tomatoes. To her left, a fridge hummed, keeping its stock of meats and cheeses cool. Eve grabbed a wire basket from near the door and chose some farmhouse cheddar and stilton, along with mushrooms, leeks and broccoli, and more pasta.

The first customer had paid for their goods now, and walked out of the store, setting the bell jangling again. She took her place in the queue and found herself listening to the exchange between the woman ahead of her and the storekeeper.

Moira – assuming it was the person Viv had mentioned – was leaning forward and grimacing.

'*My poor Polly.* We really feel for you. Such a shock. And I suppose you'll be looking for a new position now?' There was more than a hint of relish in her voice, which was also heavy with curiosity. If this was about Bernard Fitzpatrick's death, Eve could tell one person at least was treating it as a soap opera.

Polly… she rallied her mental resources. Yes, she was sure that was the name of Fitzpatrick's current publicity manager; the one who'd only been in post for a short time. She was an image to behold, even from the rear. She was wearing a figure-hugging black sundress that showed off her curves, and her high-heeled sandals were just as impractical as the shoes Eve had donned that morning. Her gleaming gold-blonde hair cascaded down her back in waves.

'Yes, it's knocked all the staff for six, naturally.' Her voice was tight.

Moira looked disappointed when she didn't elaborate. 'You'll have been visited by the police, I suppose? It must be quite horrifying, to be interviewed about something like that.'

'I haven't spoken to them yet. I imagine they'll approach people who knew Bernard the longest first. I suppose *you* must have known him a lot longer than me, Moira. Have they been to talk to you yet?'

Neatly parried. Moira's eyes opened wide and she put her hands on her hips. 'Oh, dear me. It hadn't occurred to me that they would.' She sounded quite excited.

'I'm sure they'll be along. How much did you say I owed you?'

The storekeeper was a bit pink in the cheeks now. 'Fifteen pounds sixty,' she said, breathlessly. Taking the woman's proffered twenty-pound note, she scrabbled in the till for the correct change.

As the woman called Polly turned to leave the store, Eve saw she was just as attractive head-on as she was from behind: heart-shaped face, delicate eyebrows and huge grey eyes. Her features were hard at that moment, irritation etched into them – but Eve could hardly blame her for that.

The storekeeper sighed as Polly left the premises, her gaze still on the departing woman, but in a second her attention switched to Eve.

'Good afternoon,' she said, in polished tones. 'Do forgive me, we've had a little local tragedy here and that poor girl is involved. That is to say, she worked for the famous musician who lived here and died just recently. Bernard Fitzpatrick – you might have heard of him? The shocking thing is, it turns out he was murdered!'

Her words had come out at high speed, robbing Eve of the chance to chip in any sooner. She introduced herself, and explained why she was in the village.

Moira's mouth formed an O. 'I should have guessed – but at this time of year we get some passing trade from tourists too.' She paused, then smiled. 'I'd heard you were an American.'

Eve wasn't sure what to say to that – or who might have told her. But of course, Viv had warned her that the news of her arrival would already have travelled.

'So' – the storekeeper drew the word out, her eyes full of anticipation – 'you're right in the thick of things, then. Tell me,' she leaned over the counter conspiratorially, 'how is poor Adam Cox bearing up?'

It was clear Eve would have to be on her guard each time she came in. 'I was only there on a professional basis – I'm afraid I don't know him well enough to judge.'

It took Moira a moment to rally. 'The police were still there, I suppose, when you visited? I heard that was this morning.'

Viv was absolutely right – she'd have no secrets in Saxford St Peter. London was so anonymous by comparison. For a second, she wondered how the villagers stood it. But of course, it cut both ways. If she could absorb Moira's information like a sponge without talking out of turn herself, she might be very glad of her as a source. 'I didn't see them,' she said, carefully, 'but of course, I was focused on my work.'

At that moment, the man who must be Paul shrugged himself still further into his jacket, muttered something indecipherable and disappeared through the side door.

Moira didn't even glance in his direction, so Eve guessed he was exhibiting standard behaviour. Instead, she smiled her lipsticky smile, introduced herself and explained that the man who'd departed was indeed her husband, Paul.

A second later they both heard a shout from the rear of the store. 'Get her to buy some of his stuff!'

Moira shook her head and raised her eyes to heaven. 'I've already told him that's all sorted,' she said. 'He's hoping you might want to take Bernard Fitzpatrick's regular order off our hands. It had just come in when we heard he'd drowned, and most of it's not the kind of goods the regular villagers will want.'

He must have been one of the people who'd managed to gain favour with the couple over the years then, Eve thought, remembering what Viv had said. Either that, or the income from the mark-up was just too tempting. It was time to turn the tables on Moira and ask some questions of her own. 'What kind of things did he ask you to supply?'

'He had a taste for champagne and caviar!'

'Not the kind of thing I normally go in for.' She didn't usually get the chance.

The woman nodded towards the door her husband had exited through. 'Of course; I quite understand. It's just that – you know – with you being a city media type and all that, Paul probably thought…'

Eve imagined Moira Squires' face if she could see her tiny terraced house in Kilburn, or her office at the inner-city state school where she did battle with paperwork and parents. 'But in any case,' Moira continued, 'it's all sorted out. I've cancelled his order for next month, and the vicar's taking most of the current supply off our hands.'

Interesting.

'He'll be holding a memorial service for Bernard, and he said he thought it would be "fitting" to serve food and drink that he would have enjoyed.' She sniffed. 'Seems a bit peculiar to me. Champagne at a memorial service? But that's the rector all over. There's some as would say he's not as pious as he should be. Not me, of course.'

Eve mentally added the vicar to her list of people she'd want to see. He sounded intriguing.

'And apart from *those* goods,' Moira went on, ringing up the prices for Eve's shopping, 'there's his specialist whisky. He liked an eighteen-year-old Bowmore.' She made a huffing noise. 'One bottle a month – regular as clockwork. I did think we'd be out of pocket there since it costs over a hundred pounds a bottle, but' – she gave Eve a look – 'the vicar said he'd take that too, which, say what you will' – and she would, Eve felt sure, to anyone who would listen – 'was a generous gesture. That just leaves a month's supply of Patum Peperium.' She wrinkled her nose. 'You know, the anchovy paste that goes on toast. *Very* strong and salty. But that's all right because Daphne Lovatt eats it too. She lives at Hope Cottage, diagonally opposite to the place you're renting. Shares the house with Sylvia Hepworth. Sylvia's a lady photographer and Daphne's a potter.'

Lady photographer? What century was Moira Squires living in? And she'd named Daphne's profession as though it explained everything, including the liking for anchovy paste.

Moira Squires started to weigh her vegetables on a set of old-fashioned scales with weights on one side. It would have driven Eve crazy, but the woman clearly had an experienced eye and knew almost exactly what combination of weights would be needed before she started each operation.

'How long have you had the store?' Eve asked.

'Nigh on thirty years.'

That explained it. 'You must be the hub of the village.' She felt her comment sounded like a transparent attempt to curry favour. Paul Squires' manner would hardly tempt the crowds in… but she could tell from Moira's expression that her words had been well received.

'Oh yes, we are. Everyone comes in here.'

Captive audience, thought Eve.

'We feel very involved when the village is hit by something like this.'

'I could see that from the way you spoke to the customer who was here before me.' Eve knew she was prying herself now, but she would need to talk to Polly the publicity manager, so it was all useful background.

Moira smiled and looked towards the front of the store again, as though the young woman had only just walked out. 'Poor, dear Polly. And she'd only just got her feet under the desk, so to speak. She can't have been there for more than a month.' She shook her head. 'I was interested when Bernard employed her. I'd heard that there were several *very* senior applicants for the role, whereas Polly, as you saw, is quite… youthful.'

'Plenty of energy and dedication, perhaps.'

Moira gave her a meaningful look. 'I'm sure you're right.'

'Was there much of a gap between Mr Fitzpatrick's previous publicity manager leaving and Polly taking up the role?' Eve was wondering just how many alternative applicants the cellist had turned down.

The storekeeper put her head on one side. 'There *was* quite a hiatus, as a matter of fact. His previous lady, Fiona Goddard – Fi – got a swanky new job offer. Publicity director at Thrushcroft Hall, where they do all the outdoor concerts. But in the end it fell through. I thought she might work for Bernard again at that point, but it didn't happen.' She looked frustrated at not having the full background. 'He continued to advertise for a replacement, and it was three or four months before Polly turned up.' She put all of Eve's shopping into the tote bag she'd brought with her for the purpose. 'I suppose he had something very particular in mind when he was looking for a replacement for Fi. Those senior applicants from further afield just didn't have it. Whatever *it* was.'

But it was quite clear that Moira had a firm idea of what Fitzpatrick had been after. It was all interesting, but it looked as though Fi Goddard had been good at her job if she'd landed a new role as a publicity director – even if it had fallen through. And there was nothing to say Polly was any less effective, despite her youth. Eve would need to find out more if she wanted to get to the truth.

As she walked outside to find Gus, she made a mental note to write down everything Moira had said. She felt as though she'd been thrown a tangled ball of wool. If she could pull out some of the strands and get them straight, she might understand a lot more about Bernard Fitzpatrick's relationships.

The take-home point for Eve was that Fi Goddard hadn't gone back to the PR job when her new position had fallen through. Or maybe Bernard Fitzpatrick hadn't invited her to, for some reason. Could she have been pushed, rather than walking of her own accord?

CHAPTER EIGHT

Gus leaped up from the shade where he'd been lying the moment Eve left the store, his tail wagging on overdrive. She unfastened his leash, waited while he had one more noisy drink of water, then walked with him across the green towards home.

'Well, she was easier to deal with than I'd thought,' Eve told him, after checking there was no one in earshot. All the same, she didn't like to imagine what Moira Squires might say about her to the next customer who walked in. She seemed to have a bad word for everyone – dressed up in the form of casual, harmless observations. If someone was going to be rude, Eve preferred them to be upfront about it.

As they entered Haunted Lane, she peered at Hope Cottage. Sylvia and Daphne were the occupants, then: a photographer and a potter. And one of them – Daphne, she thought, suddenly remembering the words she'd overheard the previous day – played the violin. She wondered if she'd get to meet them. They didn't relate to Bernard Fitzpatrick, as far as she knew, but they sounded interesting. One of their windows was open, but all was quiet at the moment.

Back at Elizabeth's Cottage, she paused briefly to unload the shopping and put it away, while Gus pottered to and fro, making his presence felt.

'I'm not reneging on my promise!' she said, as he got under her feet and fixed her with a series of appealing glances from odd angles. 'We'll be out of here again in two minutes, but it would be quicker if you didn't keep trying to trip me up. Honestly – there's no trust in our relationship.'

At last she let them out of the house, locked up the cottage again and turned right onto Haunted Lane, towards the estuary. On her phone, she checked the map she'd found in the article detailing the discovery of Bernard Fitzpatrick's body. After two minutes' walk, the lane, with its honeysuckle-covered hedgerows, petered out and they went beyond it, onto the path that ran towards the water.

'It's called Elizabeth's Walk, according to the map here,' Eve said to Gus. It was eerie to think that they were following in the footsteps she had taken, the night she'd smuggled Isaac to safety. Perhaps the woman had also gone back there afterwards, to look out over the water, and wonder if the boy had found a new home.

The vegetation changed as Eve walked on. At first, she and Gus made their way between spiny gorse bushes, their bright yellow coconut-perfumed flowers looking hot under the sun, but before long they were surrounded by reeds, lower on their left, between them and the estuary. On the mudflats, which were just covered by the water, Eve could see crowds of birds. She'd downloaded an app just before lunch so that she could try to identify the local wildlife. Consulting the section on waders, she spotted oystercatchers – with their black and white plumage and long red bills – and avocets – also black and white, with bills that turned upward at the end. Their cries filled the air. They were all out of Gus's range, safely across the water, so she let him off his leash and he bounded ahead of her, disappearing out of sight as the path turned to run alongside the widening River Sax, towards the sea.

After another five minutes' walk, Eve reached the spot identified on the map in the newspaper article, and called Gus back.

'We can carry on to the sea *in a minute*.' He knew 'in a minute', but she had to repeat it several times for emphasis all the same. 'This is important. Or at least – it might be.'

When she'd first looked at the image that appeared alongside the map, it had seemed fairly anonymous – reeds, water and mud – which would be an accurate description of most of the estuary. But now she examined it more closely, she saw there was a disused concrete mooring block, almost submerged in the silt. It was easier to spot in real life than it was in the picture. The news report said the pathologist had concluded that Fitzpatrick had gone into the water close to where he was found. As well as the damage from the fatal blow to the side of his head, his body displayed bruising, likely inflicted immediately post-mortem, consistent with striking an obstruction in the area of water where he was discovered. Initially it was thought he'd fallen in by accident, and that it was this that had caused him to lose consciousness and drown.

The time of death was estimated to be around midnight between the Monday and Tuesday of that week – nearly four days earlier. It was late to be out walking alone. She wouldn't risk it – even with Gus in tow. But she knew Fitzpatrick had been tall and sturdily built – if he slept badly and wanted some air, he'd probably have had no such qualms. Even if it seemed unlikely, it wasn't *impossible* he'd met with someone by chance. Her opinion hadn't changed from the previous evening though. The idea of Fitzpatrick being attacked by an opportunistic stranger still seemed far-fetched. Of course, he could have met an acquaintance coincidentally. But although Saxford St Peter was a small place, and bumping into people must be common, she couldn't imagine hordes of them tramping along the estuary path late at night.

Which left a planned meet-up. That made a lot more sense, as far as Eve could see. What other reason would he have to pick a route this far from his home?

'What d'you think, Gus? If you lived in High House, with the woods on your doorstep, and the heath and the beach just beyond, where would you go for a late-night stroll?'

Gus's look told her that he didn't care, one way or the other – he just wanted to get going.

'All right. We've seen all there is to see – go on then!'

He gave her a quick glance and sprang forward, his short legs propelling him onward at impressive speed.

As she followed him, she was sure she was right. She couldn't see Fitzpatrick crossing the village to reach the estuary path so late. That meant his trip there must have been prearranged. At his instigation? Or at someone else's? And why there? It was certainly more isolated than most places in Saxford St Peter. If the murderer had already decided Fitzpatrick's fate, that might be their reason for suggesting that location. Or if the rendezvous had been the musician's idea, then he must have wanted to keep it secret for some reason.

She frowned. Either way, he must have been happy to make for a location hidden away from prying eyes. Even if someone else had chosen the meet-up point, he must also have approved of it. He sounded as though he'd been arrogant. Had he failed to see danger where others might have spotted it?

Gus was on the beach now, tearing up and down, looking longingly at the seagulls and scampering in and out of the waves that broke on the shore. But Eve stood still and looked unseeingly into the surf for some time.

After half an hour, she knew they needed to make their way back. Viv had suggested coming to give her a knock at seven, ready to visit the Cross Keys for dinner. Eve had brought a ball to throw for Gus, and he wasn't tired of the game yet; his eyes were dancing.

'No more, buddy, but we're going out on the town tonight, and you get to play with the pub landlord's schnauzer.' Hopefully not too boisterously. She must stop obsessing about it.

Eve wondered about finding the path that led back through the heath for variety, but retracing their steps would be quicker, and she wanted some time to get ready. As before, Gus dashed ahead, nosing his way into the reeds, his back end sticking out, tail wagging. He'd just rushed on again when she returned to the spot where Fitzpatrick had gone into the water. If Gus hadn't been beyond her reach – and she'd had more time – she might have been tempted to turn on her heel and head back towards the coast. Because, there in front of her again, was the man she'd seen in the grand garden of the big house – the one whose eye she'd accidentally caught. She saw him jerk upright as Gus shot past him, but until a moment earlier, he must have been crouching down – he was tall, but she hadn't seen him beyond the reeds.

After looking in the direction Gus had gone, he turned, and his blue-grey eyes met hers, his glance cool.

She was going to speak with him this time. 'Good afternoon.' If she hadn't been so startled, she might have managed something more original – or useful. She really would want to talk to him if he'd been Bernard Fitzpatrick's gardener. But standing there, with him between her and Elizabeth's Cottage, she suddenly felt nerves tickle her insides.

He didn't return her greeting – and she didn't stop to analyse his expression. Instead, she walked swiftly past, as a crazy shiver ran through her. But however much she told herself she was being dumb, it was all she could do not to glance over her shoulder to check he wasn't following her – quite possibly with some kind of heavy object, raised high in his hand.

It was only when she got as far as the turn towards her temporary home that she dared to look. The man was nowhere to be seen, and Gus was waiting for her, halfway along Elizabeth's Walk.

She took a deep breath. *Get a grip, Eve!* Time to head inside, feed Gus and put some make-up on, ready for her evening out.

But as she stood in Elizabeth's bedroom, leaning down to apply mascara in front of the mirror that sat on a waist-high pine chest of drawers, she couldn't stop thinking of the gardener's eyes as they'd met hers. What had he been doing? Was he just a curious onlooker? After all, that was basically what she had been, even if she had good reason for her nosiness. Or was his presence more sinister?

She'd no reason to suppose he might have killed his boss, but it made sense that the murderer might revisit the scene of their crime. Unless Fitzpatrick's killer was supremely confident, they must be in an agitated state by now, wondering when the police might catch up with them. She thought again of the gardener crouching down next to the water. One cause for anxiety was bound to be the presence of any clues the killer might have left at the scene...

CHAPTER NINE

Toby Falconer's dog, Hetty, was not a miniature schnauzer. If anything, she seemed to Eve to be on the large side of standard. However, she and Gus *appeared* to be getting on well, though their antics were somewhat short of restful. For five solid minutes – it felt like longer – she'd been watching the jumbled, tumbling ball of dog, over by the window, poised to see if she'd need to intervene.

The reactions of the Falconer brothers had given Eve an instant impression of each of them.

Matt Falconer had roared with laughter but then ignored the situation and gone to talk to one of the regulars, allowing the man to buy him a pint. Toby, Matt's brother, had watched the dogs as he served, an amused smile on his face – but Eve could tell he was monitoring the situation.

Now, a Rubenesque woman in a stretchy low-cut black dress, with a red apron on top, arrived on the scene. Her hands were on her hips and her focus zoned in on the dogs as though she'd identified a target.

'Matt's wife!' Viv hissed. 'She and the boys run the place jointly.'

Eve was slightly concerned by the newcomer's expression. 'You said it would be okay to bring Gus in, right?' She'd lowered her voice.

Viv laughed as the woman marched over to the dachshund and Hetty. 'Of course it is! Don't worry about Jo. Her bark's worse than her bite. Which is just as well, in many ways…'

Jo addressed the dogs as though they were a pair of rowdy drunks.

'What on earth do you think you're playing at? Do I look the sort to tolerate this kind of behaviour in my pub?'

Eve leaped up as Gus cowered under the woman's gaze, but Toby Falconer was at Jo's side before she got near. He gave the woman a supplicatory look and she took a deep breath.

'Honestly, your puppy eyes are even more pathetic than your dog's.' There was a long pause, but at last his sister-in-law crouched down to address Gus, who'd flattened himself on the floor.

'It's all right. I wasn't talking to you!' She sounded as though she was cajoling a toddler now, but still at high volume. 'I was talking to Hetty. She knocked a glass over earlier and I could see she was about to do it again.'

Toby hung his head. 'My fault. I should have kept a better eye on her. But you're failing to see the business opportunity here, Jo.' Hetty nuzzled his hand and eyed the woman warily. 'If you let them carry on, I'll be able to sell tickets and popcorn.'

The woman's frown flickered and Toby laughed, which seemed like a risk as far as Eve was concerned. But after a knife-edge moment, Jo rolled her eyes. 'I don't know why I put up with you, really I don't.' But Eve could see the laughter behind her severe words now. Jo turned on her heel, walked back behind the bar and then through a door beyond.

Toby's wild black hair, streaked with grey, fell forward as he ruffled the fur round Hetty's neck and smiled down at her. The schnauzer tilted her head towards him. 'Hetty knows she has to quieten down once the place starts to fill up, don't you girl? But it's great for her to have some company.'

'I told Eve she shouldn't worry about Jo,' Viv said.

Toby smiled. 'That's right. Once you know what to expect it's okay. You get to sense when stormy weather's on its way!' It was clearly water off a duck's back as far as he was concerned. 'She won't normally mind the dogs having a bit of a game, so long as they don't go too far.'

The whole situation was unfamiliar to Eve. She'd never found anywhere indoors in her patch of London where she could let Gus play like that. He'd probably been repressed – which might explain his extreme excitement around Hetty.

The Cross Keys had tables laid for people to eat, but also couches in corners, bookshelves lining the walls and plenty of floor space. A grand fireplace was set into a huge chimney breast and soft lighting, shining down from lamps fixed to ancient dark beams, gave the whole place a cosy feel. The smell of good food and good cheer (in the form of local ale) filled the bar. But it was the pub's atmosphere that really set it apart. It was as though the Falconers had invited her into their home. She bet they were each exactly the same whether talking in private or to their clientele. Jo would speak her mind, without fear or favour, and Toby would welcome you calmly, as a friend, whether he'd known you ten minutes or ten years. And Matt, she sensed, would share a drink with anyone.

Gus followed Eve back to her and Viv's table, and settled down under it, though each time someone new came through the door, he emerged and was usually rewarded by a tickle on the tummy when he rolled over. Shameless hound! But no one seemed to mind. Even Jo smiled when she appeared briefly in the bar again, though with a slightly despairing shake of her head.

'She might be volatile,' Viv handed her a menu, 'but she cooks the most excellent food. I guess she channels all that passion into her meals – and the ingredients are too alarmed not to behave themselves.'

Eve scanned the menu. It was going to be hard to choose. There was a mix of seafood and dishes made with locally sourced farm produce. 'What part do the brothers play?'

'Toby helps out with most things, but the pub's bed and breakfast business is all down to him. He makes the most luxurious breakfasts, and the good news is you can come for them even if you're non-resident, so take note.' Her pink hair covered her face as she bent forward to scan the menu herself. 'Ah – and you should know that he supplies the village shop with fresh bread too. Moira started to get requests, so he expanded the batches he makes for the B&B clients. But you have to go early to bag any. He's good with the guests too; he's turned it into a very successful business.' She sighed. 'He was married. His ex, Carrie, used to work here as well. Toby's great, but I think she didn't realise she'd married the pub, as well as him, when she made her vows.'

'And Matt?'

Viv raised her head. 'Ah, yes… Matt. Well, he's the life and soul of the party, as you can see – and that goes down well with the patrons.' She paused. 'He's in charge of doing the books for the pub side of the business too. I get the impression he's not very organised about it though. Jo gives him hell when he's behind schedule.'

Eve could imagine. Matt looked the sort that might take a lot of chivvying. 'So "being generally friendly" is Matt's main contribution?' She wondered that the other two let him get away with it.

Viv smiled. 'Ah! He has hidden talents. Each of the Falconers acts as a linchpin for this place, in their own way. And, to be fair, I hate the organisational side of my business too. I put it off and off until something goes pear-shaped and then dig myself out of whatever hole I've landed in.' She laughed. 'My eldest, Jonah, used to keep me on the straight and narrow – he worked with me for a year after he finished uni, but he's opened a café of his own now, down in Kent.' She put her menu down. 'I think I'm going to have the battered skate. It's a fiddle to eat but it's always excellent.'

Eve's mouth was watering. She decided on the turkey, Blyth-burgh ham and leek pie with a red wine gravy. A moment later, they gave Toby their orders at the bar and took glasses of wine back to their table.

'I spoke to my reprobate brother earlier, by the way,' Viv said. 'His business is all sorted, so he's coming home late tonight.'

'Was his trip to do with the riding stables?' Eve remembered Viv had said he owned some, though she'd yet to find them.

She rolled her eyes. 'No, not this time. Simon's a bit of a serial entrepreneur. He was tying up a loose end to do with a business that he sold on. Watching my organisational skills at the café makes him cringe. Anyway, I expect he'll be round to say hello. I can confidently predict that by the end of tomorrow he'll have offered to take you on the Black Shuck tour.'

'Black Shuck?'

'We're back to ghosts again.' Viv's blue eyes twinkled. 'According to legend, Black Shuck is a dog that's meant to roam the coasts and countryside of East Anglia. Blythburgh's got the top story associated with him, in my opinion. Back in the 1500s, Black Shuck was supposed to have stormed into the church there, killed a man and then left scorch marks on the north door, which you can still see.' She met Eve's sceptical look and laughed. 'I know, I know. But I'm not going to ruin a good story by casting doubt on its reliability. Anyway, Simon's very fond of showing people where the beast's meant to appear here in Saxford – near St Peter's Church.'

'Hmm. Well, thanks for the warning.'

Viv grinned. 'So, I hear you visited Moira and Paul at the shop earlier.'

'Seriously? You weren't kidding when you said news travels fast here.'

'How did you get on? Moira had the frown of a woman thwarted when she spoke about you, so I'm guessing you managed to dodge her questions all right.'

It was Eve's turn to smile now. 'Yes. I had to stay very focused.'

She nodded. 'Moira was convinced you'd be the go-to person for a round-up of Bernard Fitzpatrick-related intelligence.'

'And vice versa – going to see her was a good tip, thanks.'

All in all, Eve's research was shaping up nicely. She'd checked her email before she'd gotten ready for the pub and found that Fi Goddard, Bernard Fitzpatrick's former publicity manager, had replied to her request for an interview. One phone call later, and she'd set up a visit with her for the following day. Interestingly, she lived at the large house with the silver birches and Scots pine in the garden, so she'd get to see inside the place. She'd sent another message to Adam Cox to ask for Lucas Booth's contact details. She'd explained he'd be of interest, as someone from the trust that would now run Mr Fitzpatrick's house. She still wanted to understand the dynamic between them; she needed to see the dead man in the round to make a good job of her obituary.

At that moment, Eve saw a young man approaching their table, carrying platefuls of food that smelled out of this world – rich with flavour.

'That looks amazing,' she said, when he was in earshot. The guy smiled and checked which dish was for whom before setting them down.

Viv raised her glass as he retreated. 'Cheers, bon appétit!'

Eve watched the guy walk back towards the bar and ran her eyes idly over the other clientele. It was only then that she sensed something was up. Was it her imagination, or were they all watching her and Viv's waiter too? She noticed a woman on a nearby table indicate the young man subtly with a flick of her head, whereupon she and her companion drew closer together and started a conversation. And they weren't the only ones.

Thanks to her staring, Viv turned in her seat and picked up on the interest too.

She frowned. 'What's going on? Cole Wentworth's a good-looking boy, but he seems to be causing more of a stir than usual this evening.' She glanced behind her, towards the bar. 'There's Toby again. I'm going to catch his eye and ask him.'

Before Eve knew it, the publican was at their table.

'Sit down, sit down,' Viv said, in a stage whisper. 'Eagle-eyed Eve here noticed that your handsome young barman's the centre of attention this evening.'

Eve felt herself blushing. Toby would think that's how *she'd* referred to him, now – and he was young enough to be her son. *Great.*

Toby dropped into the chair between them, gave Eve a speculative look and grinned. 'Ah – you haven't heard then?'

Viv's eyes opened wider. 'Don't tell me you've got information that I don't yet have. I hate it when news comes to light after the teashop closes. It puts me at such a disadvantage. So, what gives?'

'I shouldn't be spreading gossip about a member of staff!'

Viv gave him a severe look, before jerking her head at the other clientele. '*They* already know, clearly! I'll find out at opening time tomorrow. You might as well tell me now.'

He shook his head, a smile playing round his lips. 'All right, you win. It's just come out that Bernard Fitzpatrick was Cole Wentworth's biological dad. Sounds as though Cole's mother, Adele, moved in some of the same circles as Bernard, way back when.' He turned to Eve. 'Cole and Adele have been in the village for years now – but she'd still have been a Londoner when they got it together.'

'Wow.' It was Viv who breathed out the word, but Eve was thinking it too. The supposedly childless Fitzpatrick had been a father after all – yet still he'd left his house for the benefit of his adoring public. Could Adele have kept the truth from him? Surely the possibility must have crossed his mind.

'Do you happen to know if either Cole or Bernard were aware of the fact?' she asked. 'I won't write anything you tell me, of course, but I might ask Cole if he'd be willing to give me an interview, and I don't want to put my foot in it.'

Toby's glance met hers. 'From what Cole says, Bernard was aware, but he and Adele kept Cole in the dark. His mother's only just admitted the truth. Adele was married at the time of the affair and her late husband brought Cole up assuming he was his own. Now I know the background, I guess Adele must have moved here to be near to Bernard.'

At that moment there was a commotion at the door, interrupting their discussion. A gaggle of men and woman had appeared. They were talking loudly, laughing, swearing and ignoring the locals. Some surged towards the bar while others dallied, blocking the doorway.

'Hacks.' Toby raised an eyebrow. 'It has to be said, I shan't be sorry when the vultures fly back to London.' He glanced at Eve quickly. 'Hell. Sorry. I don't include you in that – I hope it goes without saying. But we had more in yesterday evening and you can imagine the sort of stories they're after. Ones that won't do anyone any good.'

Eve waved away his apologies, but her heart sank at the appearance of the journalists. Toby might distinguish her professional role from theirs, but a lot of Fitzpatrick's contacts wouldn't.

Toby glanced over to the bar. One of the mob had spotted Cole Wentworth and was calling out questions to him. They must have heard the gossip then. Cole was engaging with them, but the situation looked stressful.

Toby leaped up. 'I'd better go and take the heat off. He shouldn't have to cope with this on top of everything else. So long, you two.'

In another moment the press pack were discussing the copy they'd be filing, ordering spirits and making comments about the price of the food. Eve cringed, but there was nothing to be done. She'd just have to convince everyone she was different. She turned her mind to the news of Cole Wentworth and Bernard Fitzpatrick's relationship. It was more than interesting, under the circumstances. Even in the ordinary way, the situation would have made Eve curious. When you were writing about someone famous, it was rare for something completely new to come to light.

'So, have you any more background on Cole and Adele?' she asked Viv.

The woman grinned. 'There, I can help you. Cole has being doing odd jobs here in the village since he finished his studies, and she's a former high-ranking civil servant – I think she advises on various government panels now, that sort of thing. For large consultancy fees, judging by her wardrobe. A lot of people move here when they want a change of pace, so I'd always assumed that was why she'd relocated… They came a couple of years after her husband died, when Cole was in his mid-teens. After I was widowed, I sometimes wished I could decamp too. It's oppressive when everyone treats you differently because of what you're going through… But this puts a whole new spin on things. Adele's got a house right on the edge of the village on Smugglers' Lane, down in the woods, and Cole lives with her. She likes to keep herself to herself when she's here.' She looked at Eve curiously. 'What do you do, when something like this comes out?'

The rules never varied. 'I have to be sensitive, of course, but objectivity and truthfulness are important. We're not in the business of writing eulogies – but no one's after a character assassination either.' It could be hard, sometimes. You had to make it clear you weren't a bereaved person's friend, or their counsellor. Let them think that and they forgot your professional purpose. 'In a case like this, it's obviously very personal, but it's already set to become public knowledge.' She gestured to the newshounds milling round the pub. 'And I'm not yet aware that anyone will suffer from the fallout, given Adele's husband is dead.'

Viv frowned. 'I can't see that they will either,' she said at last, taking a sip of her wine.

And given that fact, Eve wondered why Adele Wentworth and Bernard Fitzpatrick had kept Cole's parentage a secret.

CHAPTER TEN

Eve let herself back into Elizabeth's Cottage, her head still full of what she'd learned that day. Gus flopped into his dog bed, which she'd put in a quiet corner of the kitchen, next to his bowls.

'Not surprised you're worn out after that scramble with Hetty, not to mention parading around in front of the locals.' She bent down to make a fuss of him. 'Shameless! But I love you anyway, so count yourself lucky.'

He stretched out, pushing his legs against the soft sides of the bed, and looked ecstatic to be where he was. Eve was strangely tired too – it must be the change of scene, or maybe the sea air. She went to sit down on one of the comfortable couches in the living room and reached to the side table, where she'd left her laptop. She needed to type up all the information she'd gathered so far; get it straight in her mind. She slipped off her pumps, put her feet up and opened her existing file, ready to run through the people of interest one by one.

She began by adding the latest information she'd gathered about Adam Cox: his previous complaints to Viv about poor pay and his new role as custodian of High House.

Fi Goddard came next. She noted that Fitzpatrick's former publicity manager's new job had fallen through, but she hadn't returned to her role at High House, despite her position still being vacant at the time. It would be interesting to know why; it might tell Eve something about the cellist. She was looking forward to adding more, once she'd spoken with the woman the following day.

After that she put in a heading for Cole Wentworth, now revealed as Fitzpatrick's illegitimate son – a fascinating potential interviewee, if he'd be prepared to talk to her. She might wait a day or two before approaching him; the poor guy was clearly under siege right now. She put his mother, Adele, in the same section. Might she speak with Eve? It would be a big ask. She'd have to see.

The fourth heading went to Lucas Booth, whose interactions with Fitzpatrick must have been so delicate, over the trust's role in High House's future, but who'd clearly lost patience with the man – at least on one occasion.

And then came Polly Cartwright – the musician's latest publicity manager – whom Moira Squires had hinted won the job for her looks rather than her talent. Eve was treating everything the storekeeper said as questionable, and if she was correct in this instance, the attraction had probably been one-sided. Polly hadn't seemed unduly cut up about her boss's death. All the same, she might have a different slant on the cellist's personality.

Lastly, she added the man she assumed was Robin Yardley, Fitzpatrick's gardener, who'd seemed so interested in the spot where Fitzpatrick had died. The addition brought her up short. It had nothing to do with the obituary she needed to write, but everything to do with the musician's murder.

And then she saw the way she'd ordered the list, with the resentful secretary Adam Cox at the top. Of course, he was the only one she'd visited so far, but he also had the clearest motive for Fitzpatrick's murder that she knew of.

Just under Adam on the list, giving in to what her subconscious had been doing, she added the mystery woman she'd overheard on the beach, with a question mark next to her. The two top suspects…

Her mind tussled with possibilities, questions and hunches.

The sound of her phone ringing almost made her jump off the couch. Ian. *Really?* She let the call go to voicemail.

She couldn't ignore the notification that sat there malignantly on her screen though. What if it was something important? She dialled to pick up his message.

'*Eve, why didn't you text back? I need to speak to you urgently. I've just heard that the musician guy you're writing about was murdered. It's made the national news. I'm sure the magazine won't expect you to carry on under the circumstances. I imagine they can get the same result by googling his background. Staying and putting yourself in danger would be reckless – but also selfish, don't you think? The police are the only people who should be interviewing the crowd who knew him. Having you blundering around will slow up their investigation.*

'*I hope you'll have the sense to get back to London and your proper job. I'm surprised the school hasn't lost patience with you for dashing off. It's not like you to be so dizzy. And I also—*'

Eve ended the call. *Blundering around? Get the same results by googling?*

No amount of googling could let you glimpse the essence of a subject's character. The fact that Ian had never bothered to understand her career was symptomatic of his attitude to her. He was wrapped up in himself. That was why he found it so hard to believe she could cope. He probably couldn't imagine anything more awful than being without him. Admitting that she was flourishing would be beyond what his ego could take.

Facing up to the facts – the ones that had been staring her in the face for years before they split up – sent adrenaline coursing round Eve's veins until she felt she could burst with frustration.

No more.

As it was, if she was careful, she could produce a first-class obituary on a very unusual subject, and even – possibly – find clues that might lead to the arrest of Fitzpatrick's killer. She wanted to be of use and true to her profession. As for Ian, he'd surpassed himself this time. He needed to butt out.

*

Eve found it hard to relax that night – and not just because of the adrenaline rush Ian's message had caused. Writing everything down was her way of shelving thoughts, knowing she'd gotten them nailed, ready for future use. But the records she made didn't usually relate to a murder victim. The information she'd gathered whirled round in her head and pulled her back from sleep each time she got close. Once again, she thought of the police who'd be working on the case. The person covering the investigation's mailbox had emailed back with admirable speed, thanking her for getting in touch and inviting her to contact them again if she heard anything she thought might be significant. *They take me seriously.* Should she tell them that she was sure his secretary, Adam Cox, must have resented Fitzpatrick, and that he'd benefited from the man's death? Or that she'd heard an unknown man and woman talking suspiciously on the beach – possibly about the news of the musician's murder?

It didn't seem right, on either count – it would be too leading, and the facts might well be incidental. But sitting on the information also felt wrong. What if she did nothing and there were consequences?

At last, she must have drifted off. But after what felt like only minutes of fitful sleep, she was awake again, her heart racing, thudding heavily in her chest.

She thought she'd heard someone running outside the window. The sound of multiple feet, thudding past Elizabeth's Cottage, down Haunted Lane. She picked up her phone and checked the time. Two thirty.

Damn the ghost story – it had eaten into her consciousness. What with the unsettling situation, she'd conjured up imaginary echoes of the past. She shook her head. How could someone as

level-headed as her fall prey to this kind of thing? She flung back
her sheet and blanket, put on the bathrobe she'd left on a chair,
and went to pull back the curtains and look out the window. All
was quiet, of course. Taking a deep breath, her heart rate steadying,
she went to her bedroom door. She might make a hot drink, and
try to get sleepy again. But as she pulled the creaking cottage door
open, she heard Gus whine. The plaintive sound was followed by
a low growl.

Of course, it was only natural that he might be disturbed too.

'We're not in Kilburn any more,' she said wryly, as she went
downstairs to stroke his fur and rustle up a hot chocolate.

CHAPTER ELEVEN

The following morning, Eve woke early and lay still in her bed, conscious of the birdsong outside. The fears of the night before felt crazy now that there was daylight and signs of life beyond the curtains. The blackbirds and song thrushes must be in the hedgerows, out on Haunted Lane, but she could also hear the more distant eerie cries of the seabirds.

It was Saturday and she knew Ian was likely still asleep, his phone on silent. She settled down to compose a message.

There's no need for us to be in touch all the time now that we're apart. Probably best for us

You, she thought as she typed it – *you!*

to take step back now. Not to cut off ties, of course,

She wouldn't want to make the twins sad…

but to move on with our own lives. Healthier that way. Don't worry about the murder. I'm getting on with my job and the police are getting on with theirs. They've asked me to let them know if I discover anything useful.

I have a role here – and they realise I might be able to help, so stick that in your pipe and smoke it.

Enjoy your weekend.

She got a quiet satisfaction out of keeping her temper under control – outwardly at least. She wondered whether to message the twins. If they'd seen reports about the murder, they might be worried. If they hadn't, then she didn't want them to focus on it, but it would be just like Ian to pass on the news.

In the end, she opted for a pre-emptive message. She made it clear that the killer was probably someone who'd had a grudge against Fitzpatrick, and that she was keeping her head down, though listening out for anything important.

Before she got up, she checked the news on her phone for mentions of the murder, hoping that the police might have a lead, but there was no comfort in the reports – they said enquiries were ongoing. There was a quote from the lead officer on the case asking for witnesses. Apparently they hadn't found the killer's weapon.

Half an hour later, she was clean, dressed in jeans and a white T-shirt, and outside her cottage with Gus. The results of a quick coffee, combined with the clear fresh air filling up her lungs, put a spring in her step and heightened her senses. There was nothing like getting outdoors for a bit of perspective. The twins had replied, urging her to take care, but applauding her efforts.

She turned her attention to Gus. 'This is not just a walk,' she said, as he trotted ahead of her on his leash, 'it's a fact-finding mission. I value you for your own sake – you know that – but it has to be said, you are also the perfect decoy for a bit of unobtrusive snooping.'

He looked at her and wagged his tail, oblivious to the way she was taking advantage of him. It cut both ways though: she frequently felt he saw her as a glorified treat dispenser.

They'd reached the village green, and she let Gus's extendable leash out as far as it would go. Viv's teashop was to her right. She glanced over to see if there were any signs of life from her cottage next door, but the curtains were still closed. She'd noted the previous day that the teashop opened for business each morning at ten, but Eve had the impression that Viv's relaxed attitude to life meant she tended to cut things fine. She smiled for a second. If she was in charge she'd already be on the premises, double-checking everything.

She took a moment to savour the tranquillity of her surroundings. Sun shone on the three oaks and wide expanse of healthy lawn in front of her. Under each tree, hexagonal wooden benches provided a quiet place to sit and think – and would give welcome shade when the summer sun was at its height. The air was full of the fresh smell of the grass. The green had four sides, but there was nothing regular about it. Three of the four were lined with houses painted in a range of Suffolk pinks as well as creams and blues, thatched roofs side-by-side with the red tiles that seemed to be favoured in this part of the world. Set in amongst the homes were Viv's teashop on one side and Moira and Paul's store on another. On the fourth side of the green was St Peter's, the church tower rising majestically above every other building. There were ruins next to it that also looked ecclesiastical. It was certainly atmospheric. For a second, she wondered whether Viv's brother, Simon, really would take her on the 'Black Shuck tour'. She shook her head, as Gus looked up at her. She couldn't make up her mind if she was horrified or amused by the idea. She guessed Viv had exaggerated the likelihood anyway.

'Right,' she said to the dachshund, peering at the folded map of the village she'd found in one of the cupboards at Elizabeth's Cottage, 'let's go down to the beach, through the woods.'

There was an extra bounce in Gus's step as they crossed the green towards the road that led east to the coast. They were going to walk along Smugglers' Lane. In amongst the trees, just before they reached the open heath of gorse and heather that separated the woods from the beach, she expected to find the house belonging to Bernard Fitzpatrick's former lover, Adele, and their illegitimate son, Cole.

The lane turned into little more than a track, the way dusty and narrow. Eve let Gus off his leash and looked ahead to see if she could pick out a gap in the pine trees that might indicate the presence of the Wentworths' residence.

Gus had dashed ahead of her when at last she reached a clearing, and saw the place that must be theirs. Trees pressed in close on the village side of the house and to the rear. It was a grand construction – modern and architect-built, she guessed: all large windows with an atrium in the centre. Out on the drive sat a shiny black Porsche Panamera and a red Mercedes. The garden had a large swimming pool in it. Viv had implied Adele Wentworth was wealthy, and given her high-powered career it made sense – but Eve hadn't expected anything quite so grand.

It was 8 a.m. now, and the curtains in the house had been drawn back. There were windows open both upstairs and down, and Eve could see that someone had started to set a variety of breakfast things on an outdoor table.

As she walked slowly on in the direction Gus had headed, she heard someone playing the cello. Was this Cole, following in his dead father's footsteps? A moment later, the woman she assumed must be Adele Wentworth appeared, holding a pitcher of orange juice. It must be Cole who was playing then. Eve hurried on before the woman caught her staring. The beautiful melancholy music faded, leaving only the birdsong and the sound of the sea somewhere ahead of her.

As the trees thinned out, Eve emerged into unbroken sunshine, lighting the pinks and purples of the heather that spread over the ground, interspersed with the bright yellows of the gorse. Ahead, she could see Gus's head rising up above the vegetation periodically as his bounding enthusiasm took him at speed towards the beach. Eve kept an eye on him, but her mind was on the Wentworths too.

She'd written down all her conclusions and questions about the pair the night before – along with the notes about Fitzpatrick's other contacts. But now she let the points filter through her mind again as she reached the dunes, stepping past a clump of yellow horned poppies and onto the pebble-strewn sand. The twinkling sea stretched wide in front of her – it looked as endless as the possibilities swirling in her head.

Toby at the pub said Cole Wentworth had been unaware of his relationship with Bernard Fitzpatrick until after the musician had been killed. Of course, if Cole had known all along – and been down to get a nice, fat inheritance from the guy – then he'd have good reason to lie. Even if he wasn't guilty of his murder it might make him look that way. But taking into account his and Adele Wentworth's house and cars, she couldn't imagine him being desperate for cash. Of course, if he'd secretly known his father's identity, he might also have resented him very bitterly – if the man had refused to acknowledge him, for instance. But did that work as a motive for murder? Why would Cole act now, if he and his mother had been living a stone's throw from Fitzpatrick for years? If Cole had found out the truth suddenly, by accident, and the pair had gotten into a fight, she could just about see it – maybe. But Eve still felt Fitzpatrick's murder had been premeditated. To assume that the cellist just happened to be in such an isolated place, late at night, with someone predisposed to turn violently angry towards him, who then just happened to find a suitable object to use as a weapon, in the dark, amongst a tangle of reeds and mud – well, that seemed way too far-fetched.

If Cole really hadn't known Fitzpatrick was his biological father, Eve still wondered why neither the cellist nor Adele had told him, and why his mother had decided to move to the village. Maybe they'd agreed it would be best for Cole not to know, for some reason, but Adele had wanted Fitzpatrick to see something of his son. Or maybe the musician had wanted nothing more to do with either of them, and Adele had taken up residence in Saxford St Peter to try to make him feel guilty. In that scenario, Adele might have a motive for murder – frustration and anger could have built up. But again, why act now?

Either way, she couldn't see why the secret should matter much. Fitzpatrick had never been married, and having an illegitimate child wouldn't have damaged his reputation – people didn't care about that kind of stuff much these days. It might have led to a few column inches of coverage, but if anything, it would probably have added to Fitzpatrick's mystique. And given Adele Wentworth's husband was dead, he was beyond hurt too.

She frowned. If Cole really had only just found out, it looked likely that it was his biological father's death that had triggered the revelation. Perhaps he *had* left him something in his will. That would explain the timing.

Gus had paused in his running up and down the beach, and turned to look at her.

'Sorry. I'm coming!' She ought to make the most of being by the sea, just as he was. In another minute, she was dashing up and down with him, laughing, her Converse rapidly shipping sand. What with the wind and the sound of the gulls, she only realised she'd received a text when she took out her phone to check the time.

It was from Ian.

What's brought this on? It's healthiest for us to still be in regular contact, surely? Never mind. We can catch up when you're back and feeling better.

Feeling better? She was feeling fine. Or at least, she had been.

A moment later, a second message came through.

As regards the murder, what happened to the level-headed Eve I used to know? I can only hope you'll see sense and reconsider.

For a second, she started mentally composing a colourful reply, her heart rate ramping up, but then she took a deep breath. *Let it go…* Unexpectedly, she found herself smiling, her irritation gone. Looking ahead at the expanse of sea in front of her, what she felt was freedom.

CHAPTER TWELVE

The sun was high in the sky and the temperature was rising by the time Eve walked Gus back towards home. But it wasn't like it was in London, where fumes hung in the oppressive air and the sheer numbers of people ramped the heat up further. There was a constant breeze in Saxford St Peter, thanks to its proximity to the coast. Mostly it was as unlike Seattle as a place could get, but the air coming off the sea was enough to remind her very gently of what had once been home.

Eve was walking slowly up Dark Lane, pausing as Gus investigated an interesting smell, when she saw two police officers in a patrol car. Dust flew up from their wheels as they pulled to a halt further up the road.

As she drew level with the house that seemed to have attracted their presence, she saw Adam Cox outside. He was talking to one of the officers who'd emerged from the car, a bulky plain-clothes man in a suit, with salt-and-pepper hair.

The secretary-turned-custodian's normal pallor was tinged with red, his mouth tight, eyebrows drawn down.

'Who called you?'

'A Mrs Lennox, who lives on Love Lane. She noticed your side window had been forced and when she knocked on your door, she didn't get a reply. You were out, sir?'

As Cox explained his new role at High House, and how he'd had to be at work on a Saturday, thanks to urgent legalities and inventories to be tackled, Eve drifted over to the other side of the lane, walking as slowly as she could. Saxford St Peter was a peaceful village. She couldn't help wondering if Cox's break-in was somehow related to the Fitzpatrick affair. She strained to hear the conversation, while surreptitiously casting her eyes towards the scene.

'And you're certain nothing's been stolen, sir?' the detective was saying.

'That's right.' Eve watched as a fleck of spittle flew from Cox's mouth and landed on the officer's lapel.

'It might be worth having one more careful look round. It's only twenty minutes since Mrs Lennox called us. You can't have had long to check.'

Cox raised his hands level with his face and spread his fingers in a gesture of what looked to Eve like despair and extreme frustration. 'It's… I…' He paused and looked over his shoulder. 'Everything's been roughed up. Disturbed. But I can't abide clutter, so I don't allow my belongings to build up. I can assure you, there's nothing missing!' His voice rose in pitch. He was getting more agitated, not less. 'That was why I didn't call you myself.'

'I understand, sir. But if your belongings have been ransacked perhaps the intruder was looking for something in particular?'

'I'm not a rich man,' Cox snapped. 'I don't have gold and silver lying about the place.' His eyes widened and he snapped his mouth tight shut.

The officer eyed him curiously. Eve had taken out her phone and was having a mock text exchange, while keeping herself as hidden as possible, standing just beyond an informal hedge of deep pink roses, their heady scent filling the air. Thankfully, Cox and the detective were too involved in their exchange to have noticed her.

There was a long pause. It looked as though Cox was trying to master his feelings.

'Can I ask, sir,' the officer said, 'what brought you back home from your work at High House? Did someone call to let you know you'd had a break-in?'

Cox opened his mouth, then closed it again. 'I – er – I realised I'd forgotten some paperwork. I dashed back to pick it up and found all this.' He gestured towards his home.

At that moment the second officer from the patrol car appeared at the doorway of Cox's house. He must have been having a look round inside.

'Graffiti on the sitting room wall, sir,' he said to his colleague.

The first detective raised his eyebrows.

'Bright red spray paint. Says: "Sucks to be you".'

The red tinge in Cox's cheeks darkened and Eve could have sworn she saw the senior officer's mouth twitch.

'So it's possible whoever broke in just wanted to create havoc, rather than to steal something. Can you think of anyone that might act in this malicious way, sir?'

Cox's jaw was working, his eyes were beady and snake-like. She saw him draw in a deep breath, but at last he said: 'No.'

'We can probably assume it was someone who was aware of your movements – knew that you'd be working over at High House this morning.'

Cox was twisting his hands together. 'I went to buy a loaf of bread at the village shop earlier. Moira Squires asked about my plans for the day and I mentioned it then.'

It could have been round the whole village in half an hour in that case. But there was a look of realisation in Cox's eyes that made Eve wonder. Had someone he knew been in the store with him?

The investigator sighed. 'We'll get our people to talk to your neighbours – see if they saw anything – but in cases like this, unless there's a witness, I'm afraid we might not find the culprit. There was a time when we'd have sent a team to dust for fingerprints, but I'm afraid our budgets don't stretch to that these days, even when something *has* been taken. It's usually a case of claiming on insurance for any losses or damage, and taking steps to increase your home security.'

Most homeowners would express outrage or disappointment, at the very least, at the lack of official action, Eve guessed. The senior officer was looking keenly at Cox, almost as though he was testing him.

'Whoever did this doesn't deserve the attention of the police,' Cox said. 'I wouldn't want to waste your officers' time with a door-to-door enquiry. I will claim on my insurance, as you suggest.'

The officers both nodded. 'As you wish, sir,' the senior one said.

Eve walked on past Cox's house as they finished their conversation, but she was close enough to the patrol car to hear the detectives' final exchange as they got in.

'So much for it being related to the murder,' the older one said. 'We shouldn't have bothered turning out – uniform would have done. Disgruntled girlfriend, I'd guess.'

The younger one gave a low chuckle. 'You're probably right, sir. I'll get you back to the station.'

Eve spent the rest of the walk, up Dark Lane and across the village green, deep in thought. If a disgruntled partner of Adam Cox's had been responsible, a police investigation and the attendant gossip would be the last thing he'd want. And he'd certainly been dead against them investigating the matter any further. But she'd gathered from Viv that Cox didn't have a partner, and that she couldn't imagine him being with anyone. That presumably meant she wasn't aware of him having had a girl- or boyfriend in the past, either. He didn't look the passionate type. And then there was his visit home, so soon after the passer-by had spotted his forced window. She glanced at her watch. She didn't buy the custodian slipping back for paperwork he'd forgotten. He was organised. She bet he normally packed his briefcase the night before and went through what he'd need systematically. Her guess was that whoever had graffitied his house had called him to rub his nose in the fact.

And then there was the desperation in Cox's voice as he'd told the police there was nothing missing – even though he'd hardly had the chance to check.

Either he understood the motive of his intruder well enough to know theft wasn't on their agenda… Or? Or he knew exactly what they'd taken, but he didn't want to make a fuss about it.

Which might mean it was something embarrassing – or something he'd come by dishonestly himself.

What on earth was going on? And how did it tie in with Fitzpatrick's murder?

CHAPTER THIRTEEN

Eve had snatched an early lunch, and was just about to google for more background on Fi Goddard when she heard the knocker go on the door of Elizabeth's Cottage. She put her laptop down on the coffee table and went to open up. Gus – who'd stopped barking and was now wagging his tail – went with her and peeked out from behind her legs as she pulled the door back.

The man in front of her was of medium height and slim build, with dark-brown hair, brown eyes and a ready smile.

'Eve?' He put out a hand. 'Simon Maxwell. I'm so sorry I wasn't here to welcome you when you arrived. I gather you've already met my weird sister?'

'You make her sound like something from *Macbeth*!'

His grin was as infectious as Viv's. In other ways though, they were like night and day. Simon had none of the rebellious quirky style of his sibling. He was wearing tailored trousers and a crisp white shirt, open at the neck. He looked rather smartly dressed for someone who owned a riding stables. Mind you, Viv had said he was a serial entrepreneur. If he was doing well at it, she guessed he had employees who were more actively involved.

'Viv left me some lovely shortbread when I first arrived, and she's plied me with free tea and cake since then, so I've been well looked after.'

'I'm glad to hear it. I'd have liked to be here myself. My hours are normally more flexible than Viv's, but last-minute business called me away. I expect she mentioned it?'

Eve nodded. 'She said it wasn't to do with the riding stables.'

'That's right. I had an interest in a property venture down towards London, but I've just sold it on. Cashflow was an issue.' He patted the doorframe of Elizabeth's Cottage with his right hand and sighed. 'That's one of the reasons we need to get this place on the market soon.'

'It's a beautiful house.'

He smiled, and she noticed the attractive twinkle in his eyes. Eve was glad Viv had warned her about him; she might have been quite susceptible, otherwise.

'It certainly is. I can send you the details if you're interested?'

'Ah – I wish.' Eve said it automatically, to be polite, but just for a second, she imagined what it would be like to actually live there. 'My life's down in London.'

He raised his shoulders – the shrug was regretful rather than dismissive. 'Ah well. So, I gather you're writing about Bernard.' His smile had faded now, and for a second he looked lost. 'I'm still not over the shock of hearing about his death, and now – to return to the news that he was murdered…' His glance met hers. 'Viv and I were saying how awkward it must be for you, knowing that the person who finished him off might be one of your interviewees. She said I should give you all the local gossip I can muster, in case it helps. Forewarned is forearmed, I suppose.' He hesitated for just a moment. 'Have you seen my stables yet?'

She shook her head.

'Perhaps I can tempt you to a walk across the village? I can show you round and give you my twopence worth on the Saxford St Peter set-up?'

Gus had heard the word 'walk' and was no longer hiding behind Eve's legs; he'd sneaked round the front and was making up to Simon Maxwell in the most shameless fashion, fluttering his bushy eyebrows. You'd think he'd be ready for a rest; he'd only been home for an hour. But the new surroundings seemed to have set him on overdrive. As for Eve, after what Viv had said, she felt even a walk with Simon somehow equalled falling for his patter. But she was curious to see the stables – so long as she didn't have to get up close and personal with the horses. As far as she was concerned it was unnatural to want to climb aboard skittish and unreliable creatures whose backs were so far from the ground. But she was safe: she couldn't possibly be expected to ride in the fitted dress she'd changed into, ready for her visit with Fi Goddard that afternoon. And of course, getting Simon Maxwell's village gossip was tempting. Murder or no murder, finding stuff out was her stock in trade.

'That sounds nice – I mean, useful. Thanks. I'll grab Gus's leash. I just need to be back for two thirty – I've got an appointment with Fi Goddard.'

It was a mellow and glorious summer's afternoon. Out on the village green, people were now occupying the hexagonal seats under the old oak trees, and a family and their West Highland terrier were playing French cricket in one corner. The terrier's role seemed to be stealing the ball and running off with it, to much hilarity from the other players, except the father of the family, who was getting peeved. Cue more laughter from his nearest and dearest.

Simon suddenly turned to her, his head on one side. 'Would you like an ice cream?'

The question was so out of the blue – and his look so boyish – that she almost laughed. It had been years since she'd had an ice cream on a stick, out of doors. 'All right – that sounds nice.'

She waited with Gus in front of the village store while Simon went inside. Two minutes later he reappeared with a pair of Magnums. Beyond him, over his shoulder, she accidentally caught the eye of Moira Squires. That was that then. She and Viv's brother might have only just met, but their low-key walk would be all over the village within the hour. She could imagine what Viv herself would say.

'Here we are,' Simon said, handing her the ice cream with a smile. He reached down to make a fuss of Gus before opening his. They left their wrappers in Moira and Paul's bin and continued on their way.

'So,' Simon turned to her, 'what can I tell you? I should start by saying that I didn't know Bernard all that well. He didn't mix very readily with the villagers – though he did once come and ask me about learning to ride.'

Eve was surprised. 'No one's mentioned his hobbies up until now.' *Unless you included baiting people.*

'Ah,' Simon took another bite of his Magnum, 'well, don't add that one. He had a look round the stables, and within half an hour he'd changed his mind. He never took lessons.' He shook his head. 'I was relieved, to be honest. It's too easy to break something if you come off – especially if you're not used to horses. I had visions of him smashing a hand or an arm and having to give up professional playing. I felt he was the kind that might try to sue.' He smiled. 'In business, you end up with a sixth sense about the sort that tend to cause trouble.'

From everything Eve now knew, she imagined Simon's instincts were sound.

They'd left the village green behind and were walking down Dark Lane, past Adam Cox's house. All was quiet there now. Eve guessed he must have secured the forced window and gone back to work; presumably he'd have a lot of tidying up to do that evening.

After checking again for any signs of movement, Eve turned to Simon. 'Do you know Adam Cox at all?'

He frowned. 'Not well, but I bump into him quite frequently – at fundraisers at High House, in church and so on.'

'Do a lot of the villagers attend St Peter's?'

Simon grinned. 'A higher percentage than you might imagine these days. Have you met our vicar?'

'Not yet, though I've heard a bit about him.' She remembered Moira Squires' comments about him taking Bernard Fitzpatrick's regular order off their hands.

Simon laughed. 'I'm not surprised. He divides opinion, but he's remarkably good at drawing in the crowds. Enter his orbit and you'll see what I mean!' His look turned sober again as he met her eye. 'You mentioned you're seeing Fi Goddard this afternoon. The dynamics between her and Adam Cox are interesting.'

'Really?'

'Adam always told everyone he was in overall charge of the staff at High House, at least administratively – but I never got the impression the balance of power was that way round between him and Fi.' He sighed. 'He's a bit of an oddball, I can't deny that, but there was no excuse for the way she wound him up when they worked together. I thought she might give it a rest, once she left Bernard's employment, but no. Just last week, she was at it again. I can hear her now, after he tripped over a gravestone outside St Peter's: "Dear old Adam, you *do* keep us all amused!" His expression afterwards really struck me. It wasn't anger; it was hatred.' He shook his head. 'And yet he never lets go – bottles his feelings up.'

For a moment Eve's mind slid to Ian. She'd battened down her feelings too, but now she'd acknowledged what she really felt, there was no going back. Maybe one day Adam would lose the firm control he had over his emotions. Or perhaps his boss had pushed him over the edge, and he already had.

Was it likely? It depended on exactly what had gone on between them, but based on character she could see it. She'd covered obituary subjects with similar temperaments to Adam in the past. In her experience, that sort could cope with all kinds of frustrations without giving anything away, but if they finally cracked, the results were dramatic. One guy she'd written about, the patron of an international charity, had been unremarkable for years, then finally made the front pages when he'd lost it in front of an audience of politicians and minor royalty. She'd seen the footage. If it had happened in another setting, she could imagine he might have turned violent. She had a feeling Adam Cox had been cast in the same mould.

'You've heard the news about Cole Wentworth, presumably?' She ate more of her ice cream, hoping she could manage the bottom section without spilling cracked bits of chocolate down her dress.

Simon's eyes widened. 'Too right, I have. Another shock. It's funny,' he went on, 'I've lived in this place since I was kid, and I've always thought it was so dependable, somehow. I love the tranquillity of the Suffolk countryside. But then, within the course of four and a half days, everything I thought I knew has been knocked out of kilter. All that time, there were undercurrents running just below the surface, and I was totally unaware.' He shook his head. 'It makes me wonder what might happen next. Viv said you live in London, so I suppose you see crime all the time.'

Eve nodded, and hastily ate the last precarious bit of ice cream. She was feeling pretty pleased with herself. Sticky fingers and dress spillage avoided, thank you very much. 'It's true, I guess there's bound to be more crime in a big city.'

'It makes sense.' Simon looked thoughtful for a moment. 'But in a way, I shouldn't be surprised that something so violent has happened here.'

Eve glanced at him. 'Why?'

'Everything's concentrated in a village. If things get out of hand, there's nowhere to run to. People are forced together in a way that they aren't in London.'

'That's true.' Eve had always thought of cities as her spiritual home, when it came to opportunities for people watching. Her whole career was built on being able to intuit the way their minds worked, so she could ask the right questions and pinpoint the information she needed. But in some ways a village had more to offer. Instead of having the sheer numbers and variety of people that you got in London, you saw a smaller, tightly interknit group up-close – under a microscope. The interactions you could monitor gave a lot away. That effect must be accentuated if you were present all year round, and understood the history behind the relationships.

'Going back to Cole,' she said, 'I gather he's working in the village now that he's finished at university?'

Simon nodded. 'That's right. He read music up in Manchester – which of course makes even more sense, now we know Bernard was his father. Must be a family talent. He graduated a couple of years ago, then went off travelling, I seem to remember. After that he came home, and he's been doing odd jobs ever since. He took on a stint for me at the stables in fact, mucking out the horses, grooming and suchlike. He seems bright, very reliable. I wondered why he wasn't applying for anything more permanent, but it might be that he's waiting for his big break in music. Perhaps if you really mind about your art, you'd rather just do dead-end jobs to get some pocket money, and keep all your energies for what you love best.'

'Could be.' She knew all about dead-end jobs for pocket money.

'And if you've seen the Wentworths' house, you'll know that he and his mother don't need the cash. He probably likes to earn something to have some independence, but I doubt his rate of pay means much to him.' He laughed. 'It certainly won't be my wages or the ones he gets at the pub that paid for that Porsche in their driveway. That belongs to him. Even the insurance must cost an arm and a leg.'

It made Eve think. 'I wonder if Bernard Fitzpatrick could have been contributing towards Cole's upbringing – via his mother – even if they kept the relationship secret.'

Simon frowned. 'It could be – but I hear that Adele comes from a wealthy family. Add to that her past earnings as a government official, and what she gets now from after-dinner speeches, consultancy work and the like, and I'd say she wouldn't have needed his money.' They weren't that far from the Wentworths' house now, and he moved a little closer to Eve. 'She's a formidable personality – the absolute opposite of needy.' His voice was low.

Eve wondered again if there was any chance the woman would give her an interview. But to be fair, would Eve be willing, under the circumstances? Some lovers wanted to feature in an obituary if they felt the need for acknowledgement or validation, but Adele Wentworth didn't sound like that sort.

At that moment, Eve looked up and caught sight of a figure she recognised, across the lane from where they were standing. He was at the door of a small cottage with a beautiful, informal front garden, crammed with foxgloves, hollyhocks, roses and night-scented stock. She hadn't seen him walk up the road, so presumably he must have been tending the plants before letting himself back into the house.

She caught Simon's eye and gave a very slight nod towards the man. He raised an eyebrow in return. They turned off Dark Lane then, and Eve followed Simon along a dusty track, edged with cow parsley, and sporting the occasional pile of horse manure, leading her to guess they'd almost reached their destination. 'Was that Robin Yardley – Bernard's gardener?'

'And just about everyone else's too,' Simon agreed. 'Yes, that's his cottage.' There was a curious look in his eye. 'Have your paths crossed already?'

Eve explained about Adam Cox's list of contacts and how she'd seen Yardley tending what she now knew to be Fi Goddard's garden.

Simon nodded and smiled. 'You see, there you are again. Everyone knows everyone here. There are umpteen little connections – the difficulty is working out which ones are significant, I suppose.'

'That's what I'm finding. It's not my role, of course, but getting a handle on the set-up here feels like a sensible precaution.' She thought again of Ian's ridiculously alarmist message. She was going to tackle things her own way – and that simply meant being thorough with her research and going into things with her eyes open. It would be fine. 'What's Robin Yardley's background? Has he been in the village long?'

Viv's brother frowned. 'A good while. Ten years or thereabouts? As to his background – that is a village mystery. It's as though he has no past. I haven't the foggiest idea what he did before he came here. Even Moira at the shop doesn't know, which as far as I'm concerned means no one does.' He rubbed his chin. 'The one exception, I suspect, is the vicar. He and Yardley appear to know each other, and Jim Thackeray – that's our rector – vouches for him.' He sighed. 'That's enough for some people. And I – well, I want to believe that too. But I don't know. Surely it's a bit unnatural for someone to be so secretive? The fact is, Jim likes his good causes. I can't help wondering if Yardley was in trouble once, and Jim has taken him under his wing. That's great – obviously. Everyone deserves a second chance. But it's hard not to speculate about what he might have done in a past life. And he's in and out of everyone's gardens the whole time, of course. Anyway, here we are, and at last I can provide you with a compost bin for that ice cream stick.'

Eve dropped it into the green barrel-shaped container that stood next to a red-brick house with climbers up its walls. 'Thanks.'

'This is my place.' His tone was warm. 'Let's go and see the horses.'

A narrow drive ran between Simon's house and a field, behind which was the stable yard. Eve took in a palomino and a bay grazing outside, more animals in the stalls and a chestnut in the yard being groomed by a young blonde woman. Each of the animals would tower over her if she went up close, so she decided not to do that.

Horses had a mean streak. Gus had no such qualms. It was just as well she'd got him on his leash. The blonde woman looked up and smiled.

'You might like to come over for a ride one day,' Simon said.

'Mmm. I'll bear it in mind. Thanks.'

He met her eye. 'Not a fan?'

'The last horse I went near trod on my toe and tried to eat my scarf. It's somewhat personal now.'

He laughed. 'Not to worry then.' He paused for a moment. 'By the way, has anyone told you about our local legends yet?' His engaging smile was present again, worryingly effective. Just as well Eve knew what was coming. She was ready.

'Well, Viv's told me about the footfalls you're meant to be able to hear out in Haunted Lane.'

'What about Black Shuck?'

She couldn't suppress a giggle.

Simon raised his eyes to heaven. 'Don't tell me my wicked sister mentioned I might ask?'

Eve nodded.

'She is *such* a tease. Honestly, it's just as well we're good friends, or I might go and take one of her cupcakes and—' He was laughing. 'I don't suppose you'd like to come along and see where the dog's meant to appear anyway? It's an atmospheric walk.'

If he hadn't laughed so hard when he realised Viv had set him up, she might have said no, but in truth it was quite tempting. She certainly wasn't going to take Simon Maxwell seriously, but after all, she was partly on vacation. It felt like a long time since she'd let her hair down.

Simon must have sensed weakness. 'It's best as an evening walk, but there's supposed to be a storm coming in tonight – and tomorrow the vicar will be holding his post-evensong drinks. What about Monday? I could come and pick you up at nine? Sunset's around then. And after we've explored we could nip to the Cross Keys for a quick drink.'

She nodded at last. 'Okay.'

'Excellent. And I'll have another think between now and then. See if I can dredge up any more local knowledge that might be useful to you.'

As Eve walked home, she banished all thoughts of ghostly dogs and spirited Simons from her mind. It was time to go and find out what Fi Goddard might reveal about her former boss. After what Simon had said about her relationship with Adam Cox, Eve wondered what to expect.

CHAPTER FOURTEEN

At two thirty on the dot, Eve walked past the silver birches and Scots pine to reach the door of Fi Goddard's home, Melgrove Place. She was curious to see inside, and to get a second report on Bernard Fitzpatrick from a former employee. She'd have to consider the background when listening to Fi Goddard's opinions though. The woman had left her job with the musician for the role that had fallen through, and when she'd found herself out of work, he hadn't taken her back. It might not have been that way round, of course – the decision not to return might have been hers. But to an outsider, it looked as though she'd suddenly become less desirable as an employee, for whatever reason. If Fitzpatrick had caught her in some act of wrongdoing, which had then leaked out and scuppered her chances elsewhere, she might have complex feelings towards the dead man.

Eve smoothed down her black fitted dress, straightened the matching jacket, and knocked on the door.

It was all she could do not to react when she saw the woman who opened it. Fi Goddard was one half of the couple she'd overheard on the beach, the day she'd arrived in Saxford St Peter. She might have only seen her from behind, but there was no mistaking the gleaming red hair and that hourglass figure. In that moment, the disturbing conversation came back to her. And then she thought of the notes she'd made on Fitzpatrick's contacts, and how she'd subconsciously put them in order, listing the ones she thought most likely to be guilty of his murder first.

The mystery woman on the beach had been second – because of that overheard exchange – and Fi Goddard third, as a result of the oddities around her departure from the cellist's employment. That hadn't seemed like much – just a vague notion that might be relevant. But now it turned out the second and third suspects on her list were one and the same person.

She tried to squash the thoughts. There was no time to consider it now; she needed to think straight and cover her feelings. 'Thanks so much for seeing me.'

Fi Goddard took her hand in hers and shook it, displaying nails that were perfectly manicured in pale coral polish. 'My pleasure. Do come in.'

There was no sign of the man she'd been with on the beach, but Eve could see items that indicated a permanent male presence in the house: a heavy grey overcoat, a trilby hat on a stand, men's formal lace-up shoes, and a traditional golfing umbrella. Was the companion she'd been with her husband? A moment later a photograph on the mantelpiece in the living room answered the question. There they were together, around ten years earlier perhaps: she all in white, holding a bouquet, and he in a tailcoat. Once again, Eve noticed the marked difference in age between them.

She'd only glanced at the picture momentarily, but her interviewee had caught her look. Her eyes were amused when they met Eve's.

'My husband, Andrew. He's out just at the moment, but he didn't know Bernard well, so I doubt he'd have much to contribute.'

'Of course.' But Eve couldn't help wondering if it might suit Fi Goddard's purposes not to have him around. He'd been angry on the beach; he might react oddly if he heard her say anything that worried him. Whereas Fi looked like a woman in control – of course, as a PR expert she'd be well-versed in presenting the image she wanted to get across. And she'd probably dealt with the hacks from the tabloids before Eve had caught up with her. She might feel facing an obituary writer was low-key by comparison.

'Can I get you a drink?' Mrs Goddard said. 'Gin and tonic? Vodka? Whisky?' Then she read Eve's expression and added – with a slightly sardonic look in her eye – 'or a sherry perhaps? Forgive me. You're not like any other journalist I've met.'

Eve quite liked the idea of her interviewee wading into her supply of spirits – she could see them lined up on a round table, to the right of the window. It would help the conversation flow. But caffeine or something cool and refreshing would suit her own purposes better.

'A soft drink maybe? Cold would be fine,' she said.

Fi Goddard looked amused. 'If that's what you'd rather.' She left her alone.

Her absence gave Eve a brief moment to scan the room. The furniture all looked antique and she could smell potpourri in the air. She spotted it a moment later, a quality mix of dried roses and lavender. There were several ornaments around – an ornate gilt clock sat on the mantelpiece, between brass candlesticks – but no dust. She bet Fi Goddard had a cleaner – she certainly looked wealthy enough to afford one, and she wouldn't have such pristine nails if she did much housework herself.

On a mahogany chest of drawers, Eve spotted a range of high-end holiday brochures – all current, for tours with upcoming dates. For a moment her mind ran back again to the beach conversation. Fi Goddard's husband – Andrew – had agreed to give their marriage one last chance. Perhaps they were planning a romantic break together as part of the healing process. The destinations looked exotic: Fiji, French Polynesia, St Lucia. *Nice.* She wasn't sure what Fi Goddard did for a living now, but she guessed it paid better than part-time admin work in the local school.

Hastily, she moved back to where she'd been standing as her hostess returned to the room with a bottle of still, artisan lemonade – its label handwritten – and two tall glasses, which looked like they'd been in the freezer.

Fi poured a helping for each of them, but went to add vodka to hers. 'I think I might need it,' she said. 'Although I left Bernard's employment six months ago now, the news of his death, and especially the circumstances, have been a huge shock.'

Eve watched the woman's eyes closely, and she did see something there: a quick rush of emotion, damped down so fast that it was impossible to judge what was going through her mind.

Fi motioned Eve to a Regency-style chair. Everything in the room looked valuable, and there was a sedate quality to the house. It made Eve wonder if the contents represented Andrew Goddard's style, rather than his wife's. There was nothing sedate about Fi.

'So,' her hostess said. 'How may I help?'

Eve explained how she needed to supplement the official career information she had on Fitzpatrick with personal reminiscences. 'How long were you with him for?'

'Six years.'

'And what was he like, personally?'

'Full of life and passion – a perfectionist, but with huge charisma and a big personality. Lots of fun, but he could be a harsh critic too. You'd expect it, I suppose – he was a very high achiever and he got impatient if other people failed to live up to the same standards. It was because he treated people as his equals – if he hadn't it would have come across as patronising. You had to take him in the round; I didn't find it a problem.'

That last sentence made it clear some people had – as Eve was aware. 'It must have been a difficult decision to move on?'

'Of course,' Fi agreed. She nodded three times, which seemed like overkill. 'The job was enjoyable, but in the end, I decided I'd like a change. I get bored quite easily. Who wants to stay in the same position forever? That said, of course I left with mixed feelings – it was a great role, and he was an inspiring person to be around.'

That was fair enough – but the sequence of events still bothered Eve. If she'd genuinely enjoyed her work for Fitzpatrick, it looked more likely than ever that it was he who'd refused to take her back. But maybe it was simply that he hadn't liked her leaving him – some employers could be very territorial and never forgive what they saw as a betrayal.

'What's your fondest memory of Mr Fitzpatrick?' she asked. If she kept on digging, would Fi Goddard crack and say something that showed he'd been possessive or unreasonable?

But the woman's face was full of amusement again. 'That would have to be when I set up an interview with the *Daily Reporter*, where their journalist ended up referring to Bernard as "the most genial and modest man in music". He roared with laughter at that – and cracked open a bottle of champagne on the spot, to celebrate my unequalled skills.' She lounged back in her beautifully upholstered chair.

Eve smiled. 'He felt the description was a little over the top?'

'He thought it was a hoot!' Fi Goddard said, sloshing back half her vodka and lemonade in one go. 'Which shows he took himself less seriously than people might think.'

That was all very well, but he'd only done that in private – with Fi Goddard, over champagne. To the outside world, the persona she'd created for him had remained intact. What Fi was telling her now would probably come across as self-deprecating when she wrote it into his obituary. It would sound as though he'd modestly laughed at the idea of a journalist paying him such a compliment. And of course, as an expert in PR, Fi would be aware of that. But the impression Eve was getting was of a man who hid his real nature. It would fit with what the Blackforth Arts Trust member, Lucas Booth, had said to Viv about him rarely showing his true colours.

'Did you and Bernard see much of each other after you left your job at High House?'

Mrs Goddard took up her glass again. 'Not so much. Of course, he was always manically busy, and I have been too.'

There was something slightly less natural about her words now – as though she was improvising.

'It was interesting to talk to Adam Cox yesterday,' Eve said. 'I understand he'd been with Mr Fitzpatrick a number of years, like you. He obviously decided to stay on.' She was hoping the woman might respond with a telling comment – not for the obituary, but to help with the unofficial murder enquiry she'd embarked on. That was what it was, in essence. She hadn't needed Ian's message to make her face facts. The sun was shining outside, but the village that contained thatched cottages and Viv's cakes – a place where she'd found peace, for the first time in ages – was also likely home to someone who'd clubbed a man to death. She suddenly felt protective of the place, and struck by her reaction. She'd never connected with Kilburn in that way.

'Ah, Adam!' Fi stood up, and for a moment Eve thought she might be about to reach for the vodka again, but in fact she just stretched and walked over to the window for a moment, her hands on the sill, her eyes on the lane outside. 'I'm afraid his reasons for staying might not be as – straightforward, shall we say – as they appear to be.' She turned to face Eve again, silhouetted in the sunshine that penetrated the room. 'He was stuck there.'

Eve frowned. 'I'm sorry, I don't—'

Fi held up a hand. 'It was his own fault, don't be in any doubt about that.' She shook her head. 'Four years back, he made a massive mistake. Bernard was down to play an exclusive concert at a stately home just outside Milan – or so he thought. Two weeks before the performance it came to light that Adam hadn't finalised the venue booking properly. All the publicity had gone out – the

VIPs attending had been sent their directions. Of course, if it had been a traditional concert hall, it would have come to light much earlier, when someone tried to book a ticket. But Adam had issued bespoke invitations direct.' There was a twinkle in the woman's eye. 'It was the most glorious, spectacular cock-up.'

'What did you do?'

'Adam managed to arrange a back-up venue at short notice, but of course it wasn't a bit what Bernard had had in mind, and all the guests had to be sent corrections and apologies. It made us look ridiculous.'

Eve was in no doubt how badly that would have gone down with the cellist. 'Mr Fitzpatrick didn't sack Adam, though?' She was surprised, given the impression she'd gotten of the man.

Fi shook her head. 'That's right. But although he let him stay on, I don't think he'd have felt able to give him a good reference. Adam's been at High House ever since. He always claimed the error was the fault of the administrator at the venue, and pointed out how he'd never made a mistake before, but well' – she laughed – 'he would say that, wouldn't he?'

As Eve walked home, she reviewed what she'd learned at the interview. Fi's information explained a lot. Adam had made one big mistake (if it *had* been him at fault) and that had meant Bernard Fitzpatrick could hang on to him and treat him as badly as he liked, knowing he was in a position to sully his name with any future employer.

And at that moment, her mind switched to Fi herself. She'd gone for her new job, but never taken up the role – and not gone back to High House. Could Fitzpatrick have pulled the same trick on her?

If so, that left two people whose lives had been controlled by the dead musician – but now his reign of tyranny was over.

Fi Goddard had laughed a lot when she'd talked about Fitzpatrick. Eve hadn't seen bitterness in her expression. But some people could put on a good act – and a PR professional was more likely than most to be capable of that.

She needed to dig more deeply. She was on the brink, she knew that; about to cross a line. If she really wanted to find out what had happened to Bernard Fitzpatrick she'd need to go well beyond her original remit.

Blundering around… It was going to take her a long while to put that infuriating comment behind her. If Ian had wanted to put her off, questioning her professionalism had been a bum move.

CHAPTER FIFTEEN

Eve sat at the dining room table in Elizabeth's Cottage, with Gus at her feet, and indulged in a Google-fest. She made notes as she worked, and then – when it was late afternoon, and she guessed the teashop might be less busy – she went to see if she could grab a quick word with Viv. Apart from anything else, she might have heard about her interactions with Simon, and Eve wanted her to know she'd agreed to the Black Shuck tour with her eyes open. It wasn't Simon's charm that had done it. *Though he had been charming...* She might not admit that.

There were still people sitting at the iron tables outside the teashop when she arrived: a couple looking at each other over a few chocolate crumbs and empty teacups, and an elderly lady sitting opposite a young boy. A granny treating her grandson to a slap-up tea, Eve guessed.

Inside, Viv caught her eye immediately and dashed forward. 'I'm glad you're here. I gather Simon called on you!'

'Things still look busy.' Eve glanced over Viv's shoulder. There was a girl with spiky blonde hair on the till.

Viv grinned. 'That's Kirsty, Sam's girlfriend. They're both doing extra shifts before they go off on their travels – they need to make money while they can. She's got it all covered; we can chat.' She raised an eyebrow. 'And I wouldn't miss this. Simon tells me he *is* taking you on the Black Shuck tour!' She chuckled. 'He had a go at me for sending him up behind his back, too.'

'I couldn't stop myself from laughing when he suggested it. But it'll be fun.'

Viv looked severe, but then relented. 'Okay – he's a nice guy really, so long as you don't take him seriously. And' – she cocked her head – 'I get the impression some country air and activities might do you the world of good.'

Eve was faintly affronted. Did she look pasty, or grumpy or…? 'Why?'

Viv laughed again. 'Calm down! You just seem a bit tense, that's all.'

Eve felt she'd just reinforced that impression with her snappy question. And perhaps there was something in what Viv said. 'Ian – my ex – has me down as a type A person.'

'Type A?'

'The stressy sort who's more likely to self-destruct due to high blood pressure and that kind of thing.'

'Nice!'

'Like I said, he's an ex.'

'Recent?' There was a knowing look in Viv's eye.

'Divorce came through six months ago. We have twins in their twenties.'

She nodded, like a doctor whose diagnosis had been proved correct.

'Cake?' she asked. 'It's excellent for people with insulting exes called Ian. I can recommend the raspberry with orange drizzle today.'

'That sounds amazing. You must let me pay this time.'

'You can pay me in news.' Viv fetched their refreshments to save Kirsty the trouble. 'Let's sit in that corner there, out of the way. How's the interviewing going? Any more thoughts about Bernard's murderer?'

It took Eve five minutes to fill Viv in on the recent developments.

'And I've just spent an hour googling for background information on all the main players,' Eve added, taking a sip of her tea.

'Anything useful?'

'I'm not sure – but it adds to the picture. I was curious about how Adele Wentworth and Bernard Fitzpatrick met. I didn't get anything concrete on that, but Adele mixed with a high-powered set back then. It was relatively early in her career, but she was already a government advisor, sitting on important committees, reporting to cabinet ministers and so on. And Fitzpatrick had a political connection too – his brother's a lawyer who works for the Attorney General's office. So' – she shrugged – 'maybe their circles overlapped. I'm hoping to talk to the brother on Monday, so I might find out more then.' She'd called his work number earlier and left a message. 'And during that period Fitzpatrick was the up-and-coming darling of high society. He did some receptions and that kind of thing, so their paths could have crossed that way as well. After that, I looked up Adele's late husband.'

Viv sat forward in her chair. 'What's the story there?'

'He was in government. Something high up in the Foreign Office.'

'What an influential gang! As for the husband, maybe he was away a lot.' Her new friend gave her a meaningful look.

'Quite possibly.' She returned it. 'Anyway, he was a lot older than Adele, and his parents are both dead, according to Wikipedia. They were in the public eye also. But now, there really is no one left to feel upset about Cole being Bernard's illegitimate son.'

'Still wondering why they kept it from him?'

Eve nodded. 'I'm assuming Bernard left him some kind of bequest, and that's why it's come to light now.' She took a bite of her raspberry and orange drizzle cake and wished it could last forever. There was something about the mix of sweetness and tart tang that made it perfect. 'Your cakes are to die for, just in case you didn't realise.'

Viv grinned. 'I did, but thanks! So, when will you speak to Cole?'

Eve shrugged. 'Soon, I hope. I need to approach him, but I'll have to be tactful.' Still, she could do tact in the same way that Viv could do cakes. 'After I'd googled the Wentworths, I tried to find out more about what Fi Goddard's been doing since she left her job at High House. She has her own website, promoting herself as a freelancer…'

'But?' Viv sipped her tea.

'The client list is interesting. It's almost all untraceable individuals. There are only three companies mentioned, and two of those don't have a web presence.'

Viv's eyes opened wide. 'Blimey – you have been digging deep.'

Eve found herself smiling. 'Goes with being type A. I'm thorough. It's a bonus when it comes to researching my subjects.'

'Or sleuthing! So, wait a minute – you're saying Fi Goddard has invented clients for her website?'

'Looks that way.'

Viv's brow was furrowed. 'That's just weird. I mean, I always got the impression she was red-hot, professionally. Why would she need to fake something like that?'

Eve looked at her meaningfully. 'If she couldn't rely on Bernard for a reference maybe, and just wanted to give the general impression she was in demand? I can't help wondering what went on between them before she left High House, and if he had anything to do with the job at Thrushcroft Hall falling through.'

Viv nodded slowly. 'That might fit, actually. They always seemed to get on like a house on fire when she was working with him – or so I thought – but there was a bit of a scene between them at the church hall, during one of Bernard's charity dos, soon after she'd left.' Her eyes were focused on the middle distance, as though she was caught up in the memory. 'It seemed to be a spat that blew up over nothing, but there were certainly harsh words. I remember catching Fi's husband's eye accidentally. I think we both felt uncomfortable. It was like watching a soap opera.' She shrugged. 'I didn't think too much of it at the time. I mean, I already knew Bernard could fly off the handle on occasion, and Fi never does things by halves.' She met Eve's eye. 'But if Bernard stopped her from taking up her new role – wow, that would have made her angry.'

Eve just nodded and Viv's eyes opened wider.

'You think she might be guilty?'

Eve finished her first cup of tea and Viv topped her up.

'It's a possible motive, isn't it?' She sighed. 'On the one hand, Bernard's interference wouldn't have affected her financial stability, from what I can see. I looked up her husband, Andrew.'

Viv nodded. 'You know he's a retired celebrity divorce lawyer, then?'

'Uh-huh.' It had been an interesting discovery. She'd immediately thought of Andrew Goddard's words on the beach. He'd told Fi she must never muck him around again, then added something like: 'You know what I'm capable of if you do.' Eve had thought he'd been threatening Fi with violence – but had he been promising to end their marriage, and leave Fi with next to nothing? Either way, the tone he'd used made her shiver.

'It certainly explains their lavish lifestyle. But Fi struck me as the kind who'd want success in her own name. She said she got bored eventually, working for Bernard. That might have been an excuse, but I can't imagine she'd be happy sitting around at home all day, drinking cocktails. And if Bernard did have some kind of hold over her, what might he have done next?' She took a sip of tea. 'The thing is, when all this got started, I contacted the police, just to let them know I was around.' She explained the response she'd had. 'It seemed so straightforward at the time, but now what do I do? I don't feel at ease with sending them a bunch of information based on hearsay, supposition and rumours. It's the same with Adam

Cox. Fi's report suggests he was firmly under Bernard's thumb, and had been for years. Maybe something happened to make him crack. But should I really be passing on what's effectively gossip to the authorities?'

Viv nodded. 'I see your point.'

Eve thought back to the dream she'd had the night before, in which she'd heard the footfalls of the men who'd chased Isaac, out in Haunted Lane. She wasn't going to tell Viv about it. The fact that she'd *almost* thought she could still hear them after she'd woken made her sound fanciful at best. But even if she'd imagined the whole thing – and Gus had too – the thought pricked her conscience. She didn't believe in omens, but she didn't need the sound of thudding feet to tell her the village might be in danger.

'I've thought of a way I might be able to find out more about the job Fi was offered – and why it fell through,' she said at last. If she managed it, it ought to help her decide about contacting the police.

'Really?' Viv leaned forward, her eyes sparkling.

'It involves being economical with the truth.'

Her friend grinned now. 'I like it! I think you should take a walk on the wild side.'

'Hmm, thanks!'

She laughed. 'Do you think it's justified?'

Eve nodded.

'And that not doing it might be worse than going ahead?' She raised an eyebrow.

'Yup.'

'Sounds all right to me, then. Are you going to tell me what it is?'

Eve closed her eyes. 'I'll wait and see if it works, first.'

Viv heaved a deep sigh. 'I suppose I'll have to be satisfied with that, though I—' Suddenly her gaze fixed on a point somewhere over Eve's shoulder, and a look of dismay flooded her face. 'Damn!'

'What?'

'Behind you,' she hissed. 'It's April, Moira Squires' sister. I'd forgotten she was coming in.'

As Viv spoke, Eve turned to see a woman with immobile blonde curls homing in on the counter and speaking to Kirsty.

Viv winced as Eve turned back to face her. 'What does she want?'

'She's come to show me her carvings, in the hope that I'll stock them.'

Before she could say more, Kirsty ushered the woman to their table.

'Thank you,' Viv said, with a rictus smile. 'April, how lovely to see you, and to get the chance to look at your – er – art.' She got up and walked across the teashop to the crafts area, mouthing *help* at Eve over her shoulder.

It was hard to resist following, both in response to Viv's pitiful look and because Eve was curious. Viv performed the introductions, and a second later, April was pulling out item after tissue-paper-wrapped item from a blue cotton tote bag she'd been carrying. There were at least thirty pieces.

April had started to unwrap the first one with a look of excited anticipation on her face. The object she revealed was certainly wood – and it was indeed carved, after a fashion.

'Paul said he couldn't even tell what it was!' April said. 'That had me and Moira laughing!' She was giggling now, in fact.

Viv gave Eve a desperate look.

'I'd have said that wasn't the most important thing anyway,' Eve said, pulling words from the air and hoping more came after, to complete her argument. 'After all, with art it's often whether or not you feel an instant connection with a piece that makes the difference.'

April beamed. 'That's just what I think.'

It didn't help Viv though – apart from removing the need to hazard a guess as to what April had been trying to represent when she'd whittled the thing. She was unwrapping more of the items now. Some of them looked a little bit like wooden gummy bears, after they'd been sucked for some time.

Eve ran her eyes over the contents of Viv's selection of crafts. The goods were eclectic: from beautiful lustreware bowls and crackle-glazed vases in deep colours, to carefully crafted felt animals that would appeal to children. But in one corner, tucked away from the main displays, was a rather odd collection of knitwear, some dark-brown coasters, and something unidentifiable covered with feathers.

It was clear that Viv lacked the right defences to deal with the Aprils of the world.

'So, what do you think?' the woman said, with a radiant smile.

Eve knew it was time to step up – to do something in return for all the free tea and cake. 'They're unique,' she said, leaping in before Viv could open her mouth. 'Forgive me for butting in, but I'm just visiting from London, and I'm seeing your work as an outsider. What Viv has here' – she indicated the existing stock – 'as you can see, is really country crafts stuff.' She smiled. 'Nothing wrong with that of course, but your output is more avant-garde.'

April opened her eyes wide. 'Do you think so?'

Viv nodded in agreement, her face serious, then sighed. 'That is true.'

'I think you really need to look for somewhere that will put your work in front of the right potential buyers,' Eve said.

April frowned. 'Perhaps you're right.' Eve saw Viv's shoulders relax. 'Though we could try them here, I suppose,' she went on, 'just to see if they go down well.'

Eve frowned. 'I don't want to speak out of turn, but I really wouldn't. The trouble is, unless your sort of customer walks through the door, your items will hang around and people will see they're not selling. It might create the wrong impression.'

April paused for a moment but then nodded. 'I see your point.' She turned to Viv. 'I'm so sorry, but I might have to withdraw my offer after all. I hope I haven't hurt your feelings. Perhaps I'll approach some galleries next time I'm in the city.'

Once she'd gone, Viv stood in the quiet of the craft area, her shoulders shaking. 'You are a marvel, you know that?'

'I feel as guilty as heck. I should have been honest, but I didn't want to offend her. Do you have any local woodcraft tutors? She could get some proper training then.'

But Viv batted her objections aside. 'Don't you think she was being a tiny bit arrogant?' She let out another guffaw of laughter. '"Hope I haven't hurt your feelings", indeed! I tell you what, Eve – I wish you could be here *every* time I have to discuss stocking someone's work in the shop. And not just for your skills. It would be a right old laugh.'

CHAPTER SIXTEEN

The storm arrived that evening, as Simon had predicted. Eve sat in the kitchen of Elizabeth's Cottage with a meal she'd prepared from the village store ingredients, watching lightning streak the sky. The rain came down so hard that she toured the house, checking the water wasn't coming in, but the thatch was doing its job. She was relieved when the tempest blew itself out by mid-evening, and low streaks of sun broke through between the indigo clouds.

When Eve walked Gus around the village green the following morning, everything seemed lusher than before. The sky was the purest cloudless blue and the air felt fresh. She bought a local paper from the store on her way home. Inevitably, Moira tried to quiz her about her walk with Simon. There were lots of arched eyebrows and questioning notes to her observations, which Eve ignored.

Crossing the village green back towards Haunted Lane, Eve glanced up at Melgrove Place, shady behind the silver birches and the Scots pine. As she crossed Love Lane, with Gus straining on his leash ahead of her, she wondered again about the woman she'd interviewed the day before. Standing at the entrance to Haunted Lane, she caught movement upstairs at Fi's house and paused for a moment, pretending to look at a text on her phone. Gus glanced back at her accusingly. *Bear with me, buddy – I've decided I have to play detective. This might seem like nosiness, but I'm actually doing my duty…* She brought up her phone's camera and flipped it into selfie mode, so that she could sneak a look at what was going on above her. She was standing just beyond Haunted Lane's oak tree, which provided a bit of cover. A moment later, she saw a man she recognised as Andrew open the casement window wide. He was already dressed in a smart white shirt and seemed to be scanning the scene down below. An uneasy frown crossed his face and she edged forwards a little even though his eyes weren't on her.

'It's a beautiful house, isn't it?'

Eve almost jumped out of her skin. Moira Squires. And she'd caught her looking, despite her cautious approach. At least she seemed to assume it was just the property Eve was interested in.

'I forgot that there's a free supplement with today's local paper,' the storekeeper said. 'It's just a section on summer events in Suffolk, but you ought to have it in case you have any free time. Paul's holding the fort, so I thought I'd come after you with it.'

'Thank you so much!' She half wondered if the woman was still after gossip about her and Simon, and had followed her in order to have another go at getting it. If so, it was good that Eve's nosiness had distracted her.

Moira inclined her head towards Melgrove Place, 'I suppose you've been inside? To interview Fi, I mean?'

Eve was very conscious of the open window above them. She nodded. She was determined not to give Moira any information, but it was hard to blank a direct question like that.

Moira smiled. 'I went in once too, just for a drinks reception. Very beautiful. Such gorgeous furniture.' She lowered her voice. 'I thought at the time that it would be wonderful to see the whole house, but of course I would never ask. It's just that – it being such a desirable and historic residence – I couldn't help being interested.' She brightened. 'But then it went on the market, so I could browse all the photographs on the estate agent's website. Bedrooms fit for royalty – so spacious and really quite light, for the period. And the bathroom…' Her eyes were genuinely misty, but then they sharpened. 'It was valued at four million pounds!'

'It's for sale now, is it?' Eve asked, her voice low.

'Oh no!' Moira said, as though she ought to have known. 'It went up a short while after Fi left her job at High House.' She lowered her own voice now. 'Normally, I would have assumed it was because of her other job falling through, and the drop in income, but I imagine her salary would be insignificant compared with her husband's financial resources. Andrew is, shall we say, very nicely off. He's a retired divorce lawyer, you know. But Fi has expensive tastes.'

Eve glanced up at the open window again, and tried to edge Moira towards the opposite side of Haunted Lane. Meanwhile Gus was getting restless, pulling her towards Elizabeth's Cottage with the occasional stern glance in her direction.

'Anyway,' Moira went on, 'there was a lot of gossip in the village' – *Surely not*, thought Eve – 'because word got out that some pop star had put in an offer for the place!' Her face was full of concentration. 'I hadn't heard of him. Billy somebody? But everyone was very excited; apparently he's in the charts all the time. And the girl who told me about it – a junior at the estate agents, over in Southwold – got to meet him, apparently.' She heaved a sigh. 'But that fell through. Glemham and Co carried on trying to find a buyer, but in the end the Goddards took it off the market again.'

At last, Moira glanced back in the direction of the village store. 'Well, I suppose I'd better get back. We're only open until ten this morning. It gives me and Paul half an hour to get ready for church.' She gave Eve a look. 'Not that the vicar is always precisely on time. Oh dear, I almost forgot again. Here's the supplement I mentioned.'

Once Eve and Gus were back inside the house, she made coffee and toast, then stepped out into the back garden to have her breakfast at the ironwork table. She checked the chair before she sat down, but it was already dry.

Now, she spread the paper out in front of her on the table as Gus dashed down the garden in hot pursuit of whatever had caused a rustle in the bushes.

The front page was still devoted to Bernard Fitzpatrick's murder – no surprises there. There was a box about High House and its future as a museum, and an update on the police investigation, though it didn't give much away. Detectives on the case were 'continuing with their enquiries' and 'pursuing multiple angles'. Fi Goddard, Andrew Goddard and Lucas Booth were *all* listed as members of the Blackforth Arts Trust, along with a couple of other names she didn't recognise. That was unexpected. Why hadn't Fi mentioned it the day before? Eve couldn't help wondering if it was because she was reluctant for her to speak with Andrew. It seemed likely he'd known Bernard better than she'd implied.

The coverage of the case was continued on the inside pages. As she sipped her coffee she found an article on Cole Wentworth. It would probably be a while before the press left him in peace – and maybe the police too, if he'd received a significant bequest. And in fact, that was what the article referred to: there was a photograph of a smiling Cole, looking handsome and emotional. The headline was WORLD-FAMOUS CELLO LINKS SON WITH FATHER BEYOND HIS REACH.

Gus had reappeared at the table with what looked like a mouldy sock in his mouth.

'Ugh! Where did you get that? Come on, Gus – let me have it. I'll find you a treat instead.' She got up to fetch him one of the mini-snacks that were meant to be good for his teeth. 'Now, eat that, and listen to what it says here about Cole Wentworth.' She went back to the table and swigged some more coffee. 'Apparently, Bernard Fitzpatrick left Cole a private letter and the cello he used when he first performed publicly. Cole's very musical too, so the papers are loving it. "Bernard wanted me to carry on in his footsteps," says Cole, twenty-three, his eyes shining. "I only wish I'd known about our biological connection when he was alive." Despite what the papers have done to the copy, it does make me feel a little emotional. That said' – she reached down to ruffle Gus's fur as he looked up at her, no doubt after another treat – 'call me a cynic, but for a moment there I did wonder about the cello's value.' Gus nuzzled her hand, but she wasn't fooled; he just wanted to see what was in it. 'Cupboard love, eh? No, Gus – no more. Because I love you and I'm taking care of your health.' For a moment she imagined how it would be if the roles were reversed, and Gus was in a position to ration her cake intake at the teashop. It didn't bear thinking about. Though Viv's cakes were a tenth of the size of the muffins they sold at her local café in Kilburn, and fifty times nicer. 'Anyway,' she said, fussing him again, 'I don't think the cello counts as a motive for murder. The article goes on to say that the one Fitzpatrick used later in life, once he became famous, is going to the museum. Apparently it's valued at seven hundred thousand – partly for its own sake and partly because Fitzpatrick owned it. Can you imagine?' Gus got up, shook himself and pottered back off down the lawn.

The paper didn't mention the value of the cello that was to go to Cole, but an online search on her phone revealed news articles that were less reticent. One put it at £10,000. Still a lot of money, but a drop in the ocean, she guessed, if your mother happened to be Adele Wentworth.

But what had Cole thought, when he found out about his biological father? He was on first-name terms with the guy, judging by the newspaper quote, so they must have come into contact. Eve tried to imagine Cole's feelings. He'd be sore at both parents, surely, for deciding what was best for him, and keeping such a fundamental secret? But if he hadn't known then she guessed that removed him from the suspect list – and if he had, then she still wasn't sure about motive.

She must ask Cole for that interview, but her next mission was to catch the Reverend Jim Thackeray after he'd conducted the church service that morning. It was useful that she knew where to find him.

As she got ready for her mission, her mind ran over what she'd found out about the Goddards. Had it been a coincidence that they'd tried to sell their house soon after Fi's new job fell through? It was clear she and Andrew were planning their next expensive holiday, witness the brochures she'd seen in their drawing room, so it looked as though Moira was right and money wasn't a problem. Eve presumed they hadn't needed to downsize. And yet the timing was interesting. Selling up would have been another major life move for Fi if it hadn't fallen through. And it was another plan she'd had that had come to nothing.

CHAPTER SEVENTEEN

As Eve crossed the village green, ready to intercept Mr Thackeray at the end of his service, it seemed as though the whole of Saxford St Peter must be inside the church. The streets and the area of grass were deserted, the village store and the teashop closed. It felt almost surreal; it just wasn't something that happened in London – or that she remembered back home in Seattle, either. For a moment she stood there on the green, listening to the sounds of the village without any human component: just the gulls, and the blackbirds in the oak trees, together with the bees buzzing around the lavender and roses in the flowerbeds.

It occurred to Eve that the dress she had on – fitted, green and patterned with daisies – was almost like camouflage gear. She could lie down on the village green and simply fade into the lawn. Whereas in Kilburn, an outfit in fume grey would work better. Suddenly, London felt very far away. For a second, she wondered how her co-worker at the school had been getting on. She'd be covering for her again the following week. Eve didn't miss the stress and irritations that came with the job. Still, it wouldn't be long until the summer vacation started. She'd still be in work, but it simplified things.

At that moment, she picked up on movement. She wasn't the only person not attending church after all. Across the green, approaching from the direction of the coast, was Robin Yardley.

He raised his eyes to meet hers and gave a very slight nod. It was the most she'd gotten out of him so far. Did he really have something to hide? Was that why he avoided company? It was interesting that it was apparently Jim Thackeray who'd vouched for his good character. She'd half wondered if she might see the gardener exiting after the service, under the circumstances. Either way, she still wanted to talk to him about Bernard Fitzpatrick. It was time to take control, and she walked over to intercept him.

'I was wondering if you'd received my email.'

Their accidental meeting at the spot where Fitzpatrick had been killed hung in the air between them.

The man nodded. 'I did, but I don't much like talking about my clients, even after they're dead and gone. And you're not the first journalist to ask.'

Eve silently cursed the hacks, who'd no doubt coloured his opinion of her. 'I might be the first who's here to write an obituary though.'

He gave her a long look, but at last he nodded. 'You are. As far as I know.'

'I saw you tending Fi Goddard's garden.' She felt like Moira Squires.

'I do some work for most of the people in the village.'

She could only imagine the conversations he must have overheard – quite possibly without the homeowners' knowledge. At this time of year, everyone had their windows open, and voices would carry out into the gardens.

'I wouldn't want you to break any confidences.' In reality, she'd love someone to say something they shouldn't, so she could work out what was going on. 'I'm just after reminiscences from people who knew Bernard Fitzpatrick personally. It's hard to get a feel for a subject when you've only got a list of achievements and rather stilted quotes from previous press reports.'

Robin Yardley gave a slow smile. His blue-grey eyes were hard to read. 'I don't think I can provide you with fond memories of my late employer.'

'You didn't like him?'

'I didn't know him well.'

She thought he was about to walk away but at that moment he paused. 'Who have you spoken to so far?'

She told him, then added: 'And I'd like to speak with Cole Wentworth – and Adele, too – though I realise the situation's sensitive. I have an appointment with Lucas Booth, this afternoon at four.' She'd set it up after Adam Cox had performed email introductions.

Yardley nodded. 'Cole and Adele are obvious people to include, if they'll talk to you.' His voice was quiet and authoritative. It was all very well to approve of her approach, but his manner got to her. 'Did you know Lucas Booth used to live at High House?' he said, a moment later, making her forget her irritation.

'No.'

The man nodded. 'With his wife, Sophie. She was a keen gardener, so I didn't help them out back then. I only got involved after they moved to the house on the Old Toll Road. Sophie had done a beautiful job with the new garden there after the move, but then she got ill, and it wasn't long before she couldn't manage it.'

'What happened to her?'

Robin shook his head. 'She got cancer. When she became too weak to carry on, I took over and I've been working for Lucas ever since.' He was gazing into the distance. 'She died two years after they moved.'

All of a sudden his attention was back on her. Eve found it hard to meet his intense stare. 'Lucas knew Bernard from well before he got involved with the trust.'

As he walked on past her, she turned his last sentence over in her mind. It hadn't felt like a general, off-the-cuff remark somehow. And given that Robin Yardley hardly spoke at all, she guessed he wasn't in the habit of making polite conversation for the sake of it. He'd given her the information for a reason, she was sure. It made her all the more curious about his motives.

*

Walking through the lychgate of St Peter's as the congregation began to spill out into the churchyard, with the bells ringing and the organ still playing within, Eve got an attack of emotion that took her completely by surprise. Viv appeared as if from nowhere, looked delighted to see her and gave her a hug. Toby from the pub emerged just after her, with a broad grin, his sister-in-law Jo just behind him. The woman clapped her on the back and asked after Gus. Even Toby's brother, Matt, whom she'd barely talked to, recognised her and said hello. She was still more surprised when Moira Squires greeted her warmly, albeit after querying her absence at the service. Her husband Paul steadfastly ignored her, however, to wry smirks from Viv. It was a plus, as far as Eve was concerned. Adam Cox came next. He gave her a brief nod, before making a beeline for the lychgate. A moment later Viv's son Sam and his girlfriend appeared too.

'They don't always come,' Viv said, 'but I told Sam he needs all the blessings he can get before he goes off travelling. With his and Kirsty's organisational skills they'll probably get lost or arrested or something.' For just a second Eve could see the anxiety behind her banter.

'He seems pretty organised to me.'

She closed her eyes for a moment. 'Yes, yes. You're right. I hate it each time one of them flies the nest.'

Other people she recognised poured through the great wooden church door now. Simon hadn't been kidding when he said the vicar got a good turnout. Of course, people might want a chance to come together to talk about Fitzpatrick's murder, too.

After a moment she spotted Fi Goddard's husband Andrew.

Viv stepped forward. 'Andrew! Have you met Eve? She's writing Bernard's obituary!' Viv turned towards Eve. 'Andrew's on the

Blackforth Arts Trust, just like Fi. Fi's the PR brains of the team, and Andrew gives his legal expertise.'

Andrew Goddard nodded.

'I had the pleasure of interviewing your wife yesterday,' Eve said, shaking the hand he held out.

The man's eyes left hers for a moment. 'Ah yes. She mentioned it. She's not in church today – a prior engagement. Excuse me, I have an appointment myself imminently.'

Eve would have liked a longer chat, given his role with the trust, but it seemed it would have to wait. She'd contact him to find a time when he wasn't rushing.

At that moment, a young man she recognised as Cole Wentworth appeared and walked straight up to her.

'Eve Mallow? I'm Cole – I think I served you at the Cross Keys on Friday night? That's my mother, Adele.' He glanced over his shoulder towards a retreating woman Eve remembered seeing at the house on Smugglers' Lane. She was elegantly dressed in a grey silk suit that hung beautifully from her long-limbed body, swishing as she walked.

'Please forgive her for not stopping to say hello,' Cole said. 'She's only just back from London. She gave an after-dinner speech in Westminster last night at a do that went on until the small hours.'

The woman's past with Fitzpatrick and Eve's reasons for being there might have caused Adele Wentworth to beat a hasty retreat, too. If even Robin Yardley had been approached by the press, she couldn't imagine what life must have been like for Fitzpatrick's former lover.

But Cole surprised her. 'We were wondering if you'd like to visit us at Woodlands House tomorrow morning, to talk about Bernard,' he said. 'If you'd like to come at eleven, we can give you coffee. We're on Smugglers' Lane.'

Eve wondered how at ease his mother was with the idea, and accepted before he had a change of heart. 'Let me give you my card, in case you need to get in touch.'

Viv gave her a thumbs up as Cole Wentworth walked out of the churchyard. 'Good news, huh?' she said.

'Yes.'

'So why the frown?'

'Just unexpected. Maybe Cole's keen to take control of the news feed, to cut through all the speculation that's circulating.'

At that moment, the vicar appeared.

'Let me introduce you,' Viv said, stepping forward. 'Jim, this is Eve – top obituary writer and expert diplomat. Eve, this is Jim, the best vicar in town.' She laughed. 'I mean, the world.'

Jim Thackeray laughed himself then.

'We'll maybe see you down at the Cross Keys a little later, vicar?' Toby said.

He nodded and smiled. 'I'll be along, thank you, Toby.'

Viv said, under her breath. 'Jim says he always has a thirst after righteousness. He's a terrible tease, but the reasons behind his pub-going are pure. People find it easier to sidle up to him and offload their worries when he's on their turf.'

Eve had caught Moira's disapproving look though. She couldn't imagine the storekeeper appreciating his unconventional methods.

Simon appeared then, and Eve was unsettled to find she had an instant reaction to his presence. She felt the heat rise in her cheeks as he approached her.

'Eve! Lovely to see you. I'm looking forward to Monday!'

'Come along, Romeo,' Viv said to him, which made things significantly worse. 'Eve needs to chat to Jim.' She turned to Eve. 'I've just got time for a lazy lunch before I open the café for the afternoon trade. Catch you soon!' She followed her brother, son and Kirsty down the church path.

Eve turned to Jim Thackeray, a bulky, broad-shouldered but gentle-looking man with grey hair, who peered down at her from a great height.

'You didn't feel like joining the service today?' he said, smiling. 'We take visitors as well as regulars, if it's of interest.'

She hadn't thought he'd ask, given she was only there for a few days. 'I'm not really a believer, to be honest.'

The man opened his laughter-lined eyes wide. 'Well, you'll fit right in, in that case!' He held up a large hand. 'Don't get me wrong; I'm sure some of my flock believe, but I'd put most of them down as "yet to be convinced".' He grinned. 'I'd rather have them here for the after-service banter than not at all. A vicar has to start somewhere.' His blue eyes met hers. 'Yes, definitely don't let a little thing like that put you off. We'd love to have you. I'd be disappointed not to, in fact. And I must invite you to Bernard Fitzpatrick's memorial service. It's here at eleven a.m. on Tuesday, and I think I can guarantee a packed house, thanks to the champagne and caviar on offer.'

'Moira Squires mentioned you'd taken Mr Fitzpatrick's regular order off their hands.'

'I bet she did!' The laughter was there again in his eyes. 'So, as you can imagine, I already know a certain amount about you. You come highly recommended by Viv, and her opinion is gold standard.' He paused for a moment, a slight frown furrowing his brow. 'I wonder… as I opened up the church door after the service, I fancied I saw you exchange a few words with Robin Yardley.' He ended his sentence with a slight questioning note.

'I wondered if he wanted me to include his memories of Bernard Fitzpatrick.'

'Didn't get anything out of him, I suppose?'

Eve shook her head. 'Nothing personal.'

The vicar met her eyes. 'He's a good man.' His tone was firm. 'And now you want to ask me about Bernard too, I presume?'

'That would be great. Viv mentioned she attended various charity dos that he'd organised, including one at the church hall, so I guessed you must have known each other. Did he attend services?'

'He did. Don't quote me on this, but I'd certainly put him in the "to be convinced" category. But I believe he liked to feel part of the fabric of the village.'

Eve remembered Viv saying he'd wanted to be a figurehead. The overlord type. He probably wished he had a family pew to make himself distinctive. She must stop thinking uncharitable thoughts; especially in front of the vicar. His perceptive gaze made her slightly uneasy. 'And it sounds as though he did a lot for charity?'

'Ah yes.' That smile again. 'That started about six months after Fi Goddard took up her role as his public relations manager, and I'm sure the young people's music foundations he sponsored are very grateful for the steer she gave him. It would certainly be fair to record that he was a dedicated fundraiser, when you write your article.'

There was nothing catty in the way he said it; he was just a realist, Eve guessed.

'It sounds as though he got personally involved in the organisation of the events.' She remembered Viv's tale of his spat with Fi Goddard at one of the dos. Presumably he'd been on the spot then.

'Oh yes. He always kept a close eye on proceedings. I have some photographs of the fundraiser at the church hall, if you'd like to see them? They're over at the vicarage.'

Eve nodded. 'Thank you.'

He closed the heavy old door of the church and led her to his house: a wide white-painted building with leaded windows, set back on a shingle driveway. Inside was a wood-panelled hallway with wide oak floorboards.

He ushered her through to his study, which had panelled walls like the hallway, and pulled out an album from a bookcase.

'Here we are, I think… yes. There's Bernard. And these next few photos are all from the same event. I asked one of our church wardens, Julia, to stand back and capture the atmosphere. We tend to cover that sort of do in the parish magazine.'

He put the heavy leather-bound album down on his desk and walked over to the window to give her some space. It was interesting to view Fitzpatrick unposed. Every other picture she'd seen of him, she realised, had been taken during a photoshoot. She'd already gotten a firm impression of the man now: controlling, cruel even. But the pictures here also showed a livewire: an attractive and forceful presence. The third photograph she studied had both Fitzpatrick and Fi Goddard in it, each of them looking good-humoured.

'Did Mr Fitzpatrick hold more than one fundraising event in the church hall?' she asked.

The vicar turned from the window to face her and frowned. 'No. He held several others elsewhere though.'

So, this must have been the same occasion on which Viv had seen them having that argument she'd mentioned. It reinforced the impression of a man who might fly off the handle one minute, but be genial the next. And she could imagine Fi Goddard being the volatile sort too…

She went back to the album, scanning around ten more images. The other picture that caught her attention was one of Bernard Fitzpatrick in the same frame as his son, Cole Wentworth. Cole must have been working at the event – either as a volunteer or to make a few extra pounds. It fitted with his part-time work at the pub, and the job he'd had at the stables too. Cole was arranging wine glasses on a trestle table covered with a white linen cloth. He looked relaxed, but behind him, the church warden photographer had caught the cellist's look too. He was regarding his son with an expression that was partway between irritation and anger.

'Thanks very much,' she said to the vicar, as she closed the album. 'The photos help to conjure up a picture of the man Mr Fitzpatrick was.'

There was a knowing look in Jim Thackeray's eye as he moved to see her out of the vicarage. 'Yes, they do, don't they?'

As Eve walked home to find Gus, she wondered about that last photo. How had Bernard Fitzpatrick really felt about his son? Had the look he'd directed at him simply been brought on by the way he'd been doing his job? It sounded as though the cellist had been a perfectionist. Or was there more to it than that?

The man had left Cole his cello, and that bequest seemed to represent a blessing. And yet the look in his eye in that photo had been hard.

She shook her head. It seemed Fitzpatrick had been at the centre of several relationships that were probably under strain. She'd have to keep her wits about her when she visited Adele and Cole Wentworth.

Later that afternoon, after she and Gus had been for an invigorating run up the beach, she settled down at her computer to make more notes. Once she'd finished, she tapped Robin Yardley's name into Google.

The results were few and far between: something in the local paper about Saxford St Peter winning a 'Best village gardens' competition, with an acknowledgement of his expertise, and mentions in the online version of the St Peter's parish magazine, where the vicar thanked him for his work on the churchyard. None of the articles included photographs, and other than this, the man had no web presence at all: no Facebook, Twitter or Instagram, and no hint at any history whatsoever before he'd come to the village.

In this day and age, it was pretty hard to stay so thoroughly under the radar. Surely it had to be deliberate? No wonder he hadn't wanted to talk to her. What was Robin Yardley hiding?

CHAPTER EIGHTEEN

'Thanks so much for seeing me on a Sunday, Mr Booth.'

The man opposite her, who looked around forty, was of a slender build, with sensitive eyes and delicately curved brows. His hair had a slight wave and was longer on top than it was at the sides. Somehow, he didn't look like a banker – but she knew that's what he was. She'd looked him up before she came out, and seen his fund manager profile on the website of the outfit he worked for.

'It's a pleasure, and please, call me Lucas.'

'Thank you. Lucas, I understand you knew Bernard Fitzpatrick for a number of years, so it's great to be able speak with you. Someone mentioned you owned High House before him?'

Lucas swallowed. 'That's right. It was a lovely place to live, of course, but when my wife Sophie got ill, having such a large house, with so many stairs, really didn't work. We moved here, where there was space for her to have a bedroom on the ground floor.'

'I was so sorry to hear about your loss,' Eve said.

The man took a deep breath, his eyes damp. 'It was horribly bad luck, but so many people have to cope with similar tragedies, at one time or another.'

'Did you already know Mr Fitzpatrick when he put the offer in on your house?'

'Hardly at all. My wife knew him though – she did his administration before Adam Cox took over.'

Another detail that had escaped her. 'Did she enjoy the work?'

He shrugged. 'It was very much a nine to five, leave the job as you leave the office, sort of role. She didn't talk about it much at home.' He wasn't meeting her eyes.

Eve thought of the other employees of Fitzpatrick's that she'd met so far. Sophie had been a rarity if she'd really managed to separate her role from the rest of her life so easily.

'I see. So it was mainly the Blackforth Arts Trust that brought you and Mr Fitzpatrick into contact then?'

Lucas nodded. 'That and the usual village connections: passing the time of day in the shop, at church and so on.'

Though Eve didn't think Lucas had been amongst the congregation that morning. He had a distinctive face.

'I was curious to know, was it Mr Fitzpatrick who approached the trust about the bequest of his house – or did the trust go to him, to see if he was interested?'

'Ah.' Lucas looked down at his lap for a moment. 'It was actually Fi Goddard who brokered that gift. She's on the trust's board – for her expertise in public relations – as well as being a former employee at High House, of course. She still worked for Bernard when she was appointed.'

'She had the initial idea, then?'

'Ah, well – as a group we're always on the lookout for opportunities to raise funds and broaden our activities. Fi was talking about Bernard's fundraising priorities and we all – erm – we all knew him well enough to guess he'd like to leave a lasting legacy behind after his death. He was the sort who'd want to be remembered, for the way he altered the fabric of the music world. During his lifetime he felt he'd put Saxford St Peter on the map – and we all thought he'd be receptive to the idea of that enduring after his death. Fi took it from there.'

'It must have been a surprise to find that Mr Fitzpatrick had a son.' Eve wondered if Cole would have any legal grounds to contest his father's will.

Lucas was naturally pale, but he went a shade paler at that. 'Yes. It's really rather awkward. I can only suppose that Bernard knew Cole was in line to inherit his mother's fortune, which removed any obligation to name him as his heir.' He paused. 'Adele has family money, as well as what she's earned over a long and successful career.'

He looked so worried that Eve felt sorry for him. 'I'm sure that must have been it. Cole seems very touched by his father's gift of the cello – and given his fondness for music, and the fact that he won't want for anything financially, that might mean more.' Perhaps she'd be able to judge better once she'd spoken to the son and his mother.

Lucas nodded.

'Did Mr Fitzpatrick have much involvement in the plans for the museum?' He wouldn't have felt the arrangements were pressing, presumably. As far as she knew he'd been in good health when he'd died. But if he'd gotten as far as making all the right legal provisions, she guessed he might have had thoughts of how he'd like the place to be run.

Sure enough, Lucas nodded. 'That was the chief reason we were in regular contact. He told us he'd made various stipulations in his will, and we encouraged him to discuss his wishes with us. We wanted to make sure we could accommodate them.'

His voice sounded strained. Eve guessed that type of pre-death micromanagement might have been trying. Was it enough to explain his extreme dislike of Fitzpatrick, as witnessed by Viv?

'And Bernard helped the trust to raise funds too,' Lucas went on. 'He hosted a lavish party to raise money over at High House.' For a second he closed his eyes. It must have been odd for him, going back to his old home and seeing a guy he disliked strutting round in it. Maybe he hadn't known the sort of man Fitzpatrick was when he and his wife had agreed to sell him the place.

'I think I might have heard about that event,' Eve said, wondering if she could coax any more information out of him. 'I've made friends with Viv, over at the teashop, and she mentioned she'd catered for the occasion.'

'That's right.' A faint touch of pink tinged his cheeks. Was he remembering the scene she'd had described to her? He wasn't going to go into his feelings, clearly, and she couldn't blame him for that.

It was time. 'What's your fondest memory of Mr Fitzpatrick?'

Lucas seemed stuck for words. If only she could read his mind. People usually managed to come up with some kind of bland comment, even if their feelings were far from warm. 'Did you ever hear him perform?' she asked at last, hoping to give him a way out.

'Oh yes.' Lucas Booth nodded, his jaw tight. 'He expected us to support him whenever he played locally, and he tended to perform at some of his fundraising events too. He was outstanding, naturally. Of course, High House would be an inspirational place for any artist to work. Yes, please put down listening to him play as my fondest memory.'

At last, Eve left Lucas Booth in his spacious, dark house on the other side of the River Sax. He'd sat so still and quiet at the end of their interview that she said she'd show herself out.

Just as she turned right to cross back over the water towards the main village, she caught movement out of the corner of her eye, across the road and slightly further out of Saxford St Peter. She turned to look and saw the rear view of a retreating figure.

Robin Yardley.

What was he doing there? But of course, it was a small village and the weather was fine. It wasn't especially odd that she should almost run into him for a second time that day. Unless…

As she walked back towards Elizabeth's Cottage, she remembered that she had told him the time of her appointment, when they'd met that morning on the village green.

*

Back at the cottage, she opened the back door, letting in the sunshine and birdsong, and gave Gus his supper. A moment later she was at the kitchen table checking her emails, as a gentle breeze drifted in from the garden.

Mary Anderson, Fitzpatrick's cook and housekeeper, and his latest publicity manager, Polly Cartwright, must have talked to Adam Cox about her requests to interview them. He'd responded on their behalf, suggesting she go talk to them both at High House on Wednesday morning. That ought to be interesting.

She switched her attention to the notes she needed to type up. She had two documents on her laptop now – one for her obituary and a second (an Excel spreadsheet) devoted to Bernard Fitzpatrick's murder, into which she'd transferred all relevant aspects of her notes. She navigated to the Lucas Booth tab, which so far contained the snippets of information she'd gotten from Viv and Robin Yardley. Now, she added her impressions from her interview, as well as the few hard facts he'd passed on to her.

Did it give her enough to guess the root of his animosity towards Fitzpatrick? The constant need for tact when dealing with the dead man must have been wearing. One ill-judged word might have led the cellist to alter his will. But it was Sophie Booth's job with the musician that made Eve wonder. Had he treated her badly, like he had Adam Cox and – potentially – Fi Goddard? Or could he have wanted her for himself? Moira Squires had implied he'd only employed Polly Cartwright for her looks. Maybe he'd been a serial predator.

She sat back in her chair for a moment. That would certainly be enough to make Lucas Booth hate him. But it was years ago now. Resentment might have built up and reached a peak for some reason – but it was all speculation.

It was only when she read through her notes one final time that she realised something about Lucas's narrative didn't quite hang together. She frowned. The banker had said he and Sophie moved out of High House after she got ill. The stairs became too much for her. But his information didn't match Robin's. According to the gardener, Sophie had only become ill once she and Lucas were in the house on the Old Toll Road. It was then that he'd taken over the work on their garden. He'd even mentioned that Sophie had gotten the grounds looking beautiful before she'd had to give up tending them herself.

So, when Lucas claimed Sophie had been too frail to manage the stairs at High House, she'd actually still been digging and hoeing at their new place, according to Robin Yardley.

It was a weird discrepancy. There was no way Lucas would have misremembered something so emotionally harrowing. That meant that either he or Yardley had lied, and she couldn't think of any reason why the gardener would.

It begged the question, what was the real reason Lucas and Sophie Booth had decided to leave High House, and to sell it to Bernard Fitzpatrick?

Just after dinner that night, Eve took Gus for his evening walk, out along the Old Toll Road with its sweeping views of the River Sax and the mudflats. She was on her way home again when two police patrol cars passed her, skirting round the village green and down Dark Lane.

Had the police gotten a lead? She imagined how relaxed she'd feel if they made an arrest.

She was making a drink a short while later when there was a knock on the cottage door, sending Gus into a frenzy of excitement. She went to open up.

Viv's bright pink hair, which normally tied in with her rosy cheeks, now contrasted an unusually pale face. Her eyes were gleaming and red-rimmed after what Eve guessed must have been a sustained bout of crying. She held a bottle of brandy in her right hand.

'I thought I'd better come and tell you,' she said. 'And you might need this.' She held out the spirit.

Eve let her in wordlessly and her new friend sank down onto one of the couches.

'It's just going around the village. Fi Goddard's been found dead. Cole Wentworth discovered her out on the heath this afternoon, with her head smashed in.'

CHAPTER NINETEEN

Eve didn't sleep much on Sunday night. She'd given Viv a decent dose of the brandy she'd brought and talked over the shocking news. Cole Wentworth was in a terrible state apparently – the discovery of Fi's body must have brought home the horror of his father's murder too.

None of the locals seemed to know exactly when Fi had died – only that Cole had found her when he went for a walk late in the afternoon. The news hadn't reached Viv until after the teashop had closed. Of course, most of the village had been in church on Sunday morning, and it wasn't uncommon to follow that with a drink at the pub, from what Eve had overheard. After that she imagined the villagers might indulge in a leisurely Sunday lunch. It was possible Fi had died much earlier or overnight without being discovered. Eve assumed the patrol cars she'd seen had gone to join an existing police presence. She hadn't heard sirens during the afternoon, but maybe they hadn't been needed. The Saxford roads were quiet at the best of times and especially so on a Sunday.

On Monday morning, Eve dragged herself and Gus down to the beach. She was desperate to walk off her feelings: shock, sorrow – and guilt. Simon's comments on the way Fi had goaded Adam Cox had made Eve feel she'd probably been as cruel as her former boss. And although she'd found Fi a novel and engaging character when they'd met, she'd come across as amoral too. Now, Eve felt she'd been judgemental. As long ago as the previous Thursday, she'd felt worried for her on the beach, without even knowing who she was. If only she'd carried on thinking of her as a potential victim, rather than a murderer. She *needed* to get to the bottom of this. It was the one thing she could do for Fi now.

But of course, the dead woman could still have killed Fitzpatrick... and then have been killed herself, in an act of revenge. Her murderer might have decided to copy the method she'd used to muddy the waters – or for poetic justice.

In that scenario, Adele Wentworth sprang to mind as a possible perpetrator. Even if her relationship with Fitzpatrick had been over, she might still have loved him. But Cole said she'd been in London overnight on Saturday, and she'd been in church too, so she'd have had limited time. It all depended on exactly when Fi had died. Polly Cartwright was the only other person she could think of who might fit the bill, but Eve didn't buy it. When she'd seen the current publicity manager in the village store she'd seemed more irritated by Moira's intrusive questions than sad at Fitzpatrick's death.

Beyond that, Fi could have killed Fitzpatrick with the aid of an accomplice, who now felt it would be safest to have her out of the way – though no likely candidates came to mind.

Gus was back with her, wanting his ball throwing again. She bent down to make a fuss of him, then chucked it as far as she could. In a moment, her gaze was back on the waves and the view out to sea.

What were the other possibilities, if Fi had been innocent? Someone might have killed her to protect themselves, if she'd found out they were guilty of murdering Fitzpatrick. Or possibly there was someone who'd wanted them both dead.

Her mind seized on Adam Cox. Fitzpatrick had had control of his whole future – she could imagine the former secretary killing his boss to free himself. But what about Fi – would her needling have been enough to make Adam snap? Simon had implied he'd really hated her. Or could she have found evidence of his guilt and become his target that way?

And then there was Fi's husband, Andrew Goddard. She remembered his words at church the previous morning. *She wasn't able to come today. Prior engagement.* Had Fi gone off to meet someone, out on the heath, while everyone else was at St Peter's?

She was sure Lucas Booth hadn't attended – and nor had Robin Yardley.

Or had Andrew Goddard known exactly why she wouldn't be attending, because he'd been responsible for her death? He hadn't wanted to speak with Eve as he'd left the church – and he'd avoided her eyes when he'd excused Fi's absence… He'd certainly sounded volatile that day on the beach. But she couldn't believe he'd killed Fitzpatrick too. It was clear he'd suspected Fi of being involved in that crime for whatever reason. He'd said she hadn't sounded surprised – presumably at the news of his murder. Unless… unless the root of Fi's problems with Fitzpatrick had been an affair gone sour. That could have been the hold the cellist had had over her. He'd been unmarried, with nothing to lose, whereas she'd had a lot at stake. Fi could have killed him first, to keep him quiet, and then Andrew might have taken Fi's life. But the timing was odd. It seemed unlikely that Andrew would suddenly have discovered a long-since defunct affair *after* Fitzpatrick's death – and then murdered his wife in a belated act of revenge.

She shook her head. It was something to keep in mind, but so much of it was guesswork. Until she knew more, Adam seemed like the prime suspect.

The change in circumstances left Eve in a quandary about her next steps. She'd intended to investigate Fi Goddard as suspect number two. Now that the poor woman was dead, where did that leave things? The fact that Eve's planned enquiries were morally questionable, and possibly illegal, only added to her indecision.

Gus glanced at her as he approached, as though he knew she was plotting something.

'I know I'm preoccupied, buddy, but my plans are time-critical. If I don't act today it will be too late. Once Fi's name's in the papers I won't be able to snoop without attracting the wrong sort of attention.'

But Gus had already lost interest again, and was haring up the beach. Seagulls were more exciting; she could understand that.

She went round and round her dilemma, but her thoughts always brought her to the same conclusion: until she knew more, there was no way of knowing what was relevant. Fi had behaved oddly before she'd died, and knowing why might just unlock the whole case.

So, given the legality question, she needed to work out the best approach. Her own phone was out; it was too traceable. Then there was the landline at Elizabeth's Cottage. She could hide her caller ID by dialling 1471, but the person on the other end would see 'number withheld' come up on their handset. That was hardly likely to get her put through; they'd assume she'd got something to hide before she'd even connected. That left two options. She could go to see the HR manager at Thrushcroft Hall in person, giving a false name, and then disappear into the ether. (*Do a Robin Yardley*, she thought.) Or she could call from a phone box. There was one of the old-fashioned red sort in Saxford St Peter – but it was right outside the village store. Moira Squires probably had it bugged.

In the end, the phone box won. Saying she 'just happened to be passing' Thrushcroft Hall sounded too poor an excuse for turning up in person. On looking at the map, she found it was deep in the Suffolk countryside. She could claim she was using the public phone to avoid running up the bill at the cottage if anyone asked. Not using her mobile wouldn't look odd; the signal in the village was so flaky.

She took Gus home first, passing close to Melgrove Place. What must it be like for Andrew Goddard? The press were crowded round his and Fi's house, cameras trained on his door. A uniformed officer turned up as she passed. She guessed the guy had been charged with moving the hacks on, but he looked young and unconfident.

Inside Elizabeth's Cottage, she picked up her notepad and headed off to the village green, where she shut herself inside the phone box. In the back of her mind she imagined Ian's reaction once he found out there'd been a second murder in Saxford. The thought made her all the more determined. She wasn't going to let his lack of faith stop her from doing what was right.

A moment later, her adrenaline going slightly – which was ridiculous – she was asking if she might have a quick word with the person in charge of human resources at Thrushcroft Hall. There was a suspicious pause on the end of the line.

'Don't worry,' Eve said. 'I'm an HR professional too, at a similar venue, and I'm just after some advice. I'm not trying to sell advertising space.'

Her cover story worked, and a moment later she was put through.

'*Pamela Crowther speaking. I'm sorry, what venue are you from again?*'

'It's called Fieldings – we're way down in Kent, so you might not have heard of us. We have a role to fill – head of PR – and we're finding it impossible to source the right candidate. In the end I browsed the web to see if any venues similar to ours had recruited for the role recently. I'm sorry to bother you with it.'

The woman on the end of the line sounded jolly, and quite pleased to pause for a chat. '*No problem. I'm not sure how much help I can be, though. You're right, we recruited for a director of public relations six months or so back, but we struggled as well.*'

'I wondered if any of your rejected candidates were near misses – people I might approach?' Eve was aware she was on dangerous territory. Ms Crowther was far more likely to take Eve's number and pass it on to the promising ones than to hand out their personal information. She'd have to hang up if things got difficult.

'*Well, we had one first-class candidate and – between ourselves – we actually offered her the job. She was our top choice. But, well, I don't know…*'

'She didn't take up the post?'

'*She pulled out on us – and not because she'd been offered another role that she preferred, as far as I could tell. I mean, I would have understood that. But this woman – she just ditched us. She was full of enthusiasm at her interview, and she didn't hesitate to accept when I rang to offer her the job, but just two days later she called again and said she'd decided to decline it.*'

Eve frowned. So it wasn't a case of them calling in Fi's references and finding them wanting, then.

'*I could pass your details on to her, but she might be more trouble than she's worth,*' Ms Crowther said. '*And thinking back now, to her interview, although she was clearly very talented, and a high achiever, there was something about her.*' Eve heard the woman sigh. '*I suppose it was reliability that I was worried about, or maybe stability is a better word. She struck me as very mercurial, which can be a double-edged sword.*'

Back at Elizabeth's Cottage, Eve experienced an odd mix of feelings. She was elated at having gotten through the call without being found out. But the fact that she'd persuaded the woman at Thrushcroft Hall to talk about Fi, without her having any idea that she was now dead, made her feel uncomfortable.

'It's for the greater good, Gus,' she said, walking straight through to the kitchen to fix herself a coffee. 'That's what we have to hang on to.'

As she had her drink, she decided to message both Ian and the twins. Fi's murder was going to ensure Saxford had even greater media coverage than before. If she got in touch first, she'd hopefully head Ian off at the pass, and save the children from worrying. Their responses came quickly. The twins asked if she was sure she was okay, and wanted to know when she might head back to what Nick referred to as the 'relative safety' of London. He'd put a laughing emoji afterwards. Ian's told her to return to the capital immediately.

Eve's resolve was already strong, but if anything could have made it more so, it was his reply. She focused on what she'd learned from her call that morning. Had the decision to reject Thrushcroft Hall's job offer really been Fi Goddard's alone – or had she changed her mind because she was under duress? Bernard Fitzpatrick might have contacted her and advised her to withdraw her application or risk him presenting her prospective employers with whatever information he had on her.

Or none of this might be true, and Eve could have put two and two together and made five.

But there was still the matter of the fake clients Fi Goddard had listed on her website. There was *something* odd going on – and Eve couldn't help feeling it was significant. Why on earth would Fi Goddard have turned down a top job to stay home and pretend everything was going swimmingly?

CHAPTER TWENTY

Cole Wentworth had texted Eve, confirming he could still see her that morning. She was relieved to hear from him – she didn't have his number and she'd been wondering what to do. He must have spent most of the previous day with the police, and finding Fi Goddard's body would have been horrific. She'd probably have wanted to beg off if it had been her.

The woman who let Eve into Woodlands House at eleven o'clock wore a knee-length black dress with a white apron over it. Did the Wentworths seriously have a full-time maid?

The woman didn't introduce herself, and had clearly been forewarned of Eve's arrival. She stood back in the light entrance hall to allow her to enter. 'I'll take you through now.'

The outside view of the house had already captured Eve's imagination. Its modern timber frame meant it fitted in perfectly with its surroundings – looking like a smart, cavernous and luxurious playhouse in the woods. As well as the decked area where she'd seen Adele setting a breakfast table on her previous visit, today she'd noticed an upper-floor outdoor seating area too, which must give views through the treetops towards the heath and the beach.

Inside, the hallway led to an atrium that stretched up to the second floor and the glass roof. It would be spectacular in a storm. It confirmed her conclusion that Adele must be very wealthy. The upkeep of a place like this – with all that wood, so near the coast where weather conditions in winter could be harsh – must be costly.

The maid took her through to a large living room, with huge glass walls that faced out into the woods. Inside, two weeping fig trees grew in large stone pots, linking the room to the outdoors.

The maid announced her name and left her alone. For a disconcerting moment, Eve couldn't see any other occupant in the room, but then Cole Wentworth appeared, rising from an armchair in the far corner.

He smiled, put the newspaper he'd been reading down on a coffee table and walked towards her, hand outstretched.

They shook. 'Thanks so much for seeing me. The last twenty-four hours must have been terrible.' Eve remembered Viv describing him as 'handsome' in the pub – and she was right, he was: thick dark wavy hair, huge brown eyes and broad shoulders. He looked tired though – she bet he hadn't slept the night before.

'It's honestly good to have the distraction. Though I feel a bit hoarse. When I offered to have you round yesterday, I hadn't imagined I'd spend all afternoon doing a different sort of interview, with the police.' He shook his head. 'I just keep seeing it each time I close my eyes. She'd been beaten about the head, just like Bernard.' He paused. 'My father, I mean. I still can't quite get used to it. The police think the killer used the same weapon.' He shuddered.

'It's such a shock. And you must be tired.'

'Annette will come to the rescue with some coffee for us in a moment. Shall we?' He motioned Eve over to where two couches sat next to a table.

She took a seat on one of them, grabbing her notebook from her bag, and he sat back on the other. 'This is a beautiful house,' she said. 'Are the woods at the back part of your land too?' She'd been wondering about the floor-to-ceiling windows and privacy.

Cole must have read her mind and for a second his face was lit by a smile. 'Yes. No danger of Moira Squires peering in at the window!'

Eve smiled too, but then the reality of his situation was back with her. 'I suppose you must have been coping with a lot of local interest and speculation recently.' And being the one to have discovered Fi's body would only add to that.

He nodded. 'And not just from the villagers. The press have been all over us.'

'I'm all the more grateful to you for seeing me. It must have been tough to deal with: finding out the identity of your biological dad at the same time as hearing that he'd died – if that's how it was?' She was still wondering.

'It was – exactly. I found out when the solicitor called to explain Bernard had left me his cello.' He looked down for a moment.

'So, the solicitor had to explain your connection to you?'

He shook his head. 'I went to join my mother in the kitchen after I'd heard about the bequest. I was completely perplexed, but the moment I explained what had happened I could see from her expression there was something she hadn't told me. And that it was big.' He looked Eve straight in the eye. 'I guessed before she had the chance to explain. It all made sense, once I thought about it. The times I'd seen my mother and Bernard interact – the fond touches on the shoulder, the whispered conversations. There's that sort of – I don't know – shared understanding you see in someone's eyes when they have a very old, close connection.' Eve watched as his chest lifted in a sigh, under his crisp white shirt.

'Poor Mum,' Cole went on. 'She was grieving, of course, but I just stood there for a full five minutes shouting at her. It was too much to take in.' Suddenly he leaned forwards, his eyes on hers. 'You won't write all that, will you?'

Eve shook her head. 'Not at all. I just want to sum Bernard up and let those who didn't know him in life appreciate what he achieved, and get the essence of his character.'

Cole nodded. 'That's good. Thanks. The fact is, I still haven't completely come to terms with her and Bernard not telling me the truth. But I understand why that was now.'

'It might be good to include *that* in my obituary, if you don't mind?' It was the biggest question she had – and her readers would share it.

He nodded. 'Apparently it was always her plan to break it to me. She says she almost did it, many times, but she was worried about my reaction.' He sighed. 'Do you know about my dad? Sorry – I mean the man my mother married. I'm still processing it all.'

'Not a lot.' Eve wasn't going to admit to all the googling she'd done.

'He held a very senior role at the Foreign and Commonwealth Office. As I was growing up, most of what he did was simply too secret for us to talk about, but that just made him seem all the more glamorous. I idolised him – even enjoyed a bit of reflected glory, I suppose. Mum said each time she saw me meet someone new, I'd refer to him when I filled them in on my background. She worried she'd be taking away part of my identity if she let me know the truth.' He shook his head and smiled at Eve. 'Crazy really. Dad will always be Dad, of course, but I adore playing the cello and music's my life. Imagine how I'd have felt if I'd found out Bernard was my biological father.'

'And Bernard kept quiet, too.'

He nodded. 'Mum says he felt it should be her choice about when – and even if – she told me. She'd brought me up and they'd agreed to keep quiet while Dad was still alive. And then after that, Bernard didn't want to cause her pain by leaping in at the wrong moment.'

How bothered had Fitzpatrick really been, Eve wondered, one way or the other? Maybe the relaxed status quo had suited him quite nicely. From what she'd heard about him so far, he didn't come across as the sentimental type.

At that moment, the woman called Annette appeared with the coffee. There were only two cups. Cole didn't thank the maid, which surprised Eve. After all, he knew what it was like to wait on people. She did it for him and received a smile in return.

As Annette retreated, Eve said: 'Your mom's not joining us?'

Cole shook his head. 'I'm afraid not. She's still very emotional about all this, and I think she felt I'd be able to speak more freely without her present.'

Eve nodded and smiled, but she couldn't help conjuring up the picture of the woman outside the church, and the way she'd walked off so quickly. She had the impression Adele had never been onboard with the interview idea. She was disappointed but she could totally understand. Cole was probably getting the news out of his system by talking about it, but Adele might feel very differently. It was her messy past, after all.

'How did you feel when you found out Bernard had left you his cello?'

'Very emotional,' he said immediately, then took a deep breath. 'Of course, I was reacting to the news that came with it, too. The gift of the instrument seemed like a minor thing in comparison at first.

'But it's made the whole situation easier to bear now. I never got the chance to talk to Bernard as a dad – but I do know that he was interested in my musical career and that he wished me well. He wanted me to succeed.'

Eve sipped her coffee and waited to see what he'd say next.

'A few of the papers have commented on the fact that he chose to leave me an instrument that was nowhere near as valuable as the one he's left to the Blackforth Arts Trust, but they're missing the point. Financial value wasn't on Bernard's mind. Not to be crass, but' – he indicated the house around them – 'I'm lucky enough to come from a wealthy background. The instrument he left me has an exquisite tone, but the key thing is its symbolism. It was the cello he was playing when he had his big break. Having it left to me has been like feeling his embrace from beyond the grave.'

That sounded like newspaper copy. Eve wondered if Cole was starting to quote clichés back at journalists now – not that it was surprising.

'You mention your musical career. I understand you're on a gap year after your undergraduate degree?'

'I've taken a couple of years out, in fact. I got fed up with studying – I wanted the chance to take on a few dead-end jobs, and just to play during all my free hours.' He dropped his voice, even though they were alone. 'My mother would fund me to devote all my time to my music – she's hugely supportive – but I like to get out and see people, and I've got my pride. I suppose I take after her. She never relied on anyone else either – including my biological father, as I now know. I've got a place at the Royal Academy of Music to study composition, starting in the autumn.'

'Congratulations.' He really was a chip off the old block. And of course, Bernard had composed music too – though he'd never made a success of it. Maybe Cole would succeed where his father had failed. She glanced at the young man. 'You must look back on all the interactions you had with Bernard differently, now you know the truth.'

'Yes.' For a moment, his eyes were far away. 'That's right. And I had more to do with him than you might expect. That was down to my mother. She suggested I apply for part-time roles whenever Bernard was after casual staff.' He shook his head. 'I never thought anything of it. I was always picking up odd jobs, and the ones for him just added to the mix. She's admitted now that she knew Bernard would be pleased to see something of me.'

Eve remembered the photograph she'd seen at the vicarage, showing Bernard and Cole together – and how irritable Bernard had looked. Had he really wanted him around, as Adele Wentworth said?

'Did you get along well with him?'

Cole gave her a conspiratorial smile. 'He was a character. He was known – publicly – for being genial and generous. He was both those things, but he could also be unreasonable, and he had a short temper. Not just with me, I don't mean. I saw it time and again.' He shook his head. 'I remember one evening when I helped out at an Arts Trust fundraiser over at High House. Bernard was busy schmoozing a VIP, so he got Fi's husband Andrew to show some guests around on his behalf. Bernard went on about how Andrew should give them the *full* tour, as though he might be too lazy if Bernard didn't insist. I could see Andrew was irked, and who could blame him?' Cole gave her a wry look. 'Of course, as a member of the trust, he couldn't be openly rude, but he got his revenge by wilfully misunderstanding Bernard's instructions. When he brought the guests back downstairs, one of them mentioned what a fine bedroom Bernard had.' He laughed. 'Bernard was furious with Andrew for showing them somewhere so personal.

'And as well as being ferocious, he liked everything to be just so, and *hated* anyone questioning his judgement. That clearly went for sons as well as everyone else. That said, I wonder now if he did single me out for special treatment occasionally.'

Eve raised a questioning eyebrow.

'Look over here,' Cole said, standing up and leading her to a cabinet that stood against one wall. Inside was a bottle of eighteen-year-old Bowmore whisky. 'That was Bernard's favourite tipple.'

Eve remembered. Moira Squires had mentioned it when she'd gossiped about Fitzpatrick's special monthly order at the village store.

'I'd stepped into the breach at one of his events at the last minute, and he gave it to me to say thank you. Mum isn't a whisky drinker – and I never got beyond Bell's at uni – so it was only later that I found it had been a fairly generous tip, at a hundred pounds or so a bottle.' He sighed. 'I still wish my mother *had* got around to telling me. But it's no use crying over spilt milk.'

Before she left, she asked Cole if he'd ever attended Fitzpatrick's performances (yes – and he'd been overawed), and if he'd been to his house as a guest, rather than a casual worker (yes again – at the odd dinner party, as well as at larger events. Bernard had been an excellent host, though scary when he put you on the spot). Eve avoided asking him about his fondest memory; it seemed too unkind, given he could – perhaps – have had many more, if his mother had been honest with him. But would it ever have been a case of happy families?

As she walked back home to Gus, the interview filled her head. She'd learned a lot, but she'd never know exactly what had gone on in Fitzpatrick's head. Each glimpse she got was an achievement, but a tantalising one.

And at the very edge of her mind, she felt an unexplained uneasiness too. It usually meant she'd missed something, but to do with Fitzpatrick's character, or his death? Try as she might, it eluded her, resting somewhere just out of reach, on the edge of her consciousness.

CHAPTER TWENTY-ONE

Back at Elizabeth's Cottage, Eve sat in the garden with her lunch, watching Gus potter around the lawn, his head occasionally turning towards her as though he was checking she was okay. When things were grim, holding on to the happy normality of her dachshund was very sustaining. Her mind was on Fi Goddard's murder. Cole said the police thought she and Fitzpatrick had been killed with the same weapon. Unless they were wrong, it sounded like a single murderer at work.

She tried to think, but after her poor night's sleep she felt tired. When she heard the distant knock on the cottage door, and watched Gus propel himself through the kitchen, barking for all he was worth, the idea of having to move was unappealing.

The man who'd come to call was the senior of the two detectives who'd attended the break-in at Adam Cox's house. He showed his warrant card and introduced himself as Detective Inspector Nigel Palmer. His jowly face took on a resigned expression as Gus sniffed the dark-grey legs of his trousers.

'Ms Mallow? I've been informed about your email to the case coordinator for Bernard Fitzpatrick's murder – and I'm told you spent some time extracting information from Fiona Goddard on Saturday.'

Eve stood back to let him in. *Extracting information?* He made it sound as though she'd used thumbscrews.

'Mrs Goddard agreed to talk to me about Mr Fitzpatrick. She gave me some helpful material for the obituary I've been commissioned to write.'

The man raised his eyebrows.

'Do have a seat.' She gestured towards the couches. Gus remained by the man's side, his look mistrustful. 'Can I get you a drink?'

He shook his head. 'You're just one interviewee on a very long list. Normally I'd have sent my sergeant but your role here is unusual, so I've given up my time.'

Unlike the person who'd answered her original email, he spoke as though she was an inconvenience. Eve was glad Ian couldn't hear. A moment later, he produced a notebook and pen from his jacket pocket.

'Had you ever met Mrs Goddard before you interviewed her on Saturday?'

Eve shook her head, but then she thought back to the day she'd arrived, and the conversation she'd overheard on the beach.

Palmer must have read something in her eyes. 'I'd appreciate it if you were honest with me, Ms Mallow. There's a murderer on the loose. This isn't a game.'

Eve felt her blood pressure rising as she took a deep breath and explained.

'So Mrs Goddard had heard the news of Mr Fitzpatrick's death and her husband noticed that she didn't look surprised.' Palmer was already writing it all down.

'No!'

He raised a weary eyebrow.

'Andrew Goddard noted that Fi hadn't seemed surprised at some kind of news they'd both heard that day. Neither of them confirmed what that was.'

Palmer sighed. 'But it was on the day that Mr Fitzpatrick's death was revealed as murder. And most village news wouldn't cause a couple to have that kind of conversation.'

Eve remained silent. It was the police's job to draw conclusions. To be fair, she'd thought the same, but she'd also kept in mind that she might have misread the situation. She didn't like Palmer's attitude.

'And before the day on the beach, you'd never met either of them?'

'That's correct.'

The man nodded.

'Thinking back to that first sighting and reviewing everything you've heard or seen since, is there anything else you can think of that might help me with my enquiries?'

How far should she go? Admit that she'd noticed the testimonials Fi used on her website seemed to be fake? Confess that she'd called Thrushcroft Hall's HR manager to try to get information about Fi under false pretences? Speculate about the ongoing influence she suspected Bernard Fitzpatrick might have had over Fi's life?

'Moira Squires at the village store explained Mrs Goddard left Bernard Fitzpatrick's employment when she was offered a new role, but when that fell through, she didn't go back, even though her old role was still vacant.'

She wanted to stick with the facts – not the conclusions she'd drawn.

'Indicating a possible falling-out between the two of them. Except I think we can discount Bernard Fitzpatrick for Fi Goddard's murder, don't you?'

Eve paused a moment to rein in her feelings. 'I wasn't sure what Fi Goddard was doing for work these days. I always research my interviewees before I visit them, so I looked at her website. I didn't recognise any of the companies she said she'd done work for, and when I looked I couldn't find most of them online.' She was being economical with the truth, given she'd found out those details after her visit, but passing on what she'd uncovered was the main thing.

He frowned. 'Some might think it a bit odd that you went to such lengths to investigate a woman who was nothing more than an interviewee.'

Eve met his eyes steadily. 'It feels rude to move straight to asking questions about the obituary subject without showing an interest in the interviewee first.'

Palmer was tapping his pen on his notepad. 'Any other *facts*, Ms Mallow?' Appearing rude clearly wasn't something that worried *him*.

'I arrived at St Peter's just as the service ended yesterday. I noticed that Mrs Goddard wasn't present—'

'That would make sense, under the circumstances.'

She ignored his withering tone. Fi must have died earlier than that, then – in which case Lucas Booth and Robin Yardley's absence from church was probably irrelevant. 'I was *going* to say that her husband, Andrew, said she had a prior engagement.'

She'd gotten Palmer's attention now. He scribbled something down. Presumably Andrew Goddard should have known his wife was missing by that point then. It sounded as though Fi might have been killed overnight, just like Fitzpatrick.

'Will you write Mrs Goddard's obituary now?' Palmer said suddenly.

What was he thinking? That she picked people off to keep herself in work? 'We don't just latch on to the latest person to die,' Eve said. She was feeling as cynical as Palmer looked now.

'If you think of anything else, please call the hotline immediately,' the detective said, as though she might not bother.

So, the double murder was being handled by a dismissive jerk who was inclined to concentrate harder on making people feel small than on listening to them. *Perfect.* If she did uncover anything useful, it would certainly increase the kick she got out of reporting it to the police. And she sure as heck wasn't going to sit back and trust Palmer to get the job done.

CHAPTER TWENTY-TWO

Twenty minutes after DI Palmer's visit, Eve was in her Mini Clubman with Gus, heading out of town. A change of scene might help her make sense of all this. The roads were narrow and meeting a tractor almost as soon as she left the village made her remember to pay attention. Thoughts about the case would have to wait.

'What about a walk along the beach at Southwold, Gus?'

At the mention of 'walk', Gus – who was wearing his safety harness in the rear passenger seat – let out one quick, excited bark, as though it was an immediate offer. She was still such an amateur dog owner.

'Won't be long!'

They found a place to park on a side street and walked past the town's lighthouse, its brilliant white wall high and imposing against the blue sky. The pavement took them past red-tile-roofed houses in ice-cream colours with sash windows. The sound of lively chatter from the tables outside the Sole Bay Inn drifted down the road from behind them, and, on the breeze, Eve could smell the sea. They joined North Parade, which ran along the seafront, and headed south. Down on the sand she could see a row of beach huts in a multitude of cheerful colours, the North Sea beyond them.

'No good for us, though, Gus.' There was a notice saying the beach further down was dog friendly. Staring into the distance, she could see it looked much emptier. It would be a better place to think.

Eventually, they climbed the steps from Ferry Road, and went over a bank to reach the vast expanse of sand beyond.

She could ponder her problems aloud here. No one but Gus would hear. She found bouncing ideas off him strangely helpful. After Ian, it was quite nice to have a companion that didn't answer back. She was sure Gus would talk a lot more sense, if he were able to.

'I wish I could see the police files for this case,' she said to him. 'Assuming the same killer *was* responsible for both deaths, knowing who has an alibi for either one should rule a lot of people out.' She bent down to let Gus off his leash. 'As it is, I need to take stock without the benefit of that information.' He dashed off immediately into the shallows and she felt the need to follow. Otherwise she'd just be conspicuously talking to herself, and she had some standards.

'So, we have Adam Cox. He certainly had a motive for Fitzpatrick, and quite possibly for Fi, too – especially if pure hatred counts.' She wasn't just relying on what Simon had told her about relations between the pair; Fi's tone when she'd spoken about Adam had said a lot.

Who, out of the other people she'd come across, seemed most likely to link with both deaths?

'Lucas Booth bothers me. He seems to have lied about a bit of his past that relates to his wife and Fitzpatrick. Or at least, either he or Robin Yardley did, and I can't see why Yardley would. And from what Viv said, and I observed at his interview, Lucas found the man very hard to tolerate. It's thin though. I need to find out more. But supposing he *did* kill him, his most likely route down to the site of the murder would have been via the set of steps that descends to the estuary path, near the river crossing. There are only two buildings that overlook the steps directly: Viv's teashop and Melgrove Place.' She felt a chill run up her arms. 'The teashop would have been empty, but Fi Goddard might easily have seen him.'

Gus was bouncing around like a small dog possessed, the fur under his chin dripping with saltwater. She walked along the coast by his side, as he dashed up the beach a little each time a larger wave hit the shore.

'The tone Andrew Goddard used, that day on the beach, still gives me the creeps – and Fi cried out, as though he'd hurt her in some way. But although he sets my alarm bells ringing, I'd swear he thought Fi was involved in Fitzpatrick's murder, which means *he* wasn't – and it looks like both murders were committed by the same person. Cole said the police thought the same weapon was used in both instances, and DI Palmer referred to "a" killer on the loose – singular.

'Were it not for that, I'd still have Fi on my list of suspects for Fitzpatrick's murder. It feels like he had control of her life, and that's a convincing motive.' She shook her head. 'As for Cole and Adele Wentworth, I can't discount them, but I've got no motive for either of them to kill Fitzpatrick, let alone Fi.' Their route to the spot where Fitzpatrick had died would be via the beach; it wasn't as though Fi was likely to have seen either of them even if they'd been responsible. And besides, Adele was meant to have been down in London on Saturday night. Eve sighed, her breath caught by the breeze. 'As for Robin Yardley, he's certainly behaving oddly, but again, I'm struggling to see a motive for either of the killings.'

Gus dashed up and shook himself, spraying droplets of seawater in all directions, including up her legs, bare under the knee-length dress she was wearing. *Hmm… refreshing.* The move seemed to indicate he'd had enough of wave chasing. They turned and walked back up the beach towards town as Adam Cox and Lucas Booth vied for attention in Eve's head. No one currently rivalled them as prime suspects.

They'd entered the network of streets where Eve had parked when she saw a name above a business that looked familiar. Glemham and Co. She went nearer and saw the premises belonged to an estate agent. *Of course.* It was the outfit that had tried to sell Melgrove Place for Fi and Andrew Goddard, according to that fount of all knowledge, Moira Squires.

She hesitated by the doorway, which was open thanks to the balmy summer weather. A woman who had been sitting at a counter inside got up and came to meet her.

'If you want to come in, it's fine to bring your dog.' She glanced over her shoulder, and added, in an undertone. 'Manager's out at the moment anyway!'

Without having a fully formed plan, Eve accepted her offer, hoping Gus didn't shed drying sand onto the carpet.

'I've got a dachshund myself,' the woman said. 'Smooth haired, black and tan. Can't resist them!' As so often, Eve thanked Gus silently for being so charming. 'How may I help? What type of home are you looking for?'

Eve thought of Melgrove Place and a way forward presented itself. 'I'd like a village location locally – a character property – something old, and quite large.'

'Ah.' The woman's brow furrowed. 'I'm afraid they tend to be fairly few and far between, which increases the price, of course. Families often hang on to them for years – generations even. There's one you might like out over Darsham way.'

She took the details from a blue folder, and Eve pretended to be interested. 'Beautiful.' But then she looked at the location map and sighed. 'It's just a bit far from the coast for me, unfortunately. Is there anything nearer the sea?'

The woman shook her head. 'I'm sorry. I'm afraid not at the moment.'

Eve put on her *I'm trying to think* face. 'A friend of mine mentioned a place that sounded just perfect. But it was on the market a while ago now. I suppose it probably sold.' She frowned again. 'It was in a village called something like Saxstead St Peter, I think…'

The woman's expression cleared. 'Oh yes, I know the property you mean. The village is actually *Saxford* St Peter. I remember the house, because I led on the contact we had with the client. I'm afraid she actually took it off the market again.'

Eve let her shoulders fall. 'Oh. That's too bad.' She raised her eyes, met the sales assistant's regretful gaze and forced herself to go on. Inspector Palmer would never have the time to dig like this. Nor the inclination, if Eve was any judge of character. 'I don't suppose there's any chance she might re-list it? Did she give you any indication?'

The woman frowned. 'I don't want to raise false hopes. Truth to tell, the woman I dealt with gave me the runaround. The house had been on the market for a couple of weeks when we found a buyer.' She leaned forward slightly and smiled. 'The rapper Billy Tozer, no less.'

So that was who Moira Squires had been talking about. Eve knew the name, even though her music taste was stuck a decade or two earlier. She widened her eyes. 'Wow.'

'I know. And although I mostly dealt with Mr Tozer's PA, I did get to meet him in person when we showed him round. And he was delightful, I must say. Not what you'd expect really, from the sort of press coverage he gets. A gentle giant.

'Anyway, he was mad keen and I was relieved. Houses like that can hang around for quite a while before a purchaser with the right sort of capital comes along. Mr Tozer offered the asking price straight away, and Mrs Godd— I mean, the woman who owns the house, accepted too. But about two days later she got back in touch and told me to let Mr Tozer know she'd changed her mind.' She frowned. It still bugged her, clearly, and Eve could see why.

'And that was when the owner took it off the market?'

'Well, no,' the woman said, 'that was what made it so especially embarrassing. She – or they, I should say, she was dealing with us on behalf of herself and her husband – left it on. So it must have been clear to Mr Tozer that they were rejecting him specifically. He was pretty fed up, as you can imagine, and I haven't heard from him since. And after all that, they took it off the market again a month or two later. I ask you! So, all in all, even if they were to re-list it in future, I wouldn't bank on a purchase going smoothly. It was only ever the woman that I dealt with. It's often the way – that husbands leave the admin to their wives.' She gave Eve a mischievous smile.

Eve's brain was working overtime, but not coming up with any sensible conclusions. It seemed to mirror what had happened with Fi's new job – but why?

The woman shook her head. 'To be fair, maybe there was more going on behind the scenes than I realised.' She frowned and paused for a moment. 'The woman I dealt with asked me not to discuss her rejection of Mr Tozer's offer with her husband.' She sighed. 'It was awkward. The house was in both their names, but she was the one registered with us as a client. I didn't really want to get involved, to be honest. Perhaps they had some difficulties, which resolved themselves. Maybe that's why they decided not to sell in the end.'

'What an awkward situation.'

'It was, and it got more so. Her husband rang eventually, after they'd taken the place off the market. He'd finally heard on the grapevine that it was his wife who'd sent Mr Tozer packing, rather than him withdrawing his offer, and wanted to know if it was true. At that point,' the woman went on, 'it was clear his wife had kept him entirely in the dark. My manager insisted that I tell him the full story – as it was, his wife's actions had made us look incompetent, as though the failure to sell the place was ours. I don't know what effect telling him the truth had. I haven't heard from either of them since.'

Eve caught her breath. She was thankful the news of Fi Goddard's death was only just filtering through to the local media. 'You were in an impossible position – and I'm sure if there was trouble ahead for them, it would have occurred whatever you'd said.'

The woman gave her a sad smile. 'There is that.' She still felt guilty and conflicted over the whole affair, Eve guessed, which had made her want to share.

Eve was about to leave the building when one final thought occurred to her. 'This will sound like a really crass question, but isn't Saxford St Peter the village where the famous cellist lived? Bernard Fitzpatrick? He had the most marvellous house, I hear. I don't suppose you'll be asked to sell that in due course?' It was a roundabout way of leading her on to the subject.

The woman shook her head. 'I'm afraid not. I wish we were, but it's going to be turned into a museum apparently, by some charitable trust.'

'It must be an amazing house. Did Glemham and Co sell it to Mr Fitzpatrick in the first place?'

She sighed. 'No, we didn't get our hands on it that time, either. I was a junior member of staff here back then. I remember the gossip about it – apparently the place exchanged hands over a few bottles of champagne at a private dinner party.' She grinned at Eve. 'Much cheaper than our commission, so I couldn't really blame Mr Fitzpatrick for going to the owners direct – but old Mr Glemham was very put out!'

At last, Eve said her goodbyes, encouraged Gus out from behind a rack of brochures, and left the premises.

As she drove back to Saxford, she tried to make sense of what she'd discovered. Fi Goddard had had a perfectly good buyer for Melgrove Place but she'd turned him away. And her reasons for doing so must have been something she'd wanted to hide from her husband – but ultimately, Andrew Goddard had found out she'd lied to him. Did he know why? And if so, what had the truth meant to him?

There was nothing to suggest that Bernard Fitzpatrick was involved in the failure of the house sale, and yet... and yet it seemed each major life move Fi had attempted after leaving his employment had fallen through. In both cases, she'd been the one to pull out, but why? Could he have been influencing her behaviour – blackmailing her, say, into abandoning each new plan she had? Ensuring he kept a tight hold on her life? Maybe she'd wanted to leave the area – escape his influence – but he'd put a stop to it.

Eve sighed. She couldn't work it out.

Back in the village, she parked by the green and got Gus out of his harness. At that moment, she looked up and spotted Adele Wentworth, on her way into the village store.

Eve stood by her Mini. What to do? The woman had made the decision not to talk to her and if Eve had been writing a standard obituary, she wouldn't have pushed. But Adele had been a very significant part of Fitzpatrick's life; failing to speak with her felt like a major omission when it came to investigating his death.

She made up her mind. 'I hope you're not too tired for a walk around the village green, Gus. It might just pay dividends if I can get my timing right.'

CHAPTER TWENTY-THREE

By centring her and Gus's walk around the village store, rather than the entire green, Eve manged to 'bump' into Adele Wentworth when she emerged. Cole's mom was wearing a sea-green, calf-length silk dress and expensive-looking sling-back sandals. Eve bent down to stop Gus approaching her – the silk didn't look like it would react well to close contact with dog paws.

'Good afternoon.'

The woman nodded. No smile, but it was a start.

'I was just giving Gus an airing before dinner.' She let him go now he'd calmed down and he pottered off on his extendable leash. 'It was so good of Cole to see me earlier – especially at such a terrible time. I'd be grateful if you could pass on my thanks.'

The woman inclined her head. 'I will do that.'

Eve thought she'd just walk off, and unless she followed and pestered her with questions, she'd have to let her. The woman would have been fending off approaches from tabloid hacks for days. She couldn't blame her for turning her back on the whole bunch of them.

But suddenly, Adele faced her again. 'I'm sorry for not talking to you earlier. Cole said how decent you'd been – how you hadn't pressured him. I used to have to deal with the press on a daily basis when I worked in government. One wrong word could lead to huge repercussions. It's tainted the way I see journalists, I'm afraid, and my recent experience of them hasn't done anything to restore my faith in the breed. I've been under siege.'

'I do understand. I'm sorry.'

'Cole pointed out obituary writers have a different agenda from the gutter press, but I was still cross with him for inviting you.'

'No one would blame you for that.'

The woman looked at her for a long moment. Maybe Eve's patience would win through.

'Cole was brave, talking to you, after the horror of the day before, when he found Fi's body. Perhaps I've been a coward. I can spare you five minutes, if you'd like to take a turn around the green with me.'

'That would be incredibly kind.' And possibly very revealing.

Adele nodded. 'Very well. Would you like my general thoughts, or is there anything in particular you feel is missing from your narrative?'

Eve really wanted to know what had made Adele move to Suffolk, and how her relationship had been with Bernard once they'd occupied the same village. How could she put it without sounding like just the sort of hack Ms Wentworth despised?

'I was interested in the fact that you moved to be near Bernard again, after your husband's death,' she said cautiously. If they'd ever taken up where they'd left off, it was part of Fitzpatrick's life story.

Adele gave a tight smile. 'That wasn't the reason I moved. But it's a fair topic; I'm prepared to explain. When Bernard and I had our affair we both lived in London. We met at a political do, where he'd been hired to play. During the course of our liaison, it was nice to get out of the city, away from prying eyes. I brought him to Saxford a few times. It was a favourite haunt of mine for quiet weekends; there was a cottage I used to hire, down at the end of Ferry Lane near the estuary. Anonymous, charming, peaceful. I'd always entertained the idea of moving to the village once I'd retired from full-time work. Only Bernard fell in love with the place too.'

She raised an eyebrow, a wry look in her eye. 'He visited Saxford again, after we'd gone our separate ways, and arranged to buy High

House. He was able to see just what a fantastic place it would be for a creative person to work in. What was I to do, when the time came for me to make my choice about where to locate? I wanted to get out of London, and I didn't see why I should change my plans. Bernard and I hadn't parted on especially friendly terms, but when Woodlands House came up for sale, I was damned if I was going to let the past rule me. And its position was perfect – well away from the main village. Our paths needn't cross much – or so I thought. In the event, of course, we bumped into each other occasionally.'

She smiled for a moment. 'Bernard actually laughed, the first time we had a proper interaction, and I ended up sharing the joke. I think he thought it was very "me" to have put my foot down and moved to Suffolk anyway, awkward entanglements or no.' She shrugged. 'He could be a devil when he wanted, and quick to fly off the handle, but he wasn't inclined to bear a grudge. Neither of us had any desire to restart our affair – what seems like a good idea in your thirties can seem like rank stupidity once you get to my age. But I suppose we each had warm memories of the fun we'd had. And of course, there was Cole. Bernard was intrigued to see his son at close quarters.'

Intrigued was an interesting word to use. Adele met her eyes as though she'd read her thoughts.

'This is one of the reasons I didn't want to do a joint interview with Cole. If I speak in confidence, can I trust you?' Her eyes were sharp.

'You can; you have my word. I can use what you say to inform my overall impression of Mr Fitzpatrick, without revealing any details in my article.'

She gave a small nod. 'I don't think Bernard was the paternal type. It doesn't alter the fact that I feel terrible now that I didn't tell Cole the truth. I just kept putting it off. He loved my late husband very dearly, and although music might have helped Cole and Bernard connect, I was never really sure that would be enough.' She sighed. 'Bernard was proud of the *idea* of being a dad, but that isn't the same as wanting to act like one. And the fact that he never forced my hand or told Cole himself bears that out. I tested the water – encouraged Cole to apply for casual work with Bernard when he had any going – but nothing I saw changed my mind.' She put her hand up to her forehead. 'But maybe I used that as an excuse. I was always worried what Cole would think of me if I admitted the truth.'

She shook her head. 'I still can't believe what's happened. But Cole and I went to a couple of social events at High House and I did wonder about the set-up. So many people seemed to have strained relationships with Bernard. Adam, Fi, other members of the Blackforth Arts Trust. Of course, making up to Lucas Booth's wife was never a sensible idea. You've met Lucas?'

Eve nodded. 'They had an affair?' She held her breath.

Adele shrugged. 'I can't know for sure, but he certainly paid her a lot of attention, and she seemed charmed. I think he broke the rules so often he'd started to feel invincible.'

After the woman turned to walk back home, Eve returned to Elizabeth's Cottage with Gus; he looked ready for a rest.

'It's not conclusive proof,' she said, bending down to spoon food into his bowl in the kitchen, 'but an affair between Fitzpatrick and Sophie Booth would give Lucas a compelling motive for murder.' It didn't explain why Lucas had lied about his and his wife's reasons for moving out of High House though – assuming Eve was right, and it was he, not Robin Yardley, who'd tweaked the truth. And why would Lucas act now, after years of resentment? All the same, her pulse quickened each time she thought of the man. She imagined the banker, making his way stealthily down the steps to the estuary path the night of the cellist's death, watched from above by Fi Goddard.

It would explain Fi's lack of surprise when the news of the murder broke.

CHAPTER TWENTY-FOUR

Eve had time to squeeze in one last job before she cooked dinner. She tried again to reach Bernard Fitzpatrick's brother. This time she succeeded, but the interview was frustrating. None of the questions she asked elicited anything new. Like Adele Wentworth, he'd initially assumed she was just after dirt on Bernard, hence him not calling her back. He told her very firmly that he'd known nothing about his brother's affair with Adele (even though she hadn't asked). All the spluttering on his part made it clear he disapproved. Other than that small outburst, every word he uttered was bland and measured. It made her feel there was more to unearth. Siblings normally had firm opinions about each other – positive or otherwise. If she'd been able to chat to him in person she might have gotten more, but apparently work commitments would keep him away from the memorial service the following day. If she wanted additional clues about Bernard Fitzpatrick's childhood, she'd have to ask elsewhere. Shame there were no other living relatives who'd known him back then.

The heat of the day had given way when Eve got ready for her trip with Simon Maxwell. He'd called her on his parents' old landline to check she was okay and still happy to go out, soon after she'd returned from her talk with Adele Wentworth. He'd remembered she'd been interviewing Fi just after she'd walked to the stables with him, and guessed she was probably shaken up. He might be a flirt, but he was a thoughtful one.

The evening air – when she tested it, in the back garden – was mild. She decided to wear a cropped emerald-green cardigan with three-quarter length sleeves over her fitted black dress, and went on to consider footwear. It would have to be her low-heeled sandals, rather than something more height-enhancing. Walking around the village in high heels would look ridiculous. Heck – why was she even thinking about it? She didn't care what Simon thought of her. And he was too young for her, anyway. She didn't know his precise age, but she reckoned he was several years her junior.

As they headed out, she looked at him surreptitiously, taking in his mischievous half-smile and his mop of dark hair, with just the odd – attractive – strand of grey. Had he styled it like that deliberately? It wouldn't surprise her. She smiled inwardly.

She felt like a teenager. She didn't believe in the ghost of Black Shuck, and she was quite sure he didn't either, but it was clear they were meant to keep up the pretence, or the whole planned exploit would lose something. It left her feeling awkward – she always found play-acting embarrassing. Her worst nightmare was visiting historic houses where you had to engage with staff dressed in costume, speaking as though they'd stepped straight out of Elizabethan times. Then again, she'd play-acted with the best of them that very morning when she'd called Thrushcroft Hall, and again at the estate agents. Maybe she could carry this off after all.

'It's quite spooky outside St Peter's as the sun goes down, even without Black Shuck,' Simon said, grinning as he gave her a sideways glance. It was as though he'd read her cynical thoughts. 'Something about standing in the grounds, next to the ruins, and looking up at the church tower against the darkening sky.'

'What are the ruins?' That was something concrete and factual that she could latch on to.

'They're what remains of the previous church on this site. It fell into disrepair and bits of it were used to construct the present-day building. The move from the old position to the new one was supposed to have disorientated Black Shuck, and now you can see him skirting the old ruined walls, before he finds the new church and prowls along the nave.'

'The "new" church looks ancient.'

Simon smiled. 'It was built in the mid-1600s.'

A breeze chose that moment to stir the leaves in the oak trees on the village green, causing the light from the street lamp on the other side of the grass to dim for a moment as foliage blocked it. Eve felt the hairs rise on her forearms. But it was most certainly the shifting air that had done it, not the thought of a great black dog, stealing through the shadows.

'Let's go and look at the ruins first,' Simon said, nudging her and nodding towards the church grounds.

What on earth was she doing? This was actually embarrassing. She could feel a slight quickening of her pulse as they entered the deep shadows of the tumbledown, cobble-flint walls of the old church. She imagined all the generations that had been there before them, centuries earlier.

'You haven't bribed someone to hide here and spring out at us, have you?' she asked. Best to keep a tight hold of reality.

Simon laughed. 'Damn – missed a trick there. But you'd have seen it coming anyway. Do you always anticipate everything in advance?'

'I tend to work through scenarios so I don't get caught out.' She paused. 'Nothing here's been quite as I'd expected though.'

He glanced at her, his eyes serious for a moment. 'Bernard and Fi's murders seem like part of some awful nightmare.'

'Yes. But it's not just that. Even day-to-day life here is different from what I'm used to.'

He nodded. 'Country places do surprise you. The people who've been resident for years know each other's secrets – and they've got used to the way the place functions, even if it's inherently odd. And then you get the incomers, and their reasons for settling here – it's not uncommon for people to run to the country to escape.'

They'd moved beyond the ruins now, and were looking back at them and the distant village green beyond.

'You seem to see it all in the round.'

Simon shrugged. 'I'm Saxford St Peter born and bred, but I get out of the place a lot, down to London and up to Norwich on business. Maybe that gives me a bit of perspective.'

She nodded.

'Let's stand still and see if we can sense anything.'

She gave him a withering look, which he met with a grin. They had their backs to the River Sax and as they stood, perfectly still, she could hear the curlews and – from somewhere beyond the church – an owl hooting.

'We should go inside too,' Simon said, nodding at the building and raising an ironic eyebrow. 'Just in case.'

She followed him over the tussocky grass, stepping carefully to avoid the lower bits of ruined wall, until they reached the main church door. She'd noticed how grand it looked the day before – a huge arched oak affair, with iron studs – but this evening it struck her as almost forbidding.

Simon lifted the latch and pushed it open gently. It was raised above the stone floor inside, with a ramp to ease access to the church. As it swung slowly back it was completely silent on its hinges.

It was down to that, Eve supposed, that the figure kneeling in one of the pews, right at the front, didn't hear them. Someone was at prayer – it was time to call off the mad Black Shuck hunt.

She nudged Simon and pointed back towards the churchyard. He nodded, retreated with her, and carefully pulled the door shut again.

'Bother,' he said.

'I suppose it *is* a church and everything.' Eve gave him a censorious look, and he laughed.

They'd paused amongst the ruins again, she facing towards the green, he towards the river.

'Fair point. And I can tell you're not remotely won over by my myths and legends, anyway. I have to confess, I've never seen Black Shuck. What about Elizabeth, though? I grew up in her cottage and I'd swear I heard the footsteps once, out in Haunted Lane. It was the day before a fisherman from the village was lost at sea.' Eve frowned and he looked at her intently. '*Have* you noticed something?'

She really didn't know him well enough for this sort of conversation. 'I think my mind's been playing tricks on me. A double murder's enough to make us all feel nervous.'

He continued to hold her gaze. 'Sure you're not in denial, Eve Mallow?'

She just smiled at that. But in the same moment, her memory presented her with Gus, whining downstairs, the same evening she'd thought she'd heard the footfalls.

She was distracted by the sudden appearance of a figure, who'd just emerged from the church and was looking to left and right. Had the person heard Simon closing the door after all, and come outside to see who had disturbed their peace? She moved to look through a gap that had once been a window in the old church, keeping to one side so she wouldn't be seen.

It was Lucas Booth.

It was almost completely dark now, but the light from the moon allowed her to see his distress. He wiped his eyes with the back of his hand, and she heard him take a gulp of air.

Simon had caught her sudden stillness and turned to look too, but the man was moving off now, so he didn't see his face.

'Was that Lucas?'

She nodded.

'Well, the vicar will be pleased he's putting in overtime.'

She laughed.

'Joking apart, he's never got over the death of his wife, I guess.'

Eve nodded. 'Poor man – awful to lose someone so young.' And if his marriage hadn't been in good shape, that would only have intensified his anguish.

Simon sighed. 'Too right. Sorry – I've put a dampener on things. How about heading over to the Cross Keys to warm up?'

The pub was crowded, despite it being a Monday night. People were huddled in groups, their faces serious.

Toby was at the bar and poured them their drinks. 'People tend to congregate in here when something affects the whole village,' he told Eve. 'Viv's probably had crowds over at Monty's too. Everyone wants to share their sorrow and shock – and people are frightened as well.'

A community under threat – villagers with a close bond, not knowing who they could trust and who the next victim might be. Anger rose in Eve's chest as she and Simon went to take a table in a corner. She wondered what progress Palmer had made that day, and if anything she'd found out was relevant. It was all taking too long…

She could see why people in need of comfort came to the pub. The Falconers would never let you feel alone. Toby was a calm, quiet presence at the bar, but Matt was circling round the tables. He still had a pint in his hand, but the uproarious laughter of her previous visit was gone. He was engaging with each of the customers, a friendly hand on someone's shoulder, an understanding nod for another. She remembered Viv saying he had hidden powers. Meanwhile, Jo must have spent all evening whipping food into shape in the kitchen; a lot of the clientele had empty plates in front of them.

The decor was comforting too: there were paintings with picture lights on the yellow wall behind Simon, and a small candle, burning in a tealight holder between them on the table. The cosy chairs were upholstered in red. It wasn't smart, but it was well cared for and loved.

'I like this place,' Eve said.

'It's the best,' Simon agreed. He peered towards the bar. 'Looks as though Cole Wentworth's not working tonight. I can't imagine how he must feel after discovering Fi's body.'

Eve nodded. 'And having a public-facing job must be terrible at a time like this – from the press attention to gossiping neighbours.'

'True.' Simon leaned forwards over his pint of Adnams IPA – produce of the Southwold brewery – and met her eye. 'On that note, have you heard the latest whispers going around?'

Eve took a sip of her Shiraz and leaned forward too. 'You've got me. What?'

'The word is, Fi Goddard was seen near Adam's place, just before it was broken into on Saturday.' He sat back in his chair again, his eyes serious. 'It feels wrong to pass it on, in a way – I'm not saying it means anything.'

The hairs rose on the back of Eve's neck. 'But they were former colleagues and, as you mentioned, they didn't get along.' Her mind was racing. When she'd speculated about Adam Cox being responsible for both murders, she'd imagined pure hatred as his motive for killing Fi. If she'd been the one to break into his house and scrawl that insulting graffiti, it would surely have intensified his feelings. But she might have had other reasons for entering his home too. 'Sucks to be you' made it sound as though the intruder was rubbing Adam's nose in some recent failure or stroke of bad luck. If Fi had broken in, could she have taken something that proved Adam was guilty of Fitzpatrick's murder? Maybe she'd suspected him and acted for that reason. It would fit with Adam not wanting the police to investigate further. If Fitzpatrick had been controlling Fi, she probably wouldn't have wanted justice for him, but it was clear she'd never liked Adam either. Maybe she'd decided to blackmail him, or present what she'd found to the police, just to see him suffer.

Her mind ran back to the scene she'd witnessed outside Adam Cox's house. It was hard to believe that someone would risk getting inside simply to scrawl the rude message. They could have spray-painted an exterior wall instead, especially if they'd gone under cover of darkness. And Fi had told Eve she got bored easily – taking matters into her own hands sounded like her style.

And then she remembered Adam's words, when the police had asked him who knew he'd be out that day. He said he'd gone to buy a loaf of bread in the village store and mentioned his schedule to Moira. Eve had seen a look of realisation in his eyes as he spoke, and wondered if he'd remembered someone in particular who'd overheard that conversation. It was time to follow it up. Moira might remember who'd been present.

'It's all interesting,' she said, taking a deep breath, 'even if it is only hearsay.' It wouldn't be right to share her thoughts with him, but she'd have to reassess everything later. She turned her mind back to her and Simon's previous talk, when they'd walked over to his stables. 'Speaking of fresh information, have any other interesting Fitzpatrick-related details come to mind?'

He gave her a slightly sheepish look. 'Just one – for what it's worth. I got to know Polly Cartwright a little, recently. She's the woman who took over from Fi Goddard as Bernard's publicity manager after a gap.'

Eve met his eye. *Got to know her a little, eh?*

'And she was complaining about the work Bernard gave her.'

That didn't sound unusual. 'What was her problem: long hours and not enough pay?'

He frowned. 'Not exactly. She said she'd thought it would be a step up for her, a real challenge, something she could get her teeth into. According to her, the money was okay – though nothing to write home about. But it was the work itself that left her disappointed. She said it was basic admin, not really PR at all.'

Eve frowned. That did seem odd – Fitzpatrick had courted publicity. You'd think he'd have given her plenty to do. She raised an eyebrow now, as she took another sip of her wine. 'That does sound weird. And when you say you "got to know her a little"?'

The sheepish look was back. 'I admit it, I asked her out. But she said she was involved with someone else. I haven't seen any evidence of a boyfriend though, so maybe she just didn't fancy me.' He adopted a mournful look.

'Unthinkable, surely!' Eve said, laughing.

He joined in. 'You're right. There must be some other explanation!'

Simon was good company, but after that little confession she was all the more determined to keep their friendship light. Polly was just one woman, but she could believe Simon might try it on with every new singleton that came his way.

When they left the pub, he turned to walk her back to Haunted Lane.

'There's no need to worry. I'm not afraid of the ghosts and it *is* only just around the corner. You have much further to go.'

He was doing the twinkling eyes and knowing smile thing again. 'All right – you win. By the way, I hear Bernard's friends and associates are planning a concert to celebrate his life on Wednesday. I think people who're travelling in to Suffolk to attend the memorial at the church tomorrow will stay on for it. I can't make the service, unfortunately – I've got a couple of business meetings – but I'm going to attend the concert. It's over at Snape Maltings, in the Britten Studio. Would you like to come along?'

Well, of course she would; he'd got her there. 'It sounds good – if I'm invited.'

'You will be. Jim Thackeray mentioned it. There's probably an invitation waiting on your doormat. Care to attend together?'

That smile. 'All right then. That sounds nice.'

'Excellent,' he said. 'I'll pick you up at six thirty.'

The invitation was indeed on her doormat. 'What am I doing, Gus?' she said, as he leaped up to join her by the front door. 'You and the twins are my true loves. I don't want anyone else.' And that was just as well – an additional true love wasn't on offer, just some light entertainment. She was still crouching down, having picked up the envelope. Gus rested his warm head on her knee. 'But I'm being dumb,' she said, stroking him and then rising to her feet and kicking off her sandals. 'He's invited me to a commemorative concert for a murder victim; it's hardly a date night. It'll be fine.'

She headed through to the kitchen and put the kettle on. The wine had gone to her head and she fancied a decaf.

As she sat down with her coffee, with Gus at her feet, snuggled up over her bare toes, her mind was no longer on Simon Maxwell. Instead, it had turned to Adam Cox and his break-in. She added what she'd found out to her spreadsheet, a creeping sensation running over her.

After that, her focus was on Lucas Booth. Simon could be right – maybe he went to the church alone at night because he still grieved for his wife and was looking for comfort. It would fit with his tears. It had been several years since he'd lost her, but that didn't mean anything. What struck Eve as more significant was that the man hadn't been at the church the day before for the regular service.

That made it look as though he was avoiding his neighbours and the vicar, but coming to St Peter's for secret solace. And leaving again in tears. If he'd killed Bernard, and then Fi too – overnight on Saturday – he'd have been in no fit state to meet his fellow villagers on Sunday morning. He'd have had the chance to collect himself by the time she'd interviewed him in the afternoon, but he'd certainly seemed preoccupied. She remembered how he'd sat there as she'd let herself out of his house.

Even if he wasn't guilty, he was acting as a guilty man might.

CHAPTER TWENTY-FIVE

Eve got her chance to quiz Moira on Tuesday morning, as the crowds amassed for Fitzpatrick's memorial service.

'Poor Adam looks exhausted,' Eve said, as the storekeeper paused to pick up a hymn book just inside St Peter's. 'He must be under so much strain. Have you spoken with him recently?'

Moira nodded eagerly. 'Well I have, as a matter of fact. He was in the shop the morning his house was broken into. I tried to catch him again to ask about it after church on Sunday, but I don't think he can have seen me. He dashed off without a word.'

That sounded like a natural reaction, whether he had something to hide or not.

'I was wondering how the intruder knew he'd be out,' Eve said. 'Did he mention he was working that day when he was in the store?' She didn't want to admit she knew he had, thanks to her eavesdropping.

Moira went pink. 'Now I come to think of it, he did!' She glanced across at Adam Cox and her knuckles got whiter as her grip on the hymn book tightened. 'Oh dear me, Eve! Fi was in the shop, standing right behind him. I remember because it was the last time I saw her.' She took a gulp of air. 'But what does this mean? Do you think she broke into his cottage and then he… he…' She put her free hand up to her face. 'I suppose I should tell Inspector Palmer. I happen to know the police have already interviewed Adam.' Her voice was breathless, despite the gulping. 'I understand they were with him for over an hour!'

*

Once Eve had extricated herself she went to sit near the front, where
Viv had bagged her a seat. Her mind was still on Moira's words.
She guessed it was inevitable the police would focus on Adam; it
was well known he'd had difficult relationships with both victims.
And he'd probably seen Fi behind him in the store and known or
guessed she was responsible for the break-in. The more she found
out, the more guilty he looked.

She made an effort to focus on the service. The vicar was on fine
form. He'd seen Bernard for exactly what he was, Eve was sure, but
he managed to give an honest yet positive address, packed with
amusing anecdotes. He'd come up with more since she'd quizzed
him at the weekend. She might ask if she could pinch some for her
obituary. By the end, her opinion of the dead man was teetering
once again, from viewing him as primarily cruel, to seeing him
more in the round. He'd left his mark on the village, made the
place more colourful, brought in visitors that had breathed fresh
life into the pub, teashop and store. He'd given the world the most
exquisite music and he'd never done things by halves. He'd burned
bright, even if some of his contacts had had their fingers scorched.

The vicar spoke of Fi Goddard too, paying tribute to her, and
saying a separate service would be held in her memory the following week. The mood of the congregation changed as he switched
topics – the collective shock at the latest death was a long way
from fading.

As Jim Thackeray finished his address, a recording of one of
Fitzpatrick's performances started to play, and people began to
shift in their seats. Serving staff appeared with trays of drinks and
canapés. It was time to mingle.

Viv nudged her. 'I need something light-hearted to cheer me
up, and I haven't had an update on last night yet! Simon's got

some boring clients visiting or something, so it's down to you to spill the beans.'

Eve rolled her eyes. 'All right – but I can't now! I'm working. This place is packed with Fitzpatrick's contacts. I need to watch how they interact, and then go talk to people.' Sizing them up first, before they knew they were being observed, might be informative.

Viv looked resigned, but then she brightened. 'Okay, but why don't you come to Monty's this afternoon? You can fill me in then.'

'Done.' She knew she'd never get out of it – might as well accept the situation and look forward to the cake. She ran her eyes over the room. Everywhere she looked, people were standing in closely packed groups, talking animatedly. They huddled between the pews, along the nave, in the north and south transepts and round the doorway to the tower. The white-walled space rang with a cacophony of voices.

She could see Polly Cartwright, standing next to the font, talking to Jim Thackeray. Polly was nodding, then shrugging.

'She doesn't seem that upset, does she?' Viv must have followed her gaze. 'The woman just near her, with the cowed-looking teenage granddaughter, is Mary Anderson, cook and housekeeper at High House. She cleans Elizabeth's Cottage too – did it for years for Mum and Dad. So, any cobwebs behind the bed and you know who to blame.'

'No complaints at all,' Eve assured her. 'I see Moira's enjoying herself.' She was tucking into the champagne the vicar had bought from their store – taking Fitzpatrick's order off their hands. She'd disapproved of serving it at the memorial in theory, but was lapping it up in practice. Her husband Paul stood back from the group they were with and cast regular glances at the door.

'She'll be in seventh heaven,' Viv said, 'gleaning everything she can about Bernard's famous friends and colleagues. Cole Wentworth looks nervous, doesn't he?' Eve glanced in the direction Viv indicated and saw Bernard's son, stiff in a formal dark suit, white shirt and purple tie. 'All the incomers must be sizing him up, I suppose, now that the truth's out. And Adele looks peaky.'

They'd be sizing her up too, as Bernard's former lover.

'Adam Cox doesn't look much happier,' Viv added, echoing the thoughts Eve had had earlier. 'I'd swear he smelled of alcohol when I walked past him on my way in.'

There was a certain amount of colour in his cheeks, Eve noted, but it didn't look healthy – it was more as though someone had slapped him. His eyes were darting over the guests. If he was guilty he might be checking the locals' expressions for any hint of suspicion. But perhaps he just felt a sense of responsibility, as the man who'd taken over High House and was tasked with presenting Bernard's memorabilia to the public. If he'd had a drink before the service, for Dutch courage, it suggested he wasn't coping.

'By the way,' Viv said, 'have you met your neighbours yet?'

'Sylvia and Daphne, right? A photographer and a potter?'

Viv's eyes widened.

'Moira Squires gave me a thorough overview. I even know Daphne likes to eat anchovy paste. Moira's nothing if not detailed. I almost don't need to meet them in person – but I'd like to. They sound interesting.'

Viv nodded. 'They are, and they're over there.' She inclined her head towards the other side of the packed church, where Eve saw two women: one around her own height, with short, layered light grey hair and beautiful grey eyes, the other considerably taller with a long plait, streaked light and dark grey, and a twinkle in her eye. 'Tell you what, I'll invite them to tea this afternoon too, when you'll have time to talk. But for now, let me further your career by introducing you to Emily Moore, the administrator for the Blackforth Arts Trust.'

Viv grabbed the woman's arm as she was passing. Ms Moore was tall, around six foot, with short blonde hair. 'Eve's writing Bernard's obituary, so you might be able to help her?'

Viv might not be a forward-planner, but she was good at operating on the spot. Eve had been about to intercept the pianist, Hugo Delaney – one of Bernard's contacts from out of town. The pair had frequently played duets at public performances. Still, she didn't want to offend Ms Moore, and talking to her would probably be useful too. She'd keep an eye on Hugo and make sure he didn't leave before she'd caught him. He'd be easy to track in the crowd, with his untidy crop of flaming red hair.

'You must have had lots of involvement with Bernard Fitzpatrick, I guess?' Eve said.

Emily Moore nodded. 'I'm a project manager by profession, so I volunteer those skills for the trust. Lucas Booth and Andrew Goddard spent the most hours with Bernard, listening to how he wanted High House to be run after his death, but I've done a lot of the administrative tasks associated with that – alongside administering the trust itself.'

She took a glass of champagne and a caviar canapé from the tray of a passing waiter, and Eve did the same.

'Bernard and Fi's deaths have come as the most terrible shock. It feels wrong to even think about practicalities at a time like this, but it has helped that Andrew was so efficient about putting the legal provisions relating to Bernard's bequest in place. That's lawyers for you, I suppose – he's habitually cautious. Bernard didn't have a healthy lifestyle, I'm afraid.' She smiled sadly. 'His love of whisky, fine wines, cigarettes and rich food was well known. All the same, we assumed he'd got years ahead of him. It was only Andrew's attention to detail that meant we could call on Adam Cox immediately, to help progress the museum project.'

Eve raised a questioning eyebrow.

'Andrew approached Adam a good six months ago now, to sound him out about taking on the role of custodian at High House, if the worst should happen when he was still in post.'

She must have seen Eve's expression. 'It's a lawyer's job to plan ahead, of course. They're trained to cover all eventualities. Poor Andrew. I can't imagine what he's going through now.'

He was absent from the service, understandably.

Eve could appreciate the lawyer's cautious approach; she was the same. But Emily Moore had misinterpreted her look. 'So, Adam knew about the trust's job offer a while back, then,' she said, trying not to give away her thoughts.

'That's right. I appreciate he's not necessarily the warmest of people,' she gave Eve an awkward smile, 'but his knowledge of Bernard and his work is encyclopaedic, so he'd be hard to replace – and he's extremely well organised.'

Eve found her eyes drawn to the former secretary, who was standing across the room, talking to the vicar. 'He does seem to be.' She was thinking back to Fi's tale of the mistake he'd made at work over the venue booking, and perhaps her doubt had tinged the tone she'd used.

'The trust heard the story of his failing to secure a venue booking once,' the woman said. 'I asked him about that – it was my duty. But having heard his explanation there's no doubt in my mind that the other party was at fault.'

If Emily had concluded that, presumably Bernard could have too. Perhaps he'd closed his eyes to evidence that didn't suit him.

As for Adam – on top of everything else, he'd known he'd had a nice new job to go to, once his boss was out of the way. For a moment, Eve was lost in thought, but then Hugo Delaney swept past.

'I'm so sorry, please excuse me,' she said to Ms Moore. 'There's someone I must catch before they leave.'

CHAPTER TWENTY-SIX

It was clear to Eve that Delaney was one of those people who lived his life on the tip of his toes, dashing from one place to another physically and mentally. He agreed to talk to her eagerly, his blue eyes bright, red hair bobbing, but he wouldn't wait in the church.

'I know as a concert pianist I should probably be downing caviar and champagne with the best of them, but they're not to my taste. The journey up was appalling and what I'd really like now is a beer. Didn't I see a pub across the green?'

'You did. The Cross Keys. I'd love to buy you a pint there.'

He grinned. 'In that case, you're on.'

Five minutes later they were sitting at a wooden table outside the pub, and Hugo was taking a long swig of his Adnams Southwold bitter with a show of great appreciation. He perched forward on his seat. 'So, tell me – how can I help?'

She explained her overall mission. 'And your viewpoint will be quite different, of course, from people he knew around here. When did you see Bernard last?'

Hugo put his pint down for a second and fished a phone from his trouser pocket, opening the screen and peering at his calendar. 'Not long ago at all. Around a week before he died. He and I were planning to do a recital in a few weeks' time. We were nailing down the programme. It feels eerie now, because Fi was there too.'

Eve paused, the St Clements she'd ordered from Matt Falconer halfway to her lips. 'Excuse me?'

'Fi was there to organise some PR around the event. I can't believe she's gone as well.' He frowned, his red hair falling into his eyes. 'Is there something wrong?'

Eve put her drink down on the pub table and glanced over her shoulder, her instinct for caution kicking in before she replied.

'But Fi Goddard left her job with Bernard six months ago.'

The pianist frowned. 'Well, they mentioned she was working from home now. When I called her, it was on her mobile, not on the phone at High House.'

Eve realised her mouth was hanging open and closed it. 'But I understand Mr Fitzpatrick had employed a new publicity manager in Fi's place.'

Hugo looked bemused. 'Polly what's-her-name? He said she was just a junior, learning a few tricks of the trade.'

Eve took a sustaining swig of her St Clements to rid herself of the last feeling of sleepiness the late-morning champagne had induced. 'Fi had gotten herself another job. That was why she left.' Only of course, she'd turned it down at the last minute…

Hugo shrugged. 'I didn't know about that. It all seems very odd. She was carrying on as normal when I saw her.'

'And how did she and Mr Fitzpatrick seem together?' It was a pretty personal question, but her confusion must have stopped Hugo from seeing it as unreasonable.

'Fine. I mean – they always got on brilliantly. To be honest' – he rolled his eyes – 'I was sure they were having an affair. But please don't quote me on that.'

Her head was starting to spin. 'I won't. Fi spoke warmly about him when we talked, but she didn't seem devastated by the news of his death.'

Hugo shifted in his seat, took a swig of his beer and frowned. 'Oh well, I wouldn't read anything into that. She wouldn't have seen him as her one and only, I'm sure. I'd expect her to be upset, but not heartbroken. She was a livewire who lived for the moment; you must have noticed that. I remember Bernard saying she was married to some dull old duffer and I suspect their affair spiced things up.'

A dull old duffer, but a clever one. Eve suddenly remembered his area of expertise. 'Her husband was a celebrity divorce lawyer. He's retired now, but he was at the top of his game, apparently.' She gave Delaney a look.

His eyes opened wider. 'Oh my word. Do you suppose she pretended to give up her job when he got suspicious?'

That was exactly the idea forming in Eve's mind, but it seemed incredible. And of course Fi had genuinely applied for and got the role at Thrushcroft Hall. Wouldn't it have been simpler to just say she was going freelance?

Maybe they'd decided to part company to put Andrew Goddard off the scent, and Bernard had only thought of the plan to keep Fi on after she'd been offered the new job.

She nodded slowly. 'Maybe.'

'It would fit.' He sat even further forward on the bench now and swigged some more of his drink. 'I mean, without being unkind, I imagine she saw Bernard as some sugar and spice to keep her life sweet, and her husband as the one to keep her in diamond necklaces in her retirement. Crazy really. She could have been entirely independent if she'd moved on to a better-paid role. She certainly had the skills – but I suppose she was having too much fun with Bernard to want to do that.'

So she'd invented her own business, created her website and populated the client list with fictitious companies...

'It won't have been because she couldn't bear to give Bernard up,' Hugo said, 'or vice versa. It'll be the adrenaline rush that had her hooked. They'd have done it for kicks, to see what they could get away with.' He nodded. 'I'll bet that's it. Sneaky old devil!' He grinned and shook his head, nostalgia in his eyes.

'If he'd still been paying her salary direct from his account, I'd imagine the police would have been onto it, given what's happened.' Of course, they might have been, for all she knew.

Hugo shrugged. 'Maybe he paid her cash in hand. I can imagine they'd have thought that was a hoot, too. She must have been on her toes all the time, making sure she didn't give anything away when she talked on the phone. A challenge with a hint of danger – just the sort of thing Fi would have liked.'

The more he'd gone into detail, the more amused he'd seemed, but suddenly all levity dropped from his expression.

'Do you think Andrew Goddard found out?' His worried blue eyes were on Eve's.

She swallowed. 'If he did, he had all the expert knowledge to end his marriage in the courts.'

They looked at each other. She guessed Delaney was thinking the same as she was. If fury had gotten the better of him, Andrew Goddard might have chosen a more violent way out. He'd sounded full of menace, that day on the beach... Had he pretended to suspect Fi of involvement in Fitzpatrick's murder to make himself look innocent, and lull his wife into a false sense of security? Eve thought back. He'd sounded so convincing. But then she considered his profession: lawyers had to be good actors. They dug for evidence, then sold it to their audience, be it judge, magistrate or jury. And then suddenly she remembered Cole Wentworth's anecdote about Andrew showing a party of guests round High House. Bernard had gone on about how Andrew should give them the full tour, treating him like a lazy schoolboy who might do a rushed job. In revenge, Andrew had taken Bernard at his word, even escorting the guests into Bernard's bedroom. What if he'd seen something of Fi's there? An abandoned bit of clothing, her lipstick on his dressing table or some other item? Maybe all the time Fi and Bernard had been laughing at him behind his back, he'd been well aware of their antics. The thought made her shiver, despite the heat of the sun.

'I suppose you must have talked with Fi regularly over the years,' she said at last.

Delaney took a swig of his beer. 'Yes, I got to know her quite well in the end. She was frequently around at post-performance parties and the like.'

Andrew's jealousy would have had a chance to develop and fester over time, then.

'Despite what I said about her doing things for kicks,' Delaney went on, 'I'm sure she was genuinely fond of Bernard. He showed me a gold cigarette case she'd bought him once – engraved with a very sweet message from her, I seem to remember.' He frowned. 'Oh heavens, I wonder where that's got to. It could give away their affair if it goes on display in the new museum!'

Eve felt her skin prickle as his words brought back a memory. It must be the case she'd seen in Fitzpatrick's study, the day she'd interviewed Adam Cox. She remembered him tidying it away as soon as she'd set eyes on it. It hadn't struck her as odd at the time; he'd moved to clear away an ashtray just afterwards. But now she thought about it, wasn't it weird that it was the beautiful case he'd rushed to hide first? If she'd been responsible for the state of Fitzpatrick's workroom she would have made straight for the ashtray. Given Cox's relationship with Fi, he was hardly likely to have removed it to protect her reputation. He must have had another reason. His expression that day came back to her: his eyes blinking rapidly. It was a sign of nerves… She couldn't make sense of her thoughts, but she'd return to them later.

Her mind ran over other facts now, and how the bits of the puzzle she'd been amassing might fit together. What about the sale of Melgrove Place, and her theory that Fitzpatrick had somehow exacted pressure to stop Fi getting rid of it? She'd been way off there.

And yet the situation was still odd. Perhaps Andrew had wanted them to sell up and leave Saxford St Peter. If he'd suspected his wife of having an affair with her former boss, he might have instigated the move, allowing her to handle the admin side of things, as the estate agent had suggested. Perhaps Fi had pretended to embrace the idea of a fresh start to allay his fears.

But knowing that she'd carried on working for Bernard secretly – and probably sleeping with him too – made it likely she'd wanted to stay in the village. Word had gotten out that Billy Tozer had put in an offer, so Fi must have had to accept it, initially, for the sake of appearances. She couldn't have kept it from her husband. But after that, she must have taken matters into her own hands, in secret. Moira had told Eve the sale had 'fallen through'. Fi had probably given everyone the impression that it was Tozer who'd pulled out. And, of course, she'd asked the estate agent not to discuss the details with her husband. Initially, the truth had stayed under wraps.

And maybe it wasn't just her desire to remain in the village that had driven her actions. She met Delaney's eyes.

'Hugo, what do you think Bernard's reaction would have been if he'd found out that the rapper Billy Tozer was going to buy a house in the village?'

The pianist looked taken aback, then laughed. 'Is this some weird way of getting to the heart of Bernard's character, by asking left-field questions? Well, I don't want to be disloyal, but I'd say he'd have hated it! Can you imagine? Saxford St Peter has become world famous – in musical circles at least – as his home. Someone like Billy Tozer moving in would have completely overshadowed him. Let's face it, pop stars get a lot more media attention than classical musicians; even I've heard of Tozer.' He shook his head.

It all figured. She bet Fitzpatrick would have encouraged Fi to turn Tozer down, for more reasons than one. And it wouldn't have been a big ask, if she didn't want to move anyway. And then a couple of months later, Fi and Andrew had taken Melgrove Place off the market altogether. Maybe Andrew's desire to move away had waned, as Fi appeared to have distanced herself from her supposedly former boss. And then Andrew had finally gotten the truth about the Tozer offer from the estate agents. What had he thought about it? And had Fi known he'd uncovered her secret? Or had Andrew stored the information, suspecting the worst but waiting for proof?

As Eve made her way back towards Elizabeth's Cottage, past bees buzzing round buddleia, roses and honeysuckle, she reviewed the facts. She wanted to know it all, but in reality, she ought to be satisfied. The take-home point was that Fi had still been intimately involved with Bernard, right up until a week before he'd died.

She was due at the teashop in an hour and a half, and she needed to walk Gus, but the new knowledge she had wouldn't wait. She'd stumbled on a definite, deliberate deception involving the two murder victims – a hard fact, as opposed to the speculation she'd been dealing in. Whatever Fi had gotten up to in life, she hadn't deserved to die. The killer who'd robbed her of her future needed to be brought to justice, and maybe Eve's evidence would help.

One person, at least, looked a heck of lot more suspicious than they had done. And then her mind turned to the other reason she'd been digging: to use her professional skills in a new way. Her thoughts moved to Ian for a second as she let herself into Elizabeth's Cottage, her pulse quickening.

The moment she got inside, before grabbing Gus's leash, she flipped open her laptop. The details seemed too incredible – and too involved – to pass on to the police by phone. As soon as she'd emailed her update she called the hotline, though. She wanted to let them know her information might be important.

CHAPTER TWENTY-SEVEN

Eve arrived at Monty's a bit pink in the face, having dashed Gus out to the coast and back after emailing the police. She was now aware that nothing annoyed a dog more than being given a sniff of the sea, only to be dragged away again at high speed.

She found Viv serving, alongside a teenager with chestnut-coloured hair pulled up into a bun.

'Don't worry,' Viv said, making a beeline for Eve. 'Angie's expecting me to take a break, so I can catch up with you. I've bagged us that table in the far corner, in case you want to talk about the murders. Sylvia and Daphne are joining us soon, but I wanted you to myself first!'

Eve rolled her eyes. 'Nothing happened with Simon. We just went on the Black Shuck tour, and then for a quick drink at the Cross Keys. He was charming, but he admitted that he'd asked Fitzpatrick's new publicity manager out for a drink. She turned him down, but I'm guessing that was recent. She's probably more the type he's after; someone who's closer to him in age. How old is he, by the way?'

'Forty-three. Come on! You can't be much older than that.'

'Forty-nine.'

'Blimey. What moisturiser do you use? Anyway, six years is nothing. I'll bet Polly is more than six years younger than him.'

'That makes me feel so much better! Either way, I'm not getting dewy-eyed.' She put her head on one side. 'I'm not the kind of person who would, anyway.'

Viv raised an eyebrow. 'Sure? It might do you some good, one day – but not with Simon, perhaps.'

'He's offered to take me to Bernard Fitzpatrick's commemorative concert tomorrow. Are you going? I was wondering if we might all head over together.'

'Can't be your chaperone, I'm afraid,' Viv said. 'I've been seeing this guy over in Wickham Market. Been going on for a bit, just occasional meet-ups. But tomorrow's one of them – carefully timed, as Sam won't be around. He's coming over to mine. What about your investigations? How are they going?'

Eve smiled. 'My obituary research, you mean?'

'Call it what you like.'

Was it enough to swear Viv to secrecy and tell?

'If you're after payment in food, I can inform you that Angie should arrive with tea and Pimm's cupcakes shortly. Tangy citrus sponge, infused with Pimm's syrup, with a mint and strawberry icing. Perfect for a summer's day.'

'Okay, you win – but this isn't to go any further. Promise?'

Viv nodded, and Eve explained everything she'd found out since she'd last caught her up. Her new friend put her hand over her mouth when she got to the bit about Fi and Bernard's deception.

'I understand. My lips are sealed. But goodness – in my wildest imagination I hadn't expected that.'

'Same. I contacted the police to explain.' She was already wondering what Palmer's reaction would be. Finding out the truth was paramount, of course, but she also longed to wipe the sneer off his face.

At that moment the two women Eve had seen at the memorial service came through the teashop door, causing the bell to jangle and a soft breeze to reach her. The girl called Angie appeared with a tray, laden with the cakes, a generously sized pot of tea, milk, sugar and cups.

'You're an angel, Angie. Thank you!' Viv said, standing up at the same time as Eve, and pulling out chairs for the newcomers.

Eve's neighbours were both elegant and rather beautiful, but in totally different ways. Sylvia was tall, her thick mane of hair still tied into the loose plait. It fell below her shoulders. She had a mischievous smile and an ironic look in her eye. Daphne had kind, interested grey eyes and a lively face. Her short layered haircut looked even more stylish close up. They both held out hands to Eve at the same time, and then laughed.

'Poor Eve!' Sylvia said. 'Let's not be formal – that will solve the problem. Delighted to meet you!'

'Absolutely delighted,' Daphne agreed. 'I can't believe we haven't bumped into you yet. I had thought of knocking, just to say hello, but I remember when we arrived in the village, decades ago now, the constant unexpected appearance of neighbours was hard to get used to, so I held back.'

They all sat down.

'I think I heard you playing the violin, the day I arrived,' Eve said.

Daphne blushed and Sylvia gave a quirk of a smile, the laughter in her eyes again.

'I'm very fond of it as a pastime, even if I'm not all that good!' Daphne said.

'It sounded great to me.' Eve ignored the bum note she'd heard at the end of the piece the woman had been playing. 'I imagine it's a very difficult instrument to master.'

Daphne nodded. 'Surprisingly so.'

'Takes many decades, it seems,' Sylvia said drily.

'You are rotten!' But Daphne was laughing.

'You can't be good at everything – it would be too annoying.' Sylvia turned to Eve. 'Daphne's a potter. Have you seen the crackle-glazed vases and jugs, here in the craft market?'

Eve turned to Daphne. 'Those are yours?' She'd been coveting them ever since the day Moira Squires' sister April had brought her carvings in. 'They're beautiful. Such elegant shapes, and those intense colours!'

Daphne's blush went far deeper this time. 'Thank you. But you should know about Sylvia's photography too. Her work appears in the top magazines, and it sells very well.'

It was clear Daphne didn't like to be in the limelight, even for a moment.

'That sounds amazing. I'd love to hear more about both your careers.' Perhaps she should develop a sideline, writing about the living – though she imagined it would lead to complications.

'Your profession sounds fascinating too,' Sylvia said. 'And we hear you're writing about Bernard.' She shook her head. 'Quite an undertaking.'

Viv had poured them all tea and leaned forward now. 'I thought you two might be able to contribute your knowledge. Tell Eve your memories of him and so on.'

'I'm very fond of music,' Daphne said, 'so I used to attend any local concert that he gave. He was charming – passionate. It's a cliché, but he was larger than life. He did some fantastic question-and-answer sessions after his recitals.'

'He was a patronising so-and-so who loved the sound of his own voice! And he disguised cruel sentiment behind clever words.' Sylvia's eyes were wry.

'You couldn't expect him to take my efforts seriously. I wish Moira Squires had never told him I played the violin.'

'He wouldn't have known otherwise,' Sylvia added. 'He didn't mix much.'

'It's so interesting to discover that Cole Wentworth is his son!' Daphne put in. 'It fits – and yet I had no idea at all. Cole is quite like Bernard was, facially. And then of course there's the music connection.' Her eyes drifted to the middle distance. 'I've walked past Woodlands House and heard Cole practising more than once. It brought tears to my eyes. And I'm fairly certain he composes his own pieces too. I heard music I couldn't identify, that didn't sound like any composer that I'm aware of.'

'And she's aware of a lot,' Sylvia said, confidently. 'I can hardly fit my photography books onto the shelves in our sitting room for CDs – those and tomes about ceramics.'

'I hear Cole has a place to study composition in the fall,' Eve said.

'That would make sense.' Daphne took a bite of her Pimm's cake. 'New recipe, Viv? Phenomenal.'

Eve had been thinking the same.

'Who else have you talked to?' Sylvia asked.

Eve went through the list until she came to Lucas Booth. Today's revelations showed Andrew Goddard had a strong motive for the two murders, but the banker was still on her mind too. If the rumours of his late wife and Fitzpatrick's affair were true, he'd had good reason to hate the man, but there was more to uncover. She still needed to prove her theory that it was he who'd lied about his and his wife's move to their new home, not Robin Yardley. And she was more than curious to know why. Maybe now was her chance. 'I was interested to hear that Lucas used to own High House. I gather he sold up when his wife got ill?'

'Actually, Sophie developed cancer after they moved,' Daphne said.

Bingo. It *was* Yardley who'd told the truth.

'And it wasn't *his* house, I remember,' Sylvia put in. 'Sophie inherited it from her parents; then he moved in when he married her.'

Eve remembered the estate agent saying the place had been sold on to Fitzpatrick privately, at a dinner party. She asked if the house had gone straight from Sophie to the cellist, as far as anyone knew.

'Yes, that's right,' Daphne said. 'I remember wondering if she'd had to sell it in order to support Lucas's career.'

Viv frowned. 'But he's a banker, isn't he?'

'Wasn't back then,' Sylvia said. 'He'd started out in finance but gave it up to write poetry, when a small publisher got excited about his work.' She shook her head. 'It's always difficult to make money from careers in the arts.' She glanced from Daphne to Eve. 'We all know that. But from poetry? You're doomed to failure, unless you're a household name.'

And Sophie probably hadn't earned much either, given Fitzpatrick's reputation as a penny-pinching employer.

'I think Sophie found her work for Bernard quite intense,' Daphne put in, as though her thoughts had followed the same track as Eve's.

That was interesting. Lucas said it had been a nine-to-five role that she'd left as she'd closed the office door. Maybe she'd been more taken up with it than he'd liked to admit. Because the rumours about her and Fitzpatrick having an affair were true? Or just because she'd been dedicated? Eve was betting Lucas thought the former – why lie about it otherwise? As it was, he might have been trying to save face. Or to hide the reasons for his hatred of the cellist.

'She liked to spend money on leisure activities – sailing, skiing and so on – and she dressed nicely too. All of that must have cost a fair amount. I don't blame her for selling her parents' house to fund those things. Such a dreadful shame that she got ill.'

Eve nodded. 'Awful. Did Lucas switch back to banking immediately after they moved, or when Sophie's health failed?' Maybe the need to downsize had been a wake-up call. Or perhaps Sophie's eventual inability to work had forced his hand.

'I rather think it was between those two points in time,' Daphne said, frowning.

'It was.' Sylvia finished her tea. 'He'd just got his first step up at the bank when Sophie took a turn for the worse. He was away from the village from six in the morning until nine at night.' She gave Eve a look. 'A pretty poor show, in my book.'

Daphne clearly remembered too, though she held back from saying anything.

If he'd suspected Sophie of having an affair, maybe he hadn't been able to shelve that thought, even when she was suffering so badly. Was that why he'd turned his back on her at such a terrible time?

It made Eve wonder about Simon's theory that Lucas was still grieving. Fitzpatrick's death would have brought back memories of the old days. Maybe it was guilt that had taken him to St Peter's the night before. But for the way he'd treated Sophie? Or for something more recent?

At that moment, Angie appeared near their table. She was biting her lip and looking at Viv. 'Sorry. Work-related query and it's a bit urgent.'

They'd all finished their tea and cakes.

'We'll get out of your hair,' Sylvia said. She turned to Eve. 'Come and give us a knock if you need anything. The gin and tonic comes out at six.'

'Hope to see you soon,' Daphne said, as though she meant it.

As the pair walked to the front of the teashop, Eve found herself smiling.

Viv, on the other hand, had gone pink after a whispered conversation with Angie that Eve had failed to hear. Her cheeks didn't quite match her hair for intensity, but it was close. 'Right, right. Thanks, Angie,' she said, walking towards the door that must lead to the teashop's preparation area. Eve followed.

'Oh heck.' Viv's hair danced as she looked rapidly from left to right at the chaotic kitchen. Eve hadn't imagined it would be like this.

'Problem?'

'Something of a cock-up on my part. Thirty day-trippers are due to arrive in forty minutes for tea, only I forgot to write it down in the book. The coach driver just called to check the directions.' She chewed her lip. 'Sam's gone off to London with Kirsty for a couple of nights – something to do with a visa – so this is just a little bit tight. Angie's wonderful, but she's no cook. And I haven't got thirty of anything, let alone what I promised them.'

CHAPTER TWENTY-EIGHT

Eve could see why Viv was looking anxious. There'd be the issue of the tables too, with thirty extra customers. The teashop was packed and none of the clientele looked like they were in a hurry.

'Can I help?'

'Aaaah!' Viv ran her hands through her hair. 'Um. Maybe? Do you know how to make scones?' Then she paused. 'Oh no – you might call them something else.'

'No sweat. I know how to bake the kind you mean – I've been in the UK since I was a student, and I have an English dad, don't forget.' The British scone was another thing he'd made sure she was exposed to, along with tea. They were less buttery than her mom's, but her dad made up for that by applying a thick sweep of clotted cream and jam between two slices. She made them quite often. They were comforting, and a useful standby if she needed to produce something quickly.

There was a ray of hope in Viv's eye. 'Could you make up thirty? Here's the cutter to use. I promised them scones as part of a set plateful. I'll just rustle up some of the chocolate hearts.' She glanced feverishly at her watch. 'Then there are just the lemon tartlets, but I've got blind-baked pastry cases in the freezer.'

Eve was surprised that they managed to work intensely in the same space without getting edgy around each other. It helped that Viv didn't do full-on panic, and Eve – having been set her task – simply hunkered down, knowing she wasn't responsible for the incoming crowd. If she'd been in charge of the place, she'd have been sweating blood, but of course, if *she'd* been in charge, she would have written down their booking. There were advantages to being a control freak.

But as the minutes ticked by, she found herself feeling more and more ownership of the situation. As soon as the scones were in the oven, she went to have a look at the state of play in the teashop. It was still full of customers.

Back in the kitchen, she approached Viv, who was just putting the chocolate heart cakes into the oven. 'Erm, do you have any spare tables that we could put on the lawn round the back, maybe?'

'Hell!' Viv's eyes opened wide. 'That's a point. I've been so preoccupied with the lack of cakes, I haven't even thought about where they'll sit! Is there anyone out front that we know?'

'You're thinking we could ask them to vacate their table?'

She grinned. 'I was thinking we could ask them to help us move my garden furniture – and some other tables – out of my house and into the teashop grounds.'

'Ah.' Eve went through to the main room to have a look, then darted back to the kitchen. 'Your brother's there now, as a matter of fact, talking to a guy I don't recognise.'

'It must be one of the business contacts he mentioned; he said he had a couple of meetings today.' For a moment she smiled. 'Actually, I'm rather touched he decided to bring the guy here. But no, we can't ask him. I'd never live it down. The cakes are in. Let's dash over to my place now and see what we can find.'

As they walked through Viv's side gate, two tabby cats whizzed between Eve's feet as though they were jet propelled.

'What the—?'

'That's Scruffy and Fluffy. There are more, so mind you don't trip over them. Here.' She indicated the garden table. 'Let's take this for starters.'

*

Quite how it all worked, Eve didn't know. By the time Angie was ushering the pre-booked party through the teashop, they had a collection of tables assembled on the grass outside, all covered in spare cloths that matched the pink ones elsewhere. The chairs were a random mix, but that didn't look so very odd, thanks to the deliberately non-matching crockery. Viv was still icing the chocolate heart cakes as Eve and Angie got the group sitting down, and the cream to go with the scones and jam was a little late arriving. But all in all, the group seemed happy. The sunshine and the idyllic situation probably helped.

Back in the kitchen, she caught Viv tucking into a spare scone.

'Come on!' she said. 'I mean, I have to check what they're like!'

'How did I do?'

'You're *good*!'

'Well, don't get complacent. I can only do scones and a couple of other basics. My advice is to sort out your admin.'

Viv laughed. 'You might just have a point. But I bet you could diversify on the cake front, with a small amount of training.'

'I'll be back in London in less than a week.'

Viv sighed. 'That seems like such a bad idea. We need a buyer for Elizabeth's Cottage. You could swap your part-time job in London for one here... I'm advertising.' She thrust a sheet of paper with the details on it into Eve's hands. 'I need someone who can share the management and the cooking, so the rates aren't bad. I'm no Fitzpatrick skinflint.'

Eve glanced momentarily at the sheet and hoped she hadn't given herself away. Viv was right – the salary wasn't bad at all, but it was no good. She already had a job. And she loved London. 'It's great here, but I'm a city girl. Honestly.'

Viv didn't look in the least discouraged. 'Okay. But it was fun today, wasn't it?'

'You're weird, you know that?'

Viv grinned again. 'I take your pronouncement as a huge compliment.'

Back at Elizabeth's Cottage, Eve settled down at the dining room table, the sun streaming in through the window and Gus at her feet. It was time to get back to her real work – or at least, the investigative task she'd set herself. Sylvia and Daphne's extra information on Lucas Booth, his wife and Bernard Fitzpatrick had set her antennae twitching. There was something there – she was sure of it. Some detail that she hadn't yet unearthed. However preoccupied she'd been with Andrew Goddard, she wasn't planning on getting blinkered.

Alongside her laptop, she opened her notebook and sketched out a timeline. Robin Yardley said Sophie Booth had died two years after she and Lucas had moved into their new house, and she'd only stopped gardening a while after the move.

Daphne and Sylvia had implied that Sophie liked her luxuries, and although she had a solid job for Fitzpatrick, it hadn't been enough to allow her to maintain her lifestyle. She'd decided to sell her parents' place and downsize to release some capital. Lucas wasn't contributing much when he'd worked as a poet, but later, after the move, he'd gone back to banking and just at the point when poor Sophie was too ill to help him enjoy his earnings, he'd started to climb the career ladder.

Eve googled Sophie and found her dates via an in memoriam notice in the digital edition of the local paper. She'd died six years earlier. She'd been so young; only thirty-four. So, going by Robin's information, she and Lucas had left High House around eight years earlier.

Eve googled 'Lucas Booth' and 'poetry' and found a list of pamphlets he'd had published. He'd gotten good reviews – and from some well-known names. He'd won the odd prize and been featured in magazines. She imagined him back then: the excitement he must have felt each time someone influential had praised his work, or he was featured on the radio or in the press. Every bit of encouragement must have fed his desire to carry on. But maybe, when they'd had to downsize, he'd seen the need for a day job alongside his writing. What on earth had made him go back to banking? His hours had been so long. Maybe he'd tried to use his commute to keep up his poetry, but in Eve's experience, writing on trains was hit and miss. Oftentimes she'd found herself standing her entire journey, crammed against other passengers with the noise from someone else's earphones as an irritating backdrop.

She continued her research and found several links to examples of Lucas's work. She sat reading for some time, Gus nudging her occasionally for attention. She stroked his head. 'In a minute, buddy. Just let me concentrate.'

She'd thought she'd only want to read a couple of the man's poems, out of nosiness, but in the end, she ran through every example of his work online. The verse was sharply nostalgic and pulled at her heartstrings. It was the way he'd used the Suffolk landscape to link ideas, tell stories and pour out his soul. The view from High House – the woods and heathland, the beach and the wild sea – in all seasons and moods, forceful and elemental, featured repeatedly.

When she came to assess the online works, interviews and references as a whole, she realised the timing was interesting. It didn't look as though Lucas *had* combined writing with banking. His output seemed to have tailed off around the time he and Sophie had moved to their new house – or maybe a little later. Perhaps it had been when his wife became ill – or at the point when their marriage was breaking down. He might have worked his long hours to block out the pain (it seemed inhuman, whatever the reason), and not had the emotional capacity to carry on with anything creative.

She shook her head. She'd just spent over an hour researching the background of a man she wasn't writing about. But Lucas Booth still presented a puzzle, in terms of Fitzpatrick's murder. Her normal methods involved targeted digging – and she wouldn't stop until the metaphorical earth fell away from the object she was trying to see clearly.

She went back to her search results, to look for the last publication she could find recorded – a poetry pamphlet listed on Amazon Marketplace, produced by a small press based in Ipswich. Within a minute she'd found the publisher's website and their contact number. Time for some more play-acting…

'I'm compiling an anthology of East Anglian poets,' she said, after introducing herself to the man who answered her call. 'I've just discovered Lucas Booth's work, and in theory he'd be a wonderful person to include, but I can see he hasn't published anything recently.' She hesitated. 'I wondered if you'd dealt with him personally at all?'

The guy on the phone laughed. '*I have to confess, I'm a one-man band, so yes, I did.*'

'Ah – in that case you might be able to rescue me. Do you know if he's given up writing? I was thinking of contacting him direct, but I don't want to upset him if it's a sore subject.'

The man sighed. '*To be honest, it might be. He gave up a while back now.*'

'I heard his wife died.'

'*That's right. But he actually ran out of steam before that. He got his inspiration from the place where he lived. I visited once – he had an office where he could sit in complete isolation and look out over the landscape. In his head, for whatever reason, he needed that space to do his work. Between ourselves, when he moved to a rather more ordinary place, further from the coast, that was it. Whether he told himself he couldn't function or there was some other kind of block, I don't know. The final poem he wrote was about the old house. It's called "Last View". The grief he felt at leaving is painfully obvious. It was meant to be part of a new collection that I was to publish, but the rest of the work was never written.'*

After she'd ended the call, Eve sat on the couch, thinking. Lucas Booth ought to have been grateful that his wife was happy to support him in his early career as a poet. Selling her family home put off the need for him to get a job, at least for a little while. Maybe he had appreciated her sacrifice – but after what his publisher said, maybe not.

Maybe he felt Sophie had handed the house that had been his muse to Bernard on a plate, ignoring Lucas's wishes in favour of the man whose spell she'd fallen under... Had Lucas pictured Bernard, up in the eyrie that had once been his own creative haven, practising the cello, occasionally venturing downstairs to spend a pleasant hour or two with Sophie...? Even if the affair had been imagined, it would have eaten away at him: the idea of a man he guessed had captured his wife's affections also robbing him of his creativity – of his vocation even.

At that moment, a knock on the door of Elizabeth's Cottage made her jump, and Gus let out a series of fierce barks. She went to the window and recognised the face outside.

Another visit from DI Palmer. He must have read her email.

CHAPTER TWENTY-NINE

The inspector peered down at Gus as Eve opened the door and stepped back to let him in. He and the dachshund might have met before, but Gus didn't seem any more inclined to trust him this time. Eve silently congratulated the dog on what she felt were his excellent instincts. Palmer's heavy tread made the living room floorboards creak.

'I'm here to discuss the information you emailed to our case coordinator.' He spoke as though she was in trouble.

After Palmer's previous brusque reaction to her offer of a drink, she held back. She was guessing he wouldn't want to prolong his visit any more than she did. She invited him to sit on one of the two couches in the living room and it sank low under his bulk as she took the one opposite. Gus had given up his inspection of the bits of Palmer he could reach and sat at her feet, eyeing the man suspiciously.

'I was curious to know how you came to discover such personal information about Mrs Goddard. You're in the village to write about Bernard Fitzpatrick, not his former publicity manager – and you claimed last time I visited that you'd never met her before you arrived here.' His eyes were watchful as he waited for her answer.

'I explained it all in my message.' Eve didn't see why she should repeat herself.

'Indeed. You stumbled across the information by accident while interviewing one of Mr Fitzpatrick's musician friends.'

'Hugo Delaney.'

Palmer raised an eyebrow. 'And yet you seem to have spent your time pressing him for information on the minutiae of Mrs Goddard's life.'

'I wouldn't call it minutiae. And wouldn't you ask for more details if you found a person you'd interviewed had flat-out lied to you?' She wasn't a doormat.

Palmer sighed and shifted his large shoulders. He reached his notebook from his jacket pocket. It looked small in his hand. 'I certainly don't appreciate it when people tell me untruths.'

Eve ignored the underlying threat in his tone. 'We're in agreement, then.'

Palmer frowned. 'And you still maintain you'd never met Mrs Goddard before you arrived in Saxford St Peter – when was it – last Thursday?'

Eve nodded. 'That's right – and yes, my answer is exactly the same as when you asked me last.'

The inspector looked at her narrowly. 'I hope you understand, madam, that we have to be certain of our facts. This is – I'm sure you'll admit – a serious matter.'

Eve counted silently to ten.

'It's your moral obligation to pass any information you find on to us – and to let *us* follow it up.' He heaved himself forward in his seat.

The message that she should butt out was plain. Eve's mind ran to the call she'd made to Fi Goddard's prospective employers at Thrushcroft Hall, and the fishing she'd done at the estate agent's – but she didn't feel guilty. 'That's why I sent the information I'd stumbled across straight over to the police.'

Gus put his paws up on the cushions, nuzzling his nose into her hand. She knew she should tell him to get down – it wasn't her furniture – but his presence was comforting.

'Given what you know now, is there any other information you've withheld? Any detail, however small?'

Withheld? She'd let them know what she was up to right from the start – and sprang into action the moment she'd found concrete evidence. She sat there trying to force her mind to work through a fog of irritation. She could do with checking her notes, but she didn't want him looking over her shoulder at the Excel spreadsheet named 'murder suspects'.

Love triangles formed in her head: Andrew, Fi and Fitzpatrick. Fitzpatrick, Adele and Fi…

Should she sketch in some of the finer details Hugo Delaney had passed on? Palmer didn't deserve it, but that wasn't important. 'Mr Delaney said Mrs Goddard liked excitement, but that Mr Fitzpatrick wasn't a steady man and she'd have wanted to stay with her husband.' She paused. 'That said, he mentioned that Mrs Goddard was genuinely fond of Mr Fitzpatrick. Apparently, she bought him an expensive present.' If that was how you gauged the depth of someone's affection. It wasn't how Eve measured it. 'A gold cigarette case with an inscription on it. I believe I saw it in Bernard Fitzpatrick's work room at High House, so I assume Adam Cox has it now.' *Why had he hidden it away?*

Palmer drew himself up and frowned. 'We're already aware of the item. Our crime scene investigators found it hidden in Mrs Goddard's room at Melgrove Place on Sunday. When did you see it at High House – assuming we're talking about the same object?'

'The day after I arrived in the village – so, last Friday. Mr Cox must have returned it to her then—' She stopped mid-sentence, thinking. 'Unless…'

'Unless?'

Eve's cheeks were feeling hot at the thoughts she was having. 'I heard Fi Goddard was seen near Adam Cox's house, shortly before it was broken into.' And Eve had wondered whether Fi was looking for evidence that Adam had killed Fitzpatrick. But maybe that hadn't been her motive for breaking in…

Palmer was sitting right on the edge of the couch now. 'We've heard similar reports.' He tapped his pen against his chin. 'I shall be wanting another word with Mr Cox – down at the station this time.'

Eve could see why. If he'd hoped to blackmail Fi Goddard, and she'd broken in, stolen the cigarette case and covered his sitting room wall with a mocking message, his rage might have tipped him over the edge. It was a leap from blackmail to murder, but his plans to extort money threw his morals into question – and she'd seen the fury, desperation and humiliation in his eyes when she'd witnessed his interactions with the police. And so had Palmer, of course.

Eve sighed. She passed on what Emily Moore of the Blackforth Arts Trust had told her about the prearranged role for Adam at High House. Yet one more motive he'd had for killing Fitzpatrick.

Palmer appeared more and more confident by the second. She had a feeling he was deciding they'd got their man – there was a 'job done' look in his eye. But surely he'd investigate more thoroughly? A lot of the information on Adam Cox looked damning, but not any more so than the evidence against Andrew Goddard, as far as she knew. But, of course, Cox would be a pushover compared to a top lawyer with influential friends. She didn't trust the inspector not to follow the path of least resistance.

She showed Palmer out and stood for a moment in the doorway of the cottage, trying to take it all in. Her eyes drifted after the inspector, who'd gone to join the same colleague he'd been with the day she'd seen him outside Adam Cox's house.

It was only then that Eve's mind snapped sharply back to the here and now. The younger detective was in conversation with Robin Yardley.

They were both frowning, deep in discussion. As Palmer approached them, Yardley's expression changed. Whatever had been said last seemed to have made him angry.

CHAPTER THIRTY

Back inside Elizabeth's Cottage, Eve's mind ran over the new evidence.

The more she thought about it, the more she felt Palmer was barking up the wrong tree. Now she understood the real reason Fi had broken into Adam Cox's house, there was a question she couldn't get past. If Cox was Fi's murderer, how had they come to be on the heath together the night she'd died? If Fi had evidence of his guilt, Eve could understand it – they might have arranged a rendezvous there to discuss blackmail terms – but if it was actually Adam who'd been trying to blackmail *her*, and she'd stopped him in his tracks by stealing back the cigarette case, then that idea fell apart. Why on earth would she agree to such a meet-up? He had no further hold over her – she'd been home free.

Whereas her own husband could have managed to arrange it – suggesting a talk on neutral territory, perhaps. And what about Lucas Booth? She could imagine him working out an excuse to get her there too. He and Fi had both been members of the Blackforth Arts Trust; he could have said he needed to talk to her in private about something her husband Andrew – another trust member – had done, for instance. It would have been easy to portray it as a delicate matter he couldn't possibly have tackled at the Goddards' house – or at his own, which was close enough to Melgrove Place for Andrew to see Fi visiting. Eve thought back to the weather on Saturday night. It had been dreadful early on, but sun-streaked and beautiful again by mid-evening.

She wished she had a better handle on the time of Fi's death. If it had been late, then Andrew seemed more likely; it would have been harder for Lucas to lure her out. Unless she'd deliberately crept out after Andrew was asleep, of course. Escaping under his nose during the evening without him getting suspicious might have presented a problem.

As she entered the extra details on her spreadsheet, she made herself look again at the other key players in Fitzpatrick and Fi's lives. On paper, Adele Wentworth was still plausible, if you believed she'd committed a crime of passion, killing them both out of jealousy. But thinking back to her conversation with the woman, Eve couldn't see it. There was no sign she'd still been in love with the cellist. Her tone when she'd talked about him flirting with Sophie Booth had been totally detached. Plus, Adele was meant to have been in London the night Fi died. Her opinion of Palmer was low, but she guessed he'd have checked that out at least.

Eve rose the next morning feeling as though she'd hardly slept; her mind was just too busy. She needed to focus on the obituary she was meant to be writing. Her appointment to talk to Fitzpatrick's cook and his new, decoy publicity manager was that morning at High House at ten. She presumed Adam Cox would be there too. Despite her conclusions, she'd be watching him closely.

She wore her black jacket over the daisy dress – mix and match was the order of the day, given her limited wardrobe. Her black high heels and jet-black earrings would link the whole thing together.

The door to High House was opened by the stout woman Viv had pointed out at St Peter's. Her eyes were severe, and her grey hair was pulled back into a tight bun. She had a tic going in her left cheek. They must all be in a state of shock.

'Eve Mallow? I'm Mrs Anderson. Come in.' She looked disapproving. She was probably another person who put Eve in the same category as the muck-raking hacks who'd no doubt been knocking on her door.

'I'm so sorry to bother you at a time like this,' Eve said, stepping into the dark hall as Mary Anderson retreated. 'When I agreed to write about Mr Fitzpatrick, I had no idea he'd been deliberately killed. It's very much his life I want to ask you about – not his murder.' The woman gave a stiff nod. She hadn't unbent, but Eve hoped her message might sink in gradually.

'I gather from Viv Montague that you very kindly prepared the cottage I'm staying in,' Eve added.

The woman angled her head just slightly in her direction. 'That's right. High House is a big place, but it doesn't take up all my hours. I've seen to Elizabeth's Cottage for years now. Mr and Mrs Maxwell needed the help.' She said it as though she'd found Viv and Simon's parents wanting in household management skills. It made Eve think of Viv's workspace at the teashop. Maybe some things ran in families. 'We can talk downstairs in my kitchen.' Mrs Anderson led her to a large room in the basement. She still saw it as her domain, clearly. Eve remembered Viv describing the room as 'to die for' from a fellow cook's point of view. It was vast, and full of sweeping counters, gleaming hobs and twin butler sinks.

'Will you stay on when the house opens to the public?' Eve guessed the trust might want to sell refreshments to the visitors.

Mrs Anderson tutted. 'I will not. They asked me. They're going to turn this kitchen into a canteen and convert the storage space next door so that simple meals can be "heated up". And they'll order in sandwiches from who knows where.' Her shoulders were rigid. 'Besides, I don't "come with the house" in the same way as Adam Cox does.' There was derision in her tone. 'I worked for

Mr Fitzpatrick's parents before I worked for him. Now he's gone, I shall go too.'

'You knew Mr Fitzpatrick as a boy, then?' Eve felt a rush of excitement. If so, she'd probably know about his early relationships, including the one with his brother.

The cook nodded – still stiff in her movements. 'I joined the family when he was twelve.' There were tears in her eyes. 'I was only eighteen myself – a junior in Mr and Mrs Fitzpatrick senior's kitchen. I moved on to work for young Mr Fitzpatrick thirty years ago. I'm already at retirement age, but I was prepared to carry on for as long as I was able. It's different now.'

'Did you spend any time with him as he was growing up?' After all, there had only been six years' age difference between them. By the time he'd been seventeen, say, and she'd been twenty-three, the gap might not have felt so large.

Mary Anderson straightened in her chair and frowned. 'Certainly not. Apart from what was required due to my professional role.'

That was a shame from Eve's point of view, but surely spending that much time in the same house as Fitzpatrick had given her an idea of how his character had evolved.

'Could you tell me about the interactions you had in your professional capacity, then? Your impressions of him growing up? People reading an obituary love to understand how a well-known person developed, the experiences that formed them.'

Mary Anderson had taken a tissue from her pocket, but instead of using it to dry her eyes she was twisting and turning it in her hands.

'He was very driven,' she said, 'right from the start. I remember that. Old Mr Fitzpatrick, his father, could be cruel at times. He doubted Bern— young Mr Fitzpatrick's abilities. He had a second son and rated his talents more highly.'

That must have made the cellist resent his lawyer brother. And maybe the cool feelings had been mutual.

'Old Mr Fitzpatrick always said there was no future in young Mr Fitzpatrick's passion for music.' She wiped her eyes on the back of her hand. 'That just made him all the more determined. He had something to prove: he wanted to outshine his brother and everyone else too. There were no half measures for him.' She shook her head. 'It makes me emotional when I think of Mr Fitzpatrick leaving his cello to Cole Wentworth. He may not have made himself known to his son, but it's clear he gave him the blessing he was denied by his own father.'

'You had no idea of the connection between Cole and Mr Fitzpatrick until after his death?'

Mrs Anderson's eyes took on a wary look. 'None at all.'

Was she telling the truth? She must have been working for the cellist during his affair with Adele Wentworth. Maybe she'd sworn to keep his secret; she certainly seemed to feel a strong sense of loyalty towards her late boss. And what had she thought about his liaison with a married woman?

'What was Mr Fitzpatrick like with the staff here?' Eve said. She kept her tone even, but the man's affair with Fi Goddard and his cruelty towards Adam Cox were both high in her mind.

'He inspired devotion,' Mrs Anderson said. 'To my mind, he had a beautiful and unique talent, and by doing my small bit, I supported his efforts to bring something wonderful to the world.'

Hmm. Eve could imagine Adam Cox's reaction to that sentiment.

'I had the impression Fi Goddard felt the same, when I interviewed her.' That wasn't quite true, but Fi had implied you had to take the rough with the smooth, and that Bernard's personality went hand in hand with his superstar status.

Mary Anderson's lips disappeared and there was an angry spark in her eyes. 'I think Fi's motivation was very different from mine.'

After she and the cook had finished talking, Eve went to speak with Polly Cartwright back on the ground floor, in the office next to Adam Cox's. It was Mrs Anderson who escorted her, leaving her frustrated at not seeing the custodian. She could hear voices from his room; he must have a visitor.

'I really didn't know Bernard long,' Polly said, motioning Eve to take a seat on the opposite side of her desk. 'I found him charming at my interview, and he promised a lot.'

Eve watched her eyes. 'You never met him before you applied for the job here?'

'Never. To be honest, I hadn't even heard him play. But the role sounded like a great next step for me, so I went for it.' She pulled a face. 'I understand there's gossip about why he might have given me the job. It goes with the territory. Apparently you can't be young, female and competent at the same time.' She reached into a drawer and pulled out a bit of paper, which she pushed across the desk to Eve.

It was her résumé. And unless she'd made it all up, like Fi with her fake clients, it was highly impressive. Of course, it didn't mean Fitzpatrick hadn't lusted after her, but he'd still been in a relationship with Fi. Maybe he'd been delighted that people assumed he and Polly must be involved – it lent veracity to the elaborate fiction he and Fi had created. Eve's mind ran back to the argument Viv said the cellist and Fi had had during the fundraiser at the church hall. She'd said it had been like watching a soap opera. Perhaps even that had been staged.

'You say he promised a lot?'

'The job wasn't as billed. The duties were boring. I hadn't worked in the arts world before, so I was excited – but if you're doing really basic stuff then it's the same, whether it's for a cellist or the owner of a sock factory.'

Eve nodded.

'But he *was* a livewire. There was a certain sort of – electricity – when he came into the room.' She shook her head. 'That's the message I'd give, I guess, for your article.'

Eve thanked Polly and the woman stood up to see her out. They entered the hallway just as Adam Cox and his visitor emerged from the next-door office. Eve recognised the woman's face. It was Emily Moore, the administrator from the Blackforth Arts Trust. She opened her mouth to greet them both, but Ms Moore's eyes were still on Adam and his expression threw her off. Something had put him beyond social niceties. His face was white, his jaw slack. He had one hand on the doorframe of his room; she was quite sure he hadn't registered her presence at all.

Eve turned to Polly, whose questioning glance was on Emily Moore. But after a microsecond, her eyes were back on Eve.

'I'd better show you out.'

As Eve left the grounds she spotted Robin Yardley, weeding one of the flowerbeds. She caught his eye for a second, just before he dipped his head down.

CHAPTER THIRTY-ONE

Eve was with Gus on the beach. She'd ditched her jacket and replaced her heels with flip-flops before she'd walked down the estuary path with him to reach the coast. For a moment, she'd paused on her route and closed her eyes, listening to the reeds stirring in the breeze and the cries of the wading birds, out on the water. She'd wanted to find some balance after witnessing Adam Cox's distress, but the thought of Bernard Fitzpatrick's body, slumped in the estuary near where she stood, had invaded her headspace.

Now she was heading up the coast, well away from the village and the spot further south where the press said Fi's corpse had been discovered.

What on earth could Emily Moore have said to Adam? Gus was looking at her over his shoulder, no doubt sensing her preoccupation.

'You should have seen him, Gus,' she said, shaking a pebble out of her right flip-flop. 'I can't help wondering if they've rethought his job offer or something. Perhaps someone's come up with proof that he was trying to blackmail Fi Goddard.' Would that also mean he'd be arrested, even if the police couldn't prove he was guilty of murder? 'Either way, I couldn't possibly judge his reaction to her death. He was too busy reacting to something else.'

She took Gus's ball from her bag and threw it for him, wishing she could get it to go further. The breeze wasn't helping. He brought it back to her in seconds, wagging his tail and clearly wanting a repeat performance. As she chucked it again, a text came in on her phone.

It was Simon, checking she was still okay to attend the concert that evening. They were going to add in a tribute to Fi, apparently.

She texted back to confirm. In the intervening hours she would start to draft Bernard Fitzpatrick's obituary. The picture editor of the magazine that had commissioned her work had sent her his photos, so she could keep them in mind as she pulled the piece together. The structure was standard. After leading in with a paragraph introducing her subject, and adding some fascinating and unexpected fact, she normally followed a person's life from beginning to end to provide the narrative arc. Now she'd gotten Mary Anderson's reports on Fitzpatrick's childhood, and his relationships with his family, she was well set-up to follow that pattern. And of course, the opening paragraph in this case was destined to allude to the man's untimely end, as well as his spectacular career.

As she and Gus made their way home, her mind drifted briefly to Robin Yardley. She'd felt his eyes on her as she'd left the grounds of High House. She shook the memory away.

Back in the dining room at Elizabeth's Cottage, she opened the image she'd been sent of Bernard Fitzpatrick's childhood home – a large, forbidding-looking place with tall dark windows and a sombre, regimented garden. There was also a family group shot, taken when Fitzpatrick's brother had picked up an MBE at Buckingham Palace – presumably for his work in the Attorney General's office. Fitzpatrick would turn in his grave (or in the cooler at the mortuary as things stood) if they used that one. She remembered Mary Anderson's references to the competition between the brothers, and their father's preference for his younger son. She'd ask if they could dig up an alternative image instead. Surely there must be one of them all at an event of Bernard's? Or had the family never united to celebrate his work?

She managed to lose herself in her writing for an hour or so, but then something outside caught Gus's attention and he barked, breaking the spell. She got up to look out the window, but there was nothing to see.

She tried to return to her writing, but the moment was gone. For some reason, it was Robin Yardley's face that kept encroaching on her thoughts: the way he'd looked at her as she'd left High House that day, his presence at the site of Fitzpatrick's murder, and the information he'd given her on Lucas Booth.

And then she remembered his expression as he'd spoken with the detective on the corner of Haunted Lane the day before, just before Palmer joined them. She sighed and frowned at Gus, who raised a questioning eyebrow. An idea was forming in her head.

'I might have to go out,' she said to him, getting up. 'I won't be long. Hopefully.'

Fifteen minutes later, she was outside Robin Yardley's cottage on Dark Lane. Swallowing, she knocked on his door.

CHAPTER THIRTY-TWO

'How did you reach that conclusion?'

As Eve had said her piece – uninterrupted by any verbal response at all from Robin Yardley – she'd felt increasingly awkward. He'd looked so deadpan, she couldn't imagine what he was thinking.

She was inside his cottage. The front door opened directly onto the kitchen, and Eve was standing next to a soot-blackened fireplace set into a red-brick chimney breast. Around her she could see signs of Robin's life: a blue coffee pot on the thick oak counter with a half-drained sea-green mug next to it; a basket containing pruning shears, other tools and gloves; jackets and a long, charcoal-grey coat hanging from hooks near the door.

'The way you were examining the spot where Bernard Fitzpatrick was murdered,' Eve said at last. 'As well as the way you started telling me who I should talk to, to get the most information on him – almost as though you were running down a mental checklist.'

Robin leaned against his countertop.

'And then I saw you speaking with a colleague of DI Palmer's in Haunted Lane. It looked like you were talking as equals – not being interviewed. But your manner changed when the detective inspector joined you.'

'Hellfire!' Robin rubbed his chin. 'Just as well Palmer's not as observant as you are. How far has all this gone? Have you looked me up online?'

She took a deep breath. 'It's my job to research people. It's kind of second nature to google them. Nice work on the church flowers, by the way.'

'Thanks.' Robin Yardley raised his eyes to heaven. 'Very few people round here know about me.'

'They all seem to think you're an ex-con.'

'Yup.' The man's blue-grey eyes met hers and he shrugged. 'Pretty ironic, when you come to think about it. Had you been busy suspecting me of Bernard's murder?'

'Not exactly.' She felt the colour come to her cheeks. 'But I could see you were keeping everyone at a distance. And you were really uncommunicative the first two times I met you.'

'You kept staring at me. Each time I looked up it was as though you were there.'

This was just getting more awkward. She couldn't decide whether she was relieved or annoyed when she saw the faintest flicker of amusement behind his eyes.

'So why don't you tell the villagers the truth?' she asked.

'If the locals knew I was an ex-cop, they'd never employ me as a gardener. The police make even the most innocent people feel twitchy. And they'd still gossip. They'd want to know why I left.'

Eve took a deep breath. 'And why you went underground.'

Yardley's eyes were on hers. 'I shouldn't have gone to look at Bernard's murder site,' he said at last, 'but old habits die hard.' His ability to answer without giving a thing away was maddening, and she was pretty sure he knew it, which made it more so. 'Talking to you about your interviewees was a mistake too. But I thought you'd make more of Lucas Booth if you knew the background. He might not have volunteered it.'

'You suspect him?'

'He's been on my radar. When I started to garden for them, I mentioned my work at High House once and Lucas let rip about Bernard – couldn't seem to help himself. And at that point he and Sophie were hardly speaking. It wasn't clear why, but I'd heard rumours about Sophie and Bernard.'

She told him what Adele had said on the subject, and her own theory about how Fi might have seen Lucas access the estuary path if he'd been the one to kill the cellist.

Robin nodded. 'It would all make sense. Anyway, I wanted you to go into the interview with an idea he might be someone to watch.'

Something slid into place in Eve's mind. 'You followed me? To check I was all right?'

Robin sighed. 'I hadn't realised you'd seen me. I must be getting rusty.'

'Lucas lied to me about why he and Sophie left High House – and the timing.' She explained the background: the fact that Sophie had sold the house from under her husband and the creative block that ensued, according to his publisher. 'I still don't know if Lucas covered up the truth to save face, or to avoid admitting the extent of his grudge against Fitzpatrick.' And then Eve told Robin how she and Simon had seen Lucas leaving St Peter's in distress, on Monday night.

Robin's eyes opened wider. 'The more I hear about him, the less I like it. But of course, there are others who might be guilty too. Andrew Goddard's looking pretty interesting right now. Apparently, he claims he had no idea Fi had gone out on Saturday night, as they occupy separate bedrooms. He says she tended to drink quite heavily in the evenings. When she didn't show up ready to leave for church on Sunday, he assumed she was still in her room, sleeping it off. And then when he got back, he says he guessed she must have gone out. I'm surprised the police aren't treating him as their prime suspect, but they seem to be obsessed with Adam Cox.'

Eve wondered just how much Robin Yardley knew. 'Do you have many law enforcement contacts locally?'

'Just one: the detective sergeant you saw me talking to. On the upside, he's one of the best. I definitely wouldn't want Palmer to know my background. Occasionally I get snippets of inside information, but I left CID ten years ago now – I'm well out of the game.'

But he missed it, clearly.

'Your contact told you about Fi Goddard and her double life then?' If Andrew was on his list, she guessed it was likely.

He nodded, slowly. 'I did hear that much.'

'DI Palmer seems to think it's odd that I wanted to know more when I found out she'd lied, rather than just shrugging my shoulders.'

She could see Yardley wasn't surprised. 'He won't approve if he thinks you're deliberately digging for information on the murders. But he's not the most energetic of men. He'll be quite happy to absorb everything you tell him if it helps him crack the case and take the credit.'

Eve's blood pressure rose at the thought of Palmer using her. But that was crazy – she wanted the murderer caught just as badly as the police did. And the latest interview with Palmer had helped her; he'd told her what the police knew about the gold cigarette case.

Yardley's eyes were appraising as they met hers. 'It took you less than a week to spot me for what I am, and you've handed Palmer crucial evidence on a plate. What other conclusions have you drawn so far – just out of interest?'

She felt the colour rise in her cheeks. 'Nothing you and the local guys won't have considered already, I'd guess.' She went through her conclusions.

'That's a lot of detail.'

'I make a lot of notes.'

Yardley nodded. 'I had a feeling you might. Well, Adele Wentworth's alibi for Fi Goddard's murder checks out, I'm told. I understand the time of death was between eleven thirty on Saturday and one on Sunday morning.'

So Fi had been out walking late, then – though if it had been towards the earlier end of that window, not outlandishly so. Eve still doubted Adam had anything to do with it. It was hard to imagine her agreeing to go for a moonlit walk with him, but she could see either her husband or Lucas Booth getting her out there. If it had been Lucas, he must have come up with a good reason for picking a late hour: but as she'd thought earlier, he could have told her he needed to talk in secret. She shared the thought with Robin and he nodded.

Eve frowned. 'But maybe it's Andrew who's guilty. He made a pretty forced-sounding excuse for Fi's absence at church on Sunday. He could have been trying to save face, if he really thought she was lying in after drinking too much, but I don't know. He looked very tense, and if they're not on good terms, you wouldn't think he'd feel the need to lie for her.'

Yardley looked thoughtful. 'That's interesting. He has to be right up there as a suspect.' As she turned to go, he spoke again. 'I'd appreciate it if you didn't discuss my background with anyone. The village needs a source of intrigue and gossip. I wouldn't want to spoil the fun.'

She met his look. 'Understood.' But if he expected her to take that at face value he could think again. There was something in his expression that made her realise his request mattered. It was a secret he needed to have kept.

As she walked back to Elizabeth's Cottage, her mind was teeming with questions. Why had he left the force? He had one friend on the local police team, but he was clearly wary of the officers in general knowing his identity. If he'd changed his name, had something put him in danger? Or had he left his job under controversial circumstances, to run away and look for a fresh start?

Whatever it was, it had to be big, if it was still affecting him ten years on.

CHAPTER THIRTY-THREE

Eve was getting ready for the commemorative concert over at Snape Maltings when the knock came on the front door, sending Gus into a barking frenzy. She had one eye done in dark greys for a smoky effect, the other completely untouched. Not ideal. She went to open up.

Emily Moore, the administrator for the Blackforth Arts Trust, was standing in the doorway. Eve was still holding her eyeshadow in one hand, in the hope of conveying a 'this isn't really a convenient time' subliminal message, but at the sight of the woman she stepped back into the living room and invited her in.

'I'm sorry to disturb you,' she said. 'You're getting ready to attend the memorial concert? I'll be going along too.'

She was probably wondering why Eve needed an hour and a half to prepare. That and judging her outfit, though she might assume Eve had yet to change. The event was black tie, but her limited wardrobe meant she was relying on her smartest jewellery to turn one of her interviewing outfits into something vaguely suitable. Thank goodness she'd brought the shot-silk dress with her.

'It's no problem. Come and take a seat.' She put her make-up down. 'Can I get you a drink of anything?'

Ms Moore shook her head. 'I'm fine, thank you. I just needed to have a quick word on a slightly delicate matter.' She sighed. 'It might affect the obituary you're writing, and I didn't know when you'd file the copy, so I wanted to catch you sooner rather than later.'

Eve nodded as they took seats on the couches that faced each other. 'Of course – go ahead.'

The woman hesitated. She was wondering where to start, Eve guessed.

At last, she put her shoulders back and spoke. 'The plans to turn High House into a museum won't be going ahead after all. The trust has declared it is unable to accept Bernard's bequest.'

Eve caught her breath. That was more fundamental than she'd guessed when witnessing the aftermath of her interview with Adam Cox.

'Goodness! I'm sorry. That sounds like a big disappointment for all concerned.'

She nodded. 'I'm sorry I didn't acknowledge you just after I'd broken the news to Adam. I feel so terrible about what's happened. Given his reaction, I thought I should leave High House as quickly as possible, to save him having to explain. We hadn't made his job offer official yet, but I certainly regarded it as a firm arrangement – especially as it had been suggested months ago.'

The former secretary's response to the news flashed across Eve's mind again. 'What went wrong?'

'I'm afraid that's confidential.' Emily Moore's shoulders sagged. 'Some publicity about the plans for the museum has already gone out, and we've had quite a lot of coverage, so it's a case of damage limitation.' The woman's eyes were damp. 'Fi would have managed it all brilliantly, of course, as our PR expert. I still can't believe she's gone. I can see her, shaking her head at the mess we've got ourselves into.'

Eve leaned forward, wishing she could do something. 'I'm so sorry. Do you know what will happen to High House now?' Taking a step back, that was the crucial thing from her point of view.

Ms Moore dabbed her eyes with a tissue as she shook her head. 'Andrew Goddard liaised closely with Bernard over his plans, as the trust's legal brains, but I can't ask him, of course – not at a time like this. And Adam might know too, but I didn't query it when we met. He was too stunned.'

Eve could understand that.

After she'd shown the woman out, she picked up her eyeshadow again and went back upstairs to Elizabeth's bedroom. At the mirror, tackling her second eyelid, she considered the possible implications of what she'd just heard.

Might the house now go to Cole Wentworth, as Bernard's direct descendent? Now *that* would be a motive, if Cole had secretly known about their relationship. He might come from a wealthy background, but High House must be worth a heck of a lot of money.

But even if Cole were the new beneficiary, it was hard to imagine how he could have known the trust would turn down its bequest. And he'd have to have been aware of the contents of Fitzpatrick's will, too. All the same, she liked her information to be complete. Would Adam Cox be at the memorial service that night? She wasn't sure he'd be in a fit state, the way he'd looked that morning. And asking him about something so delicate in public wouldn't be great.

Before Simon was due to pick her up, she wrote a carefully crafted email to Adam, sympathising with his situation, and asking whether he knew – for the purposes of her article – what would happen to High House now.

CHAPTER THIRTY-FOUR

Simon Maxwell scrubbed up well. Eve couldn't help admitting that – incorrigible flirt or not – he looked more than decent in a tuxedo.

'I'm parked opposite Monty's,' he said. 'I couldn't get near the green on this side.'

Eve raised an eyebrow.

'You'll see in a minute.'

As they reached the end of Haunted Lane, Eve understood. The press were back. A large gaggle of hacks leaned over Andrew Goddard's garden wall, cameras trained on his door. Their vehicles had been parked carelessly on that side of the green. One car's door hadn't been closed properly.

'What on earth's going on?' It looked like they must have gotten new information on the man – but what? Were they expecting an arrest? If so, how the heck had they got information before the police arrived?

'It's a bit of a mystery. If the shop was open I've no doubt Moira would come and fill us in, but I suppose she's probably putting her feet up – or on her way to the concert too.' His eyes met hers. 'Maybe we'll get news there.'

'Maybe.'

As Simon drove his Mercedes down the country lanes that led from the A12 out towards Snape, he turned to grin at her.

'I'm glad you could come. I can't imagine what it'll be like, after Fi's death as well. We can hold hands if things get too awkward or depressing.'

Hmm. 'You look more than capable of tackling anything anyone throws at you.'

He laughed. 'As a matter of fact, so do you.' There was an admiring tone to his voice. 'My sister admitted you came to the rescue at the teashop yesterday.'

'She was calm in a crisis too.'

He laughed. 'No sense of urgency – that's Viv. It's one thing not to panic, another to let it all wash over you and knowingly trust to luck.'

They drew into the Maltings and followed the gravel driveway round to the car park. The place was stunning, with the River Alde running next to it and a tall ship moored to their left as they entered the complex. The grounds were full of sculptures, and beyond the main buildings the reeds stretched away as far as the eye could see, the river snaking its way through them.

'The Aldeburgh Festival will be on here in a week,' Simon said. 'Hugo Delaney spearheaded tonight's event. He was lucky to get the venue at such short notice.'

They left Simon's car and made their way to the Britten Studio, showing their invitations to the young woman on the door who nodded them through, with instructions to sit anywhere from the third row back.

They entered a large concert hall with raked seats. Down at stage level was a grand piano and various music stands already set up with sheet music in front of glossy black chairs. The ambient noise in the room was high. People were greeting old friends, with the usual expressions of regret at having been brought together by such sad circumstances, coupled with fondness. She could hear snippets of the attendees catching up on each other's news. ('Really, since last year? I hadn't heard.' '… had to detour en route to New York. I'm flying out tomorrow.' 'I'd wondered too – but honestly, it's fake!')

Eve spotted Polly Cartwright sitting with Mary Anderson, but as she'd half expected, Adam Cox was nowhere to be seen. Andrew Goddard must be lying low too, thanks to his recent bereavement and the press camped outside his house. Eve wondered again what they were doing there. Maybe his next public appearance would be in court.

She and Simon found seats near the right-hand aisle as they faced the stage, and Eve excused herself to visit the bathroom. It seemed like a wise precaution, but she also wanted the chance to check her email without looking rude. If Adam Cox wasn't at the concert hall, he might have had the chance to reply to her message. She didn't relish having anything in common with the man, but he was definitely type A, just like her. He probably had the desire to zap responses straight back without delay.

Standing outside the bathroom in the queue, she unlocked her phone and checked her messages. Sure enough, there was his reply. She opened it.

High House wouldn't go to Cole Wentworth or to anyone else of interest. It was to be sold and the proceeds (together with the capital Fitzpatrick had left) donated to a London music school to fund an ongoing concert series in his name. Adam had noted that Fitzpatrick could have suggested another trust take over as the back-up option and hinted that Andrew Goddard might have influenced his decision improperly. Adam said Goddard was the sort who wouldn't want a rival trust benefiting. Eve could feel his bitterness, and understand it too. Maybe she'd been too harsh on him. He'd attempted to blackmail Fi, but Fitzpatrick had effectively done the same to him by trapping him in a terrible job. Adam had been used, over and over again.

As she returned to her seat, she saw Simon talking to Polly Cartwright in one of the aisles. The woman glanced up at her, nodded, then returned to the row where she'd been sitting.

Simon came to join Eve. 'Polly's just told me the Blackforth Arts Trust won't be taking on High House after all.' He saw her eyes. 'You already knew?'

'Yes.' Half her attention was still on Adam Cox's email – and maybe just ten per cent on seeing Simon and Polly together. 'I only heard right before you came to pick me up. Emily Moore told me the reasons behind it are confidential. I don't suppose Polly knows what went wrong?'

Simon grimaced. 'Emily hasn't got a hope in hell of keeping it quiet. She must have told Adam the truth at least – I suppose she felt he had the right to a proper explanation. But if she asked him to not to pass it on, her instructions have been ignored. Polly says he was stunned into silence at first, but then she fetched him some brandy. Adam came across with all the grisly details after a snifter.'

Eve held her breath.

'The trust is in trouble financially, I gather. They made a couple of bad investments and now they can't afford to pay Adam or supply the set-up costs the place would need. The word is, the capital Bernard left wasn't substantial. Polly says he was high-earn, high-burn.' He sighed. 'I wonder what Adam will do now.'

'Good question. I don't suppose there are many openings for him close by.' As Eve assimilated the new information, people were still milling round in front of the piano, but a second later there was an abrupt hush as though someone had turned down the volume. She looked up to see Hugo Delaney standing at a lectern to one side of the stage. A group of musicians had taken their seats and were doing some final tuning up. A moment later Delaney pointed out the fire exits, then invited them all to turn off their phones. Eve checked hers to make sure it was set to silent, but was distracted by a newsflash that had popped up on her screen.

CELEBRITY DIVORCE LAWYER, ANDREW GODDARD, HAS ALIBI
FOR WIFE'S MURDER

She nudged Simon as the lights went down and opened the full news story, angling the screen so they could both read it.

A police spokesperson has suggested Andrew Goddard, 68, will face charges for wasting police time amid reports that he lied about being home alone on the night of his wife's murder. Mrs Fiona Goddard, 35, was found dead on heathland in the Suffolk village of Saxford St Peter on Sunday. It transpires that at the time of her death, her husband was in the company of Ms Wendy Golightly, 28, at the Beaufort Lodge Hotel just outside Diss. Mr Goddard has refused to comment but a friend and former colleague, who has asked not to be named, speculates that he stayed silent to protect Ms Golightly's reputation.

Hmm. Right. And his own. The press would have him for breakfast, given his wife was killed while he was playing away.

'Andrew was innocent of his wife's murder, and knew he couldn't identify her killer,' the friend said. 'He would have seen no necessity to speak out unless it became imperative in order to prove his innocence.'
    A member of staff at the Beaufort Lodge Hotel recognised Mr Goddard's picture in news reports following the murder and contacted the authorities. The manager of the hotel said guests' privacy was normally paramount, but...

The woman next to Eve was staring pointedly at her glowing screen. Hastily, she put her phone into her bag. Her eyes met Simon's.

'What a selfish idiot!' he whispered.

Eve nodded. She could barely imagine the look on DI Palmer's face when he found out one of his suspects had had a cast-iron alibi all along. She wondered how long Andrew Goddard had been cheating on his wife, and what excuse he'd given her for his absence. What had he thought the following morning when he'd returned home and discovered Fi was missing? Maybe that she'd found him out and stormed off. That would explain why he'd made vague excuses for her in church. He'd have wanted to save face. She mentally readjusted, crossing Andrew off her list of possible killers.

At last she managed to return her focus to the here and now. Hugo Delaney had begun to speak about Bernard Fitzpatrick's career and their friendship. After a moment, he broadened his address to pay tribute to Fi Goddard, and to rue what had happened to each of them. While he spoke, Eve caught sight of Lucas Booth sitting in the front row next to Emily Moore.

As the music started, Eve felt the hairs on her forearms rise, and a shiver dance its way down her spine.

High House would have to be sold now, thanks to the hole in the Blackforth Arts Trust's finances. And Lucas Booth – poet turned banker – was the trust's financial advisor, just as Andrew Goddard covered legal matters and Fi had looked after publicity. If the bottom had fallen out of their finances, it was likely to be Lucas's decisions that were to blame.

What if…?

The trust might be virtually bankrupt, but if Lucas wanted to move back to High House all he had to do now was to wait for it to go on the market. It didn't look as though he was *personally* poor. He could sell his place and probably exchange all that cash he must have earned, via his long hours in the city, for the home he'd always loved. Maybe he thought he'd be able to write again. All he'd had to do was deliberately muck up the trust's investments.

Emily Moore hadn't known what would happen to High House if the bequest to the trust fell through, but Lucas had probably been aware. It sounded as though Fitzpatrick had relied on Andrew Goddard for legal advice, despite the potential conflict of interest, and that and financial planning went hand in hand.

And Fi? Eve guessed either she'd seen Lucas descend onto the estuary path, the night he'd killed Fitzpatrick, or that she'd somehow stumbled across his deliberate mismanagement of the trust's investments. As another trustee, that was entirely plausible.

By the time Fitzpatrick's closest contacts in the industry had finished playing one of cellist's unpublished compositions, Eve was twitching in her seat, her palms sticky, heart rate ramping up.

'That sounded dreadful to me,' Simon whispered. 'I mean, I'm no expert, but it was reminiscent of someone sawing the leg off a table with a rubber band.' He laughed but then caught her look. 'Are you okay?'

'What do you think of Lucas Booth?'

Simon shrugged. 'All right. A bit bitter and intense at times, perhaps. Viv once told me—'

'About his reaction when Fitzpatrick laid into her?'

Simon's expression was bemused. 'Yes, that's right. Why?'

Eve decided not to share her thoughts with him. Without the full background, the idea sounded crazy, but everything fitted. It explained the delay between him being forced out of High House and killing Fitzpatrick, and perhaps even his move into banking. He'd have needed to save up so that he could afford to buy his former home back.

'Doesn't matter. They're handing round refreshments. Should we go and help ourselves?'

He nodded, still with a curious look in his eye.

They ended up standing in a group with the vicar, Polly Cartwright, Mary Anderson, Emily Moore and Lucas Booth himself.

Eve noticed that Lucas and Emily both sounded stilted. Eve said something about the music, and the banker caught her eye. She was desperate not to give her suspicions away. He couldn't possibly guess – could he? But something about his look made her wonder. His eyes were sharp. Simon had turned to have a word with another Saxford St Peter resident, and Emily Moore was speaking with the vicar. With Polly and Mary Anderson involved in their own conversation, Lucas moved towards Eve.

She took an involuntary step back; she couldn't help it. Adrenaline was making her heart race. She didn't like the look in his eye now. She saw anger there. What should she do? She had no proof, just a jumble of facts.

CHAPTER THIRTY-FIVE

Eve stuck with the crowds for the rest of the interval to avoid being on her own with Lucas. Each time there was any distance between her and Simon, the banker made his way nearer to her. Was he hoping to talk to her, to gauge what was on her mind?

In the distance, she could see Sylvia and Daphne from Hope Cottage, but she put off going to talk to them in case Lucas caught her on her way over.

It was impossible to concentrate during the second half. Simon whispered the odd comment and she managed to respond, but her mind was still on the banker. She was checking and rechecking every fact she'd gathered, and each one seemed watertight.

Cole Wentworth was up on stage now, holding the cello Bernard had left him. He thanked the musician's executors for letting him use it for the evening, in advance of the legal formalities going through. Even at that distance she could see the emotion in his eyes. Hugo Delaney was at the piano and they began to play. She came to for a moment and noticed the reactions of the audience around her. Lots of tears, and lots of applause afterwards. And then four of Fitzpatrick's other collaborators – a conductor and three people on strings whose faces she recognised – took their places and played another piece.

'This is more like it,' Simon said.

To her left, across the aisle, Eve saw Daphne and Sylvia's reactions. Daphne's eyes were glistening; Eve could tell the potter was entirely caught up in the music.

At the end, one of the performers took Cole's hand and raised it high in the air, squeezing it hard as more applause came. Cole was just about holding it together, with Adele looking on from the front row. How must she be feeling?

After the musical programme ended, Eve wished she'd come in her own car. She had a strong desire to get back to Elizabeth's Cottage and think. Gus was the only company she wanted right now. Should she be calling DI Palmer to pass on her thoughts? But they were all based on supposition and circumstantial evidence. What hard, provable facts did she have? She doubted he'd take her seriously.

'Are you okay?' Simon asked, following her down towards the stage area, where the guests were being served canapés and more champagne.

'Yes, thanks. Just an emotional occasion, I guess.'

'Of course.' He put a sympathetic hand on her upper arm for a moment. He didn't sound put out, just concerned.

She ended up sticking close to his side, which wasn't her usual MO at all. She was a bit worried in case he took it the wrong way, but each time she glanced up she saw Lucas, his angry eyes on hers. She had a horrible feeling he'd read her mind.

She and Simon were in conversation with the vicar when Emily Moore came and stood at her elbow.

'Excuse me, Eve, could I have a quick word?'

She excused herself and turned to face the trustee. Lucas was beyond the woman, his eyes on them both.

'I'm responsible,' she said.

'Excuse me?'

'For the Blackforth Arts Trust not being able to accept Bernard's bequest. I should have said when I called in, even if I couldn't explain the details.' She was twisting her hands together. 'Only I feel so terrible about it. And now – well, Lucas has the impression word has got out about what's happened.' She glanced momentarily in Polly Cartwright's direction, her lips white. 'He's worried people will blame him. He took me to one side, just a moment ago, and said you'd been looking at him in a funny way all evening.'

Eve didn't bother covering up the gossip she'd heard. 'You mean it wasn't he who decided where the trust should invest its money?'

Emily Moore shrugged helplessly. 'He picked the funds and sent me the details, but he was always changing his mind, and asking me to move money from one place to another. As the administrator for the trust, it's my job to sort out the paperwork whenever one of the trustees makes a recommendation. And I was a couple of manoeuvres behind with the finances. I had no idea the matter was so urgent. Lucas had noticed that several of the funds were vulnerable, and he'd told me what to do about it. I delayed, so it's thanks to me that the trust has lost one of its most exciting opportunities and Adam Cox is out of a job. That's why I broke the news.'

The woman was in tears. Eve put a hand on her arm, avoiding Lucas Booth's eye. The conclusions she'd been drawing came tumbling down. His previous lies must have been down to pride, after all. He hadn't wanted her to know that his wife had sold her family home to rescue them, financially. Or that she had (perhaps) fallen for another man. Thank goodness Eve hadn't called DI Palmer. The mystery of Bernard and Fi's murders was back to being just that. She left Emily Moore and made her way back to Simon.

'Hello, you!' he said. 'Thought I'd lost you. What's up with Emily?'

Eve explained.

'Awkward.'

'You said it.'

'By the way, Jim Thackeray said we ought to have been given one of these on our way in.' He handed her a programme. The front cover had a photograph of Bernard Fitzpatrick laughing, his vivid brown eyes dancing. A slip had been added to the inner pages that showed Fi Goddard's picture. She looked just as vibrant as he did. It seemed almost impossible that they were gone for good.

'That last piece was a composition of Cole's, dedicated to Bernard,' Simon said, turning the pages in her hands to find the right part of the programme. 'I thought it was rather good.'

Someone at Eve's elbow leaned in towards them. Eve had seen the man on television. She knew he was a big star, though she couldn't recall his name. 'Cole's monumentally talented,' the guy said. 'I'm so glad we've discovered him. I feel bad, because he sent me a recording of his work a year ago and I never got around to listening to it. It was only when he contacted Hugo to ask to be involved with the concert that I made the connection.' He shook his head and laughed. Eve had the feeling he'd had a lot to drink. 'Fancy him being Bernard's natural son. God rest his soul, but it was hard to stay tactful when he played me *his* compositions. He was a first-rate cellist – he performed with unmatched passion – but he had nothing to offer when it came to writing his own music. Whereas Cole, well' – he nodded at Simon – 'you just heard his work. He's got a place to study composition in the autumn, but the tutors will be learning from him. I've invited him to New York before he starts. He'll be world-renowned, just like his father – only more so.'

Over the man's shoulder, Eve caught sight of Cole and the purest thrill of suspicion and fear went through her, like ice-cold water rushing through her veins.

There he was, the centre of attention, glowing, rapt in the adoration of his new-found audience.

For a moment, Eve was spellbound. She failed to look away, and Cole's eyes met hers. She gave him a smile and a thumbs up.

He beamed back and held his hand up in small wave. Thank goodness he hadn't read her expression. Smiling still, Eve turned back to Simon and managed to take a breath, but her pulse was racing.

If she'd lacked evidence on Lucas, that was nothing to the situation with Cole Wentworth – and yet, just standing there, she had a horrible feeling she'd finally identified Bernard's killer.

What the heck was she going to do about it?

CHAPTER THIRTY-SIX

Simon carried on being charming all the way back to Saxford St Peter, but Eve couldn't focus. As he left her at Elizabeth's Cottage, he suggested another drink at the Cross Keys before she went back to London. Her other life seemed a million miles away.

'Are you sure you're okay?' he said, as she started to close the door.

'I'm good, thanks.' So long as Cole didn't know she suspected him, she'd be fine. She just needed to hold on to that fact. And then take a deep breath and think.

Simon nodded, his dark hair blown by the breeze, and left her to walk back to where he'd left his car by the village green. She bent down to stroke Gus and found herself giving him a hug. It wasn't that unusual, but the dachshund looked surprised. She must have gripped him harder than she'd meant.

She locked the front door and went to make herself a coffee, but her hands shook as she put the grounds into the cafetière. She let Gus come upstairs with her, guessing Viv and Simon wouldn't mind too much. Pulling the curtains shut, she settled down on the bed with her laptop. The tab on her spreadsheet devoted to Cole and Adele Wentworth included the notes from her visit to their house, and other details too.

She needed to get it all straight in her head.

This evening, she'd seen with her own eyes how Fitzpatrick's death had affected Cole's future – and it wasn't something money could buy. Powerful contacts at the top of the music world were noticing Cole's talent. The man she and Simon had talked to that evening had admitted himself that he'd ignored Cole's approach when he thought he was just another eager young composer. It was only when the family connection came out that he'd paid attention. Cole could have spent his entire life as a might-have-been, but thanks to his biological father's death he was suddenly in the limelight, on the map. He'd be famous before he ever finished that postgrad course of his.

Bernard had known Cole was keen on music – hence the bequest – but the fact that he hadn't acknowledged his son before he died meant Cole had had no help with his career.

What if, far from Adele Wentworth encouraging Bernard to keep quiet about their secret child, it had been Bernard who'd been determined to stay silent? It would have been only natural for Adele to have glossed over the truth. Pride and protectiveness could have made her hide Fitzpatrick's real attitude towards their son. And Cole had probably repeated his mother's version of events to Eve.

But what if Cole had secretly known Bernard was his father – and seen the doors the man could have unlocked, if only he'd acknowledged him?

She got up and paced around the room, Gus following her anxiously. 'It fits,' she said to him. 'Fitzpatrick would have hated sharing the spotlight. Hugo Delaney said he'd never have wanted Billy Tozer to move to the village for that reason. And he planned for his house to be kept as a permanent memorial to his own genius. Just imagine what it would have done to him if it had come out that his son lived in the village – and was not only also a virtuoso cellist, but a far better composer than he would ever be?'

Gus gazed up into her eyes.

Had Fitzpatrick identified Cole as a rival, right from when he and Adele had first moved up to Suffolk? She double-checked the dates. Adele's husband had died when Cole was thirteen. She was betting he'd already been studying music for years by then. She could only imagine Bernard's jealousy of the boy's talent.

But even if Fitzpatrick had wanted to keep Cole in the shadows, what was to stop his son going public about his true parentage? Why had he had to kill the cellist first? Even if it was clear that Cole and Bernard didn't get on, speaking out would still have brought Cole plenty of attention from others in the music world. So why hadn't he made that move?

She couldn't imagine.

She turned her mind to Fi instead. She'd been a PR expert. Perhaps she'd seen the effect Fitzpatrick's death had had on Cole. He was in all the papers – and if she'd spoken to any of Fitzpatrick's contacts after he'd died, which was likely, given she was still secretly working for him, she'd probably picked up on their sudden interest in the young man. She'd have seen how much Cole had benefited.

Fi's body had been found on the heath, not far from Woodlands House – by Cole. He'd known where to look, and how to seem innocent by bringing the death to the attention of the authorities.

After that, she considered incidentals. To an outsider, it looked as though Bernard Fitzpatrick must have cared for Cole. After all, he'd left him his cello – the symbolic one, the one he'd been playing when he'd first found success.

But how would Fitzpatrick have viewed it? He'd owned another cello, worth hundreds of thousands, that he'd left to the trust, seemingly without a second thought. And his valuable house had also been intended for them, not Cole. Even if his pet idea for the museum fell through, he still hadn't wanted his son to have the place.

Fitzpatrick might have left him the less valuable cello as a deliberate snub. To show his son he was second best. She glanced at her notes. The newspaper mentioned Cole had been left a sealed letter along with the instrument. It was anyone's guess what that had said.

She reread all her conclusions from the day she'd visited Cole at his mother's house. When she got to the bit about the bottle of eighteen-year-old Bowmore whisky Fitzpatrick had supposedly given Cole as an impromptu thank-you present, she paused. She'd known at the time that something wasn't quite right, but she hadn't been able to put her finger on it. She had it now. Moira Squires had said Fitzpatrick ordered one bottle a month, regular as clockwork. It wasn't something the man would have had lying around unopened, ready to present as a gift. The chill that had been creeping through her tickled her stomach. Cole had shown her the whisky as evidence that Bernard had been a fond father, keeping his distance, but hiding warm feelings towards his son. In reality, she was betting Cole had bought the bottle himself.

It all hung together. But she knew what the police would say if she called them. They'd ask the same question that had stopped her in her tracks. Why hadn't Cole simply gone public, whatever Fitzpatrick thought? Without the answer to that, she couldn't expect them to listen.

She slumped back down on the bed again and stared at her laptop. She needed to work it out, and then – even if it sounded crazy – she needed to go to DI Palmer with it.

The thoughts she was after didn't come, despite the coffee. In the end, she got ready for bed and lay there, staring at the ceiling, listening to the sound of her own heartbeat. At some point she must have slept, though. She dreamed of feet, thudding outside in Haunted Lane, and woke to the sound of Gus's low whine.

Eve sat bolt upright in bed as his whimper gave way to a series of barks. She crept over to the window and eased back one of the curtains by half an inch. Peering outside, her legs turned to jelly. Cole Wentworth was down in the lane below, close to Elizabeth's Cottage.

CHAPTER THIRTY-SEVEN

'*I understand.*'

She'd called Robin's mobile phone, using the contact details Adam Cox had given her. Thank God he had signal, and hadn't had it on silent for the night. DI Palmer had been the first person to come to mind but she knew in her gut that he'd take ages to catch on.

Fear made her want to dial 999, but she forced herself to take stock. If the police currently had no proof, what happened that night might be the only thing they'd get in the way of evidence. Beyond the hedgerow, from her position on Haunted Lane, was a view over the marshes towards the Old Toll Road. Even if the police only used flashing blues, Cole would get plenty of warning of their approach. He'd be off before they got near and they'd have nothing on him. She hadn't stood her ground against Ian's interference only to give up at the last hurdle.

She battened down her feelings, and managed to keep her voice steady. 'I should get down there – into the lane – and get him talking. I ought to be safe enough out in the open. Daphne and Sylvia are only just up the road. I could run to Hope Cottage if I get into trouble.'

'*No! It's too risky. I'm on my way.*' She could hear the sound of a door creaking in the background. '*I'll get backup. Don't go outside.*'

'I can wait a few minutes to give you and anyone else time to get near the house. But if I engage with him, I think he might admit to what he's done. If you're standing by, just out of sight, you'll be an independent witness.'

'*It's way too dangerous, Eve. If he's guilty, the police will find the evidence.*'

She bit her lip. She could see his point – and fear was crawling round the pit of her stomach – but at the moment all they had was a guy, standing in a lane, where anyone had a perfect right to be.

Of course, neither of them knew what he might be planning next… 'Okay.'

'*I'll be with you soon.*'

Eve still wasn't sure of the best course of action. She went to the window again and pulled the curtain back just a fraction, as she'd done before.

Cole Wentworth had gone. She looked down at Gus, who'd quietened too, and her shoulders sagged. Maybe he *had* just been out for a walk. He'd had an emotional evening. Perhaps the whole horrific explanation she'd dreamed up was false.

But the effect of Fitzpatrick's death on Cole's life came back to her, together with the other facts she had. She was sure she was right. He must have seen the look of fear in her eyes earlier that evening after all. Where was he now? If he'd come to find her he'd hardly go straight back home again.

What if he'd had gone round the back of the house? You could reach it without going through a locked gate. Panic was biting, stopping her from thinking straight. She could hide. Isaac had escaped the hue and cry by crawling into the space under the house. But it was no good. Everyone in the village knew that story.

She needed another option, just in case, but what? Her mind was blank, her palms clammy.

And at that moment Gus turned to face Eve's bedroom door, his hackles rising, a low growl in his throat.

All the breath went out of her. Someone was in the cottage. She could hear them downstairs.

There were no locks on any of the internal doors. The bathroom had a keyhole, but she'd yet to find the key. She stood still for a moment, trying to think her way through the fear. Stay upstairs and wait for him to come to her? Or go down and talk?

In a second, she'd swapped her pjs for jeans and a T-shirt and stuffed her phone into her pocket.

'Stay!' she said to Gus, as she made her way towards the bedroom door. She wasn't sure who would do most damage, him or Cole Wentworth, but she wouldn't put her money on her darling dog. But instead of following her instructions, Gus stuck with her, almost under her feet.

She crossed the landing and began to descend the stairs, her legs shaking.

She understood Robin's original point, but the choice had been taken out of her hands. She hoped to goodness that he – and whatever backup he'd arranged – would arrive soon.

If only she could keep Cole talking for long enough. Bludgeoning someone to death would be quicker than reaching Elizabeth's Cottage from the other side of the village…

It was horrible, walking down the dark cottage stairs, the latched door below preventing her from seeing what was happening on the other side. But a second later, when she still had four stairs to go, the door at the bottom opened. Cole stood there in the pool of light given off by the living room lamp, which he must have switched on.

'Good evening, Eve,' he said. His smile and open look were just as she remembered from her visit to Woodlands House, but in his hand, he held a hammer.

'What are you doing here?'

He laughed. 'Oh, I think you know.'

'How did you get in?'

He raised an eyebrow. 'The Maxwells were always so generous, opening up Elizabeth's Cottage twice a year to visitors. One time,

I found a back-door key hidden behind a flowerpot. I guessed it might still be in place – and it was.'

Eve cursed innocent country ways. 'I don't know why you're here. Honestly.'

'Really? Oh, I'll just head off home then.' He shook his head. 'I saw it in your eyes tonight, Eve. I was hoping you hadn't realised you'd given yourself away. Even when you came to Woodlands House, I was worried I'd made a mistake. Something about that bottle of whisky made you wonder, I think. You frowned when I showed it to you, as though something had clicked – even if it was only in the back of your mind. I kicked myself. It was just a small detail but it goes to show, keeping it simple is usually best.' He sighed. 'Mum thought it was a mistake inviting you over at all, whereas I thought it would seem most guileless if we tackled you head-on.'

'Adele?' Eve caught her breath. She was still on the stairs, with Gus behind her, growling, and Cole blocking her route. 'She knows what you did?'

'Knows? It was she who killed my father.' He laughed again. 'She'd spent years trying to persuade him to acknowledge me. She knew he could unlock my career – but he was too damned selfish to do it. He blackmailed her to keep her quiet, not realising how her resentment was building up. He was a horrible man, and she killed him for love. For me.'

The heat and passion in his voice rang out. Eve's legs were shaking, mouth dry. She must concentrate – get the rest of his story out of him.

'What kind of hold did he have over your mother?'

He smiled. 'If you don't know, I'm certainly not going to tell you. Not that it will make a difference at this stage.'

'But you killed Fi – I've worked that one out.'

Robin had said Adele had definitely been in London that night.

He nodded. 'She knew all about publicity. She could see the effect Bernard's death was about to have on my career, and it turned out she'd once overheard Mum and Bernard arguing. She already knew the truth about them both – and me. And that I was in the dark. She was quick to cotton on.'

He really hadn't known about his biological father until the man's death, then. It had all been Adele's idea to start with. She'd acted her part so well – coming up with plausible reasons for keeping her distance, and throwing suspicion onto Lucas Booth.

'So when Fi guessed about the murder, she came to you and your mom instead of calling the police. Why would she do that?'

'Money,' Cole said, simply. 'She'd been having an affair with Bernard herself, and although she'd been trying to patch things up with her husband, he'd started to talk about divorce again. And divorce is Andrew Goddard's field. He would have taken her for every penny. She decided she could use us to ensure she had a comfortable future. She knew I hadn't known Bernard was my dad – or at least not when she'd overheard that argument – so she guessed it had been Mum who'd killed him. And that it would be safe to approach me.'

Eve was listening for sounds beyond where Cole was standing. Where was Robin? How close would he be? What would he do when he didn't see Cole outside? Knock, assuming he'd gone away?

She made an effort to focus on Cole again. 'So she visited you to extort money when your mother was out of the village?'

He nodded. There was a horrible, satisfied smile on his face. 'She thought she'd shock me by telling me the truth, and then get me onside, to work on Mum and persuade her to hand over money to buy her silence. But I wasn't shocked. Mum had told me what she'd done, and why. She was upset, but I was glad. He deserved to die. And so did Fi. I'd guessed she knew something when she asked to visit, way after most people would be in bed. I found the hammer Mum had used on Bernard and put it into action again. It wasn't hard to get her down to the heath without being seen. And now' – he backed away from the bottom of the stairs slightly – 'I'm ready to use the hammer one more time. We're going to go for a walk, Eve. Or I can kill you here, if you resist.'

She wanted to tell him that he was too late; that Robin Yardley knew of his guilt. But if she did that it would warn Cole of his impending arrival. He might murder her then and there, in order to be ready for Robin, who'd meet the same fate – because of her.

'You and Adele can't keep killing your way out of this. Wherever you choose to murder me, you'll leave clues. The more often you strike, the less chance you have of getting away with it!'

She could hear the desperation in her own voice.

He shook his head. 'You underestimate me. I hear Adam Cox has been drinking heavily recently; he must have been under a lot of strain. I'm going to look him up, after I've finished with you. I've already hinted I've got proof that will help clear his name. I'll take him a bottle of brandy. That and some crushed up pills. It'll look like suicide. And when I've finished, I'll leave my hammer in his house. I might even come back and plant something of his near your body. That would be a nice touch. The police already believe he's their murderer anyway.' He stepped towards her. 'Coming quietly will buy you a few extra minutes.' He smiled again. 'A chance to escape. Though you won't, of course.' He held his weapon up and reversed just enough for her to finish coming down the stairs. It was clear what would happen if she didn't.

She walked ahead of him through the living room and into the kitchen, her breath short. Once they were out in the open, she might be able to chance it and run, but Cole was a lot taller than her. He'd be faster, she was sure. If it came to the crunch, she'd have to tell him his secret was out – that she'd called to summon help before he'd gotten into the house. But would he believe her? Either way, she must use it as a last resort, to avoid putting him on his guard.

'The dog stays here,' Cole said.

She was glad of that, at least. Gus ought to be safe.

At that moment, Eve thought she heard a tiny sound ahead of her: the faintest creak. Cole heard it too, clearly. His attention was diverted for a second and Eve saw the back door handle move. She watched as Cole's jaw went slack and indecision crossed his face. He sprang towards the living room again, making for the front door.

Eve grabbed the nearest weapon she could see in the kitchen – a rolling pin from a container on the counter – and went after him.

He stood hopelessly at the front door, tugging at it, but it was double locked. The key was in a jar on a nearby shelf. Just as his eyes lit on it, she swiped at the container, knocking it beyond his reach and sending the key and shards of glass flying.

It was only then that she realised Robin had appeared at her side, armed. The fact that his weapon was a shovel – presumably from his work kit – didn't make him look any less threatening. As he rushed towards Cole, the younger man shrank away, his back against the cottage's front window.

'Open up!' an unknown male voice shouted from the direction of Haunted Lane.

In the same moment, as if from nowhere, Viv – wearing flip-flops, and what looked like a negligee with shorts pulled over the top – darted forwards from the kitchen, past her and Robin, and found the front door key.

The appearance of Robin's police contact when she opened the door, shouting at Cole to drop his hammer, completed the surreal picture.

CHAPTER THIRTY-EIGHT

'I was delighted to see you, obviously,' Eve said. 'I just don't get how you came to be there. You weren't with Robin, were you?'

Viv was sitting opposite her in Monty's. She'd brought them over a pot of tea and what she called her 'intense' cake selection – a mix of the most chocolatey brownies Eve had ever tasted and some coffee cakes with a delectable espresso syrup that soaked the sponge with bittersweet goodness. ('It's what I'd recommend for anyone who's recently come face to face with a murderer,' Viv had said. 'Perfect for inner strength.')

'Robin?' Viv looked confused. 'No! He keeps everyone at a distance.' She smiled. 'But you remember I told you I was meeting my "friend" from Wickham Market?'

'Yes.'

'He had to get back home for a work thing early this morning, so he left my house late.' There was a slightly pink tinge to her cheeks now, teaming nicely with her hair. 'I was just seeing him off when I saw Robin running hell for leather towards Haunted Lane, armed with a shovel.' She shrugged. 'It looked a bit ominous, so I pulled on some clothes and followed him. I can't sprint as fast as he can, so by the time I arrived you two had things under control.' She looked up at Eve again. 'Robin explained you'd called him because he was on the spot, and you knew he'd be able to muster some kind of weapon, even if it was a shovel. That was quick thinking! Can't blame you for not trusting DI Palmer. You have to chivvy him if you want something in a hurry. When Simon had that horse stolen, he had all the urgency of a dormouse on Valium. Just as well it was that other detective who turned up to make the arrest, I'd say.'

Eve laughed, but underneath, she felt uncomfortable. Robin had thought up a story to explain her reasons for calling him – and she'd promised she wouldn't give away his secret. But not being honest with Viv felt unnatural. She wondered again why he'd left the force, and if she'd ever know.

Viv topped up their teacups, then glanced over at the counter where her son and Kirsty were serving. They were back from London, complete with their visas. 'Are you two all right still?'

Sam rolled his eyes. 'Mum, we're leaving for India on Monday. If we can manage to travel round the world, I'm sure we can serve up a few cups of tea and slices of cake. You've got some drama to catch up on. It would be mean to stop you.'

Viv lowered her voice. 'Their ability to travel the world without mishap is still unproven. I've been putting it out of my head. It seemed like such a long way off. And now it's all happening for real on Monday…'

'They'll be fine. Sam seems sensible.'

After a moment Viv took a deep breath and nodded. 'He is really.' Her eyes slid towards Eve's at last. 'For all my protestations to the contrary, I will definitely miss their help. You wouldn't really leave me here to cope all on my own, would you? You know you love it in Saxford St Peter. You've got colour in your cheeks now. And you've discovered the importance of cake. As for Gus, I've seen how bright his eyes are each time you mention the word "beach".'

It was hard not to smile, but Eve tried to counteract the effect by folding her arms and sitting back in her chair.

'Come on! What's your job at the school got that part-time work here hasn't?'

'Well, the kids are lovely.'

'Really?' She looked shocked.

'Well, some of them are.'

Viv's eyes bored into hers.

'No, honestly – some of them really are.' Eve paused. 'Sometimes.'

Viv nodded. She knew she'd scored a point. 'And the teachers?'

'Ah, now they really are great. Almost without exception.'

'Almost?'

'The deputy head I work for is a bit of a jerk.'

'And then we come to the parents.' Her new friend leaned forwards, as though to press her advantage.

Eve pulled a face. 'Ah, well – I only get to hear from the ones who have a problem.'

'So, what you're saying is, you work with a whole bunch of kids who're pretty awful for much of the time, under a boss who's an idiot, at the beck and call of a host of unspeakable parents. Fair?'

'Somewhat fair.'

'And then there's Elizabeth's Cottage. You belong there, Eve – you know you do! You've already been instrumental in working out who was endangering Saxford St Peter – it's like you're Elizabeth's legitimate heir or something.' She caught Eve's expression. She could probably see how the idea had been playing around her mind, ever since the scone crisis. A smile spread across Viv's lips. 'You're ours!'

For a second, Eve paused. Was she? But then reality hit home. 'No. I can't possibly buy Elizabeth's Cottage.'

'Why?'

'Simon might think I'm staying because of him.'

Viv rolled her eyes. 'I know I've been bad-mouthing him, but he's not *that* big-headed. Even he wouldn't assume you're prepared to shell out three hundred thousand pounds just for the privilege of sharing a village with him.'

Put like that, her worry did sound a little outlandish.

'You're not really keen on him, are you?' Viv asked.

'He's very charming. And very good-looking. But my heart is intact. I've only known him five days. After Ian, I'm not about to rush into anything with anyone.'

For a second, she allowed herself to imagine Elizabeth's Cottage being hers. To wake up each morning to the sound of the seabirds. To open the door and wander down to the estuary. To organise Viv – a project she'd certainly relish. To sleep in Elizabeth's cosy attic room, feeling the past around her.

And it would be a fresh start.

'It's no good arguing about it now, anyway,' she said. 'I feel awful I haven't been to see Robin already. I need to thank him.'

Viv sighed. 'All right then – but this is not over!'

CHAPTER THIRTY-NINE

Eve had forewarned Robin that she wanted to drop in. She was desperate to thank him, of course, but she had questions too. With his connections, he might know the answers.

There was a half-smile on his lips as he let her in, but she didn't miss the quick glance he cast over her shoulder. She sensed he'd prefer it if no one saw her enter his house. Because they'd start asking her about him?

Inside, the cornflower-blue coffee pot steamed on the counter – a dash of bright colour in a shady room.

He motioned for her to take a seat at his kitchen table, and – after putting the coffee, cups, milk and sugar down – he dropped into the chair opposite her. She felt like a co-conspirator. Were she and the vicar the only ones in the village who knew some of Robin's history? It felt like an exclusive club. She wondered if Jim Thackeray knew the whole story.

'Thanks for coming so fast last night. Cole was trying to get me out of the house.'

Robin nodded. 'No thanks necessary. I miss my work sometimes; mucking in felt like a taste of the old days. You did well to keep him talking so long.' He poured their coffees.

She wondered if he'd ever go back to his old profession. Perhaps that wasn't an option; it seemed like the wrong moment to ask.

'Milk? Sugar?'

She shook her head. 'No, thanks.'

He had his black, like her.

She hesitated. Her head was full of questions, but she didn't want Robin to think she had selfish, ulterior motives for coming. The gratitude for his help was heartfelt. At last, she went for it. 'Has your detective friend said much to you?'

He shrugged. 'You've probably found out most things during your interview.'

But he was wrong. 'Palmer was very tight-lipped. It was all me telling him stuff.' She explained the business about the whisky. 'I was wasting my breath relating that to him, but the woman with us wrote it down.'

Robin's eyes met hers as he sipped his coffee. 'It'll probably make its way into the pack of information Palmer hands over. It never hurts to have circumstantial stuff alongside indisputable evidence. It will have been your statement that told Palmer exactly how to frame his questions. You ought to put in for expenses.'

Eve cocked her head. 'I guess it would have been hard for Cole to explain away the hammer, in any case.'

He smiled. 'Right.'

'I still don't know how Fitzpatrick was able to blackmail Adele. It's been bugging me.'

He met her eyes. 'My contact's sworn me to secrecy, but it'll be in the papers in a day or two in any case. And the police do owe you one.'

'I won't say anything. You have my word on that.'

He looked at her for a long moment, but then nodded. 'They managed to get Adele to talk. She confessed her part to protect Cole from one of the two murder charges, and to show the police she instigated the whole thing. Not that I think it'll do Cole much good.

'Way back when she and Bernard had their affair, she was working at the top of government. I guess it wasn't unnatural that she talked to Bernard about her work, but she should have been more discreet. Bernard's brother worked for the Attorney General's office – still does, in fact. And they oversee the Official Secrets Act, which Adele had signed. Bernard only had to hint at what he could pass on to his brother to keep Adele quiet.'

'How serious would it have been for her?'

'She didn't pass on information with malicious intent. If she'd been prosecuted it would have meant a couple of years in jail, or an unlimited fine. But that was enough. Her reputation would have been shot – and can you imagine a woman like Adele in prison?'

Robin's contact had shared a lot with him. Eve was glad about that, but it made her wonder, too. 'So, in the end, she chose to kill Bernard to boost Cole's future, rather than reveal the truth herself? She thought she could avoid jail and the loss of her reputation by resorting to murder?' What kind of person would make that judgement? But Eve knew from her years of obituary writing that the world's population included some seriously warped individuals.

He nodded. 'On the night she killed Bernard, she lured him out for a secret discussion by telling him Cole had found out the truth. She had one last go at persuading him to help their son by acknowledging him. But she'd taken the hammer with her, so it's clear she'd already decided what to do if he said no.'

They were silent for a moment.

'The bequest of the cello confused me,' Eve said. 'In some ways you could see it as a snub, I suppose. I wonder if that was what made Bernard pass it on to Cole.'

Robin put his cup down. 'I gather the sealed letter that went with the bequest has been found at Woodlands House. In it, Bernard said he hoped Cole enjoyed bathing in his reflected glory.'

'And he must have imagined Cole being a lot older by the time he finally inherited it.'

Robin nodded. 'He probably hoped his son would have spent years trying and failing to make a proper name for himself while Bernard basked in the fame he'd achieved. He was like that.'

'So, what happens next?' Eve asked.

'The evidence is all stacking up. Cole and Adele will both serve long prison sentences.' Robin said. 'I don't suppose we'll see them in the village again. Have some more coffee if you'd like it.'

Eve topped herself up. 'Thanks. Ironically, I was convinced it was Lucas Booth who was guilty earlier on last night.' She explained her theory about his mismanagement of the Blackforth Arts Trust's funds and how it might have helped him buy back High House. 'When I thought back to him coming out of St Peter's on Monday night in tears, it seemed to fit with him having some kind of reaction after committing a second murder.'

'Maybe he was emotional because Bernard's death brought back his resentment about High House, and reminded him of how he'd treated Sophie when she was dying. Perhaps he looked guilty because he was feeling that way – but not for the reason you thought.'

'And Andrew Goddard looked guilty, but wasn't.' She wondered just how much he'd known about his wife and Fitzpatrick's relationship. They'd never know now, unless Andrew opened up – and with Cole and Adele in custody, there was no reason he should. Either way, it was clear he and Fi had been on the point of divorce, hence Fi's decision to try to blackmail the Wentworths. Andrew had had some front, given he'd also been seeing someone else behind his wife's back.

As Eve got up to leave, Robin stood too. His blue-grey eyes met hers. 'You know what I'm going to say.'

She nodded. 'I won't share what you've said with anyone. Or tell them about you.'

As she walked along the sun-dappled lane, Robin's expression came back to her again. Secrecy was important to him, and yet one or two people knew his background. It made her think he was unlikely to be part of an official witness protection scheme. Had it been his choice to walk out of his old life and emerge as Robin Yardley, gardener? And was the old part of his life entirely in the past, or had it cast a long shadow?

CHAPTER FORTY

Eve was giving Gus his evening meal at Elizabeth's Cottage when the knock at the door came.

'Eve! I've only just heard. Are you all right? I wish you'd called me!' Simon's usual sangfroid was slipping a little, which Eve found pleasing under the circumstances. Without warning he pulled her into a quick hug. 'Sorry – I'm just so horrified at what happened after I left you.'

'Thanks. It was a little – untoward – but I'm okay. Do you want to come in?'

He was just stepping over the threshold when Viv appeared in the lane behind him. He turned and a look of exasperation spread across his face.

Eve felt momentarily disappointed too, but it was overlaid with a slight sense of relief.

'I was walking round the green, and I saw you turn up,' Viv said to Simon. 'You've arrived just at the right moment. I'm trying to persuade Eve to stay in Saxford, to work part-time at the teashop and buy this place.' She followed Simon into Elizabeth's living room.

Her brother rolled his eyes. 'All excellent ideas, but hardly fair to browbeat Eve when she was up half the night, confronting a murderer, then being grilled by the police.'

'I'd say it's the perfect time.' Viv grinned. 'Her defences are down. I'm not going to miss this opportunity.' She gave Eve a quizzical look. 'I don't imagine it happens very often.'

Eve laughed and closed the door after them. She filled Simon in on the events of the night before. In theory it ought to be hard to relive them, but each time she relayed it all aloud, she felt marginally better.

'I bumped into Emily Moore earlier, by the way,' Simon said. Eve had already told Viv about the situation with the Blackforth Arts Trust, earlier that day at Monty's. 'She was looking a heck of a lot happier than when we saw her last night.'

Eve raised an eyebrow.

'She's taken it upon herself to contact some larger arts trusts that might have the funds to buy High House.' He made a face. 'She says they're not blind to the fact that the scandal surrounding the place will make it a tempting prospect for visitors. Any organisation with the capital's likely to find it a nice little earner. The upshot is, she's got two places interested, just from the calls she's made today. And she's recommending Adam as the expert they'll need to run the place.'

'I know she felt terrible that he was out of a job.'

Simon nodded. 'I think she's on course to make up for that.'

'This is all very heart-warming,' Viv said, 'but deviating from the main point, which I insist we discuss.' She turned to Eve and smiled sweetly. 'Your continued presence in Saxford. You wouldn't turn me down, would you?'

Simon laughed. 'Viv won't have detailed the small print. For instance, if you get seriously involved with the business, you'll have to deal with her in-laws. Suit of armour and lance required.'

Viv grimaced. 'I believe I did give Eve a brief character sketch of them, soon after we first met, as a matter of fact.' She fixed Eve with her gaze one more time. 'What do you say? You could work from here on your obituaries, couldn't you, just as easily as from London?'

It was true, people were fairly indiscriminate about where they died – she often ended up working remotely. 'I guess.'

Viv grinned. 'You see!' She was fiddling with a tote bag she'd brought with her. 'Just in case you happened to say yes, I took the precaution of getting a bottle of fizz from Moira. Only prosecco – but it's good. You have to order in advance if you want champagne, so take note. The flutes are in the left-hand cupboard in the sideboard.'

As the first bubbles prickled Eve's mouth, she looked from Viv to Simon and felt happier than she had in a long time.

Eve had already texted the twins and Ian to let them know that Saxford's murderers had been caught. She'd played down the more frightening aspects of her own role, while making Ian aware that her actions had been key in providing the police with a watertight case.

That evening, Eve messaged the twins again.

What would you think if I sold up in London and moved to Suffolk? I've found I like it here, and there's a cottage going. But would it make you sad if I let the house in Kilburn go?

She couldn't *not* ask them. It had been the place where they'd grown up.

Ellen's reply only took a second:

You're kidding, right? Kilburn versus the countryside, close to the sea? Hmm. Tough choice, but yeah, fine by me.

A moment later she added:

Not that it's any of my business. I'd rather you lived in a place that makes you happy. You do know that, don't you?

Nick's response came five minutes later:

What Ellen said. Let me know when you're moving and I'll come and lug stuff.

Their messages set tears pricking her eyes. She felt a thrill rush through her at the thought of returning to Saxford, one day soon, with her own set of keys for Elizabeth's Cottage. She'd keep up traditions: open the house at midwinter and midsummer, just as Viv and Simon's parents had, and help Viv in her mission to keep the locals well fed. And at other times, she'd sit at the table in the dining room and write about her fascinating subjects in the peace and quiet of the Suffolk countryside.

But in one respect, she was absolutely determined to defy tradition. No more keeping keys to the house underneath the flower pots.

Bernard Eustace Fitzpatrick, cellist

Bernard Fitzpatrick, who dominated the world stage as a cellist for over thirty years, considered by some as the heir to Casals and Rostropovich, has died in Saxford St Peter, Suffolk. A woman has been arrested for his murder.

Friends and colleagues will remember a man who could electrify a room, both with his music and his sheer force of personality. He was a fierce, exacting and passionate genius, living life to the full and taking no prisoners. But behind the laughter and extravagance of the public-facing persona was a darker side: a man unable to deal with anyone who had the potential to outshine him, including his own unacknowledged son.

Eve stopped typing. She'd rewritten her opening paragraph so many times. No matter how hard she tried, she was never 100 per cent happy she'd nailed a subject. People were such a complex mix.

But that was why her profession had her hooked.

A LETTER FROM CLARE

Thank you so much for reading *Mystery on Hidden Lane*. I do hope you enjoyed it as much as I liked writing it! If you'd like to keep up to date with all of my latest releases, you can sign up at the following link. Your email address will never be shared, and you can unsubscribe at any time.

www.bookouture.com/clare-chase

This book marks the beginning of a new series for me. I got the idea of having an obituary writer as my heroine after listening to a fascinating interview with Margalit Fox, who fulfilled that role for the *New York Times*. It got me thinking about the unique insight obituary writers must get into a dead person's personality and how they were viewed by others. It seemed the perfect profession for an amateur sleuth! The Suffolk setting harks back to happy childhood holidays. My grandmother lived there, by the sea, and Gus is based on her wire-haired dachshund, Huw.

If you have time, I'd love it if you were able to **write a review of *Mystery on Hidden Lane***. Feedback is really valuable, and it also makes a huge difference in helping new readers discover my books for the first time.

Alternatively, if you'd like to contact me personally, you can reach me via my website, Facebook page, Twitter or Instagram. It's always great to hear from readers.

Again, thank you so much for deciding to spend some time reading *Mystery on Hidden Lane*. I'm looking forward to sharing my next book with you very soon.

With all best wishes,
Clare x

       @ClareChaseAuthor

       @ClareChase_

       www.clarechase.com

ACKNOWLEDGEMENTS

Loads of love and thanks, as ever, to my immediate family: to Charlie for the pre-submission proofreading; to George for the witty banter; and to Ros for the feedback on plot! Much love and thanks also to my parents, and to Phil and Jenny, David and Pat, Warty, Andrea, Jen, the Westfield gang, Margaret, Shelly, Mark, Helen, cousin Lorna and a whole band of family and friends.

And then, vitally, huge thanks to my fantastic editor Ruth Tross for her clear-sighted feedback, inspiring ideas and friendly support. I've thoroughly enjoyed working with her on this first Eve Mallow book and can't wait to get cracking on the next! Big thanks also to Noelle Holten, for her phenomenal promotional work.

I'd also like to express heartfelt gratitude to Peta Nightingale, Kim Nash, Alexandra Holmes and everyone involved in editing, book production and sales at Bookouture. I feel hugely lucky to be published and promoted by such a wonderful team.

Thanks to the fabulous Bookouture authors and other writer mates both online and IRL for their friendship. And a massive thank you, too, to the book bloggers and reviewers who've taken the time to pass on their thoughts about my work.

And finally, thanks to you, the reader, for buying or borrowing this book!

Lightning Source UK Ltd.
Milton Keynes UK
UKHW010618300622
405178UK00001B/158